MIRROR
DREAMS

By Catherine Webb

MIRROR DREAMS

Catherine Webb

www.atombooks.co.uk

ATOM

First published in Great Britain by Atom 2002
Reprinted 2003, 2004, 2005

Copyright © 2002 by Catherine Webb

The moral right of the author has been asserted.

*All characters and events in this publication are fictitious
and any resemblance to real persons, living or dead,
is purely coincidental.*

A CIP catalogue record for this book
is available from the British Library.

ISBN 1 9042 3300 7

Typeset in Cochin by M Rules
Printed and bound in Great Britain
by Bookmarque Ltd, Croydon, Surrey

Atom
An imprint of
Time Warner Book Group UK
Brettenham House
Lancaster Place
London WC2E 7EN

www.atombooks.co.uk

Contents

ONE

Shifting Storms

When I woke up that bright spring day in my small room of light and colour, I knew something very bad was about to happen. Don't ask me how I knew – the explanation would take up most of my story and probably require a lifetime's study of the spell books of Haven. For now just accept that every pricking thumb was screaming, 'Something wicked this way comes'. Of course that feeling was pretty commonplace around Stormpoint. Something wicked was generally eating away at my shielding night and day. Only this time the feeling was strong enough to give me an itch in my fingers and a desire to throw fire at anything that moved. That's the trouble about my little kingdom – it's too remote to merit any outside aid, but still large enough to draw a good deal of attention from monster on demon on monster.

I'd inherited Stormpoint from a particularly grumpy

mage who went for the evil-forest-ravaging-monster feel himself – probably just to impress the various monstrosities who came knocking on the gates. The moment a well-placed mage-bolt of mine had sent him into the abyss, the Key to Stormpoint – the power to control this little bubble of existence – was mine, buried deep within my soul. Really, it didn't look like much. A little sphere of magic, that just happened to make the kingdom stay in one piece, had rested itself in my hands, and I'd taken it into myself, never to be released until I either willed it so, or perished.

Then, with a proper sense of civic duty and a certain revulsion towards mess, I'd tidied the place up.

Instead of the walls of bramble and black ivy that pulled the unwary traveller to a sad demise, I established a nice, simple shield that spanned the entire country. Unlike my predecessor, who was very keen on the bemused traveller wandering down the road to his little land, I placed signs saying 'Keep Out' and 'Dragons on Patrol' everywhere I could. Believe me, the last thing I wanted was someone from the Council of Haven wandering into my realm and asking why I, as the most powerful mage ever to saunter out of Haven on some impossible quest from which I'd never come back, was hanging around inside a little sphere of customised magic.

And now the ten or so square miles of Stormpoint responded to me, and me alone. I was the king of fairies in a fairy-tale kingdom.

It was a matter of a minute to get washed and clean via the plumbing I'd insisted on having installed. Nice clean taps, steaming hot water, and a fresh towel next to the bath. Other people may like the life of quaint wells and washing in the freezing spring water – I cared nothing for it. Tradition could go jump into the Void as far as I was concerned.

The Void. It spans the edge of the island, of every island, a shimmering infinity of possibility just waiting to be filled. Powerful mages have often been known to set up their own kingdoms at the ends of the roads, just like Stormpoint, in the Void, and expand their lands towards infinity. But in these busy times people lack the patience. Kingdoms can be built from nothing, but this requires huge magical resources, an army of mages, and patience galore. It's a sad fact that these are rare resources nowadays.

I myself was quite happy with managing the little place I had. I do not know who founded Stormpoint, but they made a tough little kingdom and I am very fond of it. Naturally it is nothing to Haven, the primary kingdom, the kingdom that existed before them all, but the paperwork I had to do was bad enough just for these few square miles. Besides, places like Haven or Stormpoint attract all sorts. I had no ambition to be the target of a wandering mage determined to knock me head over heels into the surrounding Void. You fall into the Void, you fall for ever.

So, thanks to my cautious and somewhat lazy nature, there is just one road out of Stormpoint. Its twisting shape can only be seen for maybe a few hundred yards outside the luminous purple shield of Stormpoint, before it is lost in the fiery red haze of what-may-be. It runs between dense forests inside Stormpoint but, once outside, floats on a cloud of fire.

It doesn't matter, though. I know where the road leads. Through a hundred crossroads where possible destinies intersect – more than can ever be counted – the road will eventually lead back to Haven. All roads lead to Haven. Or away, depending on your point of view.

Unless you take the wrong turn, that is. Unless you follow the roads through shadier kingdoms. Unless you head west into the setting sun. Then you find Nightkeep, the other ancient kingdom, opposed in every way to its twin. You'd be amazed how many idiots can't tell shadow from light and accidentally wander into that realm of dark magic and confusion.

Think of it as a family tree. At the top are two brothers. Haven and Nightkeep. They have children – the kingdoms – which spread out quickly into the Void as more and more mages build more and more lands to call their own. Until there are now two quite definite families, glowering at each other over an infinite expanse of nothingness.

And there you have it. Haven and Nightkeep.

My little Stormpoint is on the far edge of the network of roads leading from Haven. Many mages have come here, asking if they might build their own kingdoms beyond mine, but rather than delight in the tax I could then raise from their visitors, I turn them away. I do not like the thought of two roads to watch. Just one inbound lane is good enough for me.

This stubbornness puts me eight kingdoms away from Haven, the centre of the web. That is assuming I don't get horribly lost on the road, and the eight kingdoms between me and Haven don't think, 'Let's see if we can kill this mage and take Stormpoint while he is vulnerable and passing through our lands'.

Eight is a long way out, and it makes my position in the great social network of who-bosses-whom a rather low one.

But it doesn't matter. I have been to Earth, and beyond. I have seen Nightkeep, I have fought beside kings. No one will bully me for a good while yet.

Earth. The big granddaddy of them all, lurking even higher up the family tree than Haven and Nightkeep. The one source from which all this mess stems. The place where the light kingdoms of Haven meet the dark ones of Nightkeep. The place where the dreamers – the insubstantial shadows who make the Void in their sleep – come from. So the theory runs.

I have visited that strange place, and studied it well. It's a madhouse. Somewhere so strange and unexplainable must surely be real, for I do not believe human imagination alone could conjure up such horrors and such beauty, mingled together in such terrible and wondrous detail.

Don't you dare fall asleep on me yet!

The Void is not just an empty space – it is the nothingness of sleep, made by all these humans' dreamless nights on Earth. Either that or a natural phenomenon, depending on where you stand in the academic wars that rage over this issue.

But this I can say with confidence, for I have seen it with my own eyes: Haven is not just a city – it is the city of dreams, the culmination of all those dreamers' wishes and desires. It is the golden city – heaven, if you will – where everyone wishes to be.

Nightkeep is the nightmare that sucks dreamers into its cold embrace. The dark city of hell, where people wake to find themselves trapped, unable to break free of their own despair. Why there has to be balance, I don't know. I'd have thought no one would really want it, but I guess I've no right to argue with the laws of the universe. But having a land of darkness – it's so messy.

So Stormpoint is not just a kingdom ruled by me, but a potential paradise to at least one human mind. Or if the land itself did not win the heart of the wandering dreamer, then one small aspect of it would. Just one image, one sound, one action might one day unlock paradise to someone. The creatures of my kingdom, each with their own personality and thoughts, may be the dream of someone, somewhere. And to at least one mind their presence might someday make it paradise.

And then – if the mind ever did reach Stormpoint or the part of it that would be paradise? What would happen then, I hear you cry? To tell the truth, I haven't the faintest idea. No dreamer has ever found their true paradise. They cannot see the roads between dreams, cannot manipulate the wind and fire as a mage does. They are pawns to their own indecency. Sorry, dreamer, if you are reading this, but it's true. When it comes to self-control in sleep you really suck.

So I maintain Stormpoint. I keep this one paradise alive for the dreamer who may one day find the road to it. I know that it's probably too far detached, that the minions of nightmare are too far encroached on the void, that Haven can barely maintain the barriers of light against the growing darkness – but still I wait.

As to the reality of this world or that, I know only

what my eyes have shown me. That there is a land twisted and strange where my sleeping mind can wander. That this same land can spew forth shadows who seem to start at a sight or a sound and whisper of dreams and memories as though they are one. That these same shadows can speak of wonders and sciences that I am certain were never created within my own world. That these shadows move through the Void as though it were not there. That they affect us, bringing their stories and their ideas into our world, and claiming that they have seen this tree before or that that woman there is a long-dead wife – all these are images plucked from their minds and imposed upon our world. That they affect us in this way I'm all but certain. That we affect them I also see. For when we warred in Nightkeep so there was war on Earth. When great mages raised beauteous illusions in the Void and first turned their minds out towards Earth, so minds on Earth ranged outwards to the stars. We affect them. They affect us. So closely bound are we, that we and they might almost be one.

This much I am sure of. Whether they made us, or we them, I do not know and will not speculate. I think I am real, and that is enough. Whether they are real or not I do not know. But they seem to have minds of their own, so I treat them too as real. Whether they're ghost, spirit or simply mortals like myself wandering through another world, my actions towards them will always be the same until change affects them and me both. And I'm good at waiting for change. I've had a lot of practice.

And now something wicked this way comes.

I slid down the ladder from my room high in the tower to the kitchen. Forget old-fashioned Agas and log fires, all that means nothing to me. A good electric oven (well not actually electric, electricity doesn't work well at all in a magical kingdom, but the spells I've rigged create a near-identical effect), a microwave and an immaculately clean sink made up this fairy-tale kitchen.

'Irinda?'

'Kite. Beautiful morning, isn't it?'

Irinda pushed her breakfast plate to one side and regarded me with big green eyes that could charm birds out of the trees. Of course they could – I'd made them so they could.

'Someone's coming.'

She sighed and stood up. Some mages like to make animal familiars. Some like to make elementals. Some like to make incredibly beautiful ladies, naked and willing for things best not described. I remember one mage of Nightkeep, who for several days had me locked in his dungeon, had made a lady of perfection who changed into a new woman of even more enticing beauty every day after he slept with her, just to keep his desire sated in new and interesting ways. I once looked into her eyes, a little before I escaped, and saw in their hazel depths more than just the passion of the man's creating. I saw terror. Despair. A will all of its own trying to break free. And rather than leave her to suffer another thousand years of the bastard, I'd stopped her heart then and there, and buried her on the edge of that cursed kingdom as I made good my escape. I couldn't have taken her into the Void – she would have ceased to exist the moment she crossed the border, so dependent was she for survival on the mage's magic. Of course I'd been a lot younger then – say, two hundred years – but age hasn't worn away the experience.

Irinda was my own happy version of that dewy-eyed wench. Oh yes, she was beautiful, but all I'd shaped was her body and soul. The mind, the spark of intelligence that gave her fire, was all her own, and it was more beautiful than any mere thought of mine.

'I sensed no one.'

I smiled despite myself. 'You can't sense outside the kingdom, remember?'

'But inside I sense ten times better than you.'

'Oh, and now she's proud!' It's incredible how much the average creator has to put up with from his creations.

Sighing, shaking her head wearily at the man who'd made her out of raw imagination, she stood up and began stacking plates in the nearly electric dishwasher. 'You going to stop them?'

'Only if they do anything hostile. I'll let them get maybe a few miles in, then send Arissna to see what they want.'

She frowned. 'No. Arissna is swimming with Tarmiss at the lake today – a match I've been setting up for years, believe me. Send someone else.'

'You and your match-making,' I muttered. Why does she do it? She knows that I if just imagine Arissna and Tarmiss getting together, they would! Mind you, that's cheating and we both know it. 'How about Basict?'

'He should like the break,' she agreed. 'Though I'm not sure if our guests will appreciate being met by a wolf.'

'They'll live.'

'You say that every time we get visitors.'

'Well, I can't be wrong every time, can I? I'm going to get dressed in something suitably impressive, just in case it's someone who wants to be shooed away by a great mage of magic and fire.'

She laughed like wind playing in a waterfall – a sound of purity that would have dulled any music. 'Don't forget to comb your hair this time!'

I sniffed but said nothing. Up the ladder again, into the small room that was the bathroom, glower at the neatly laid out blue robe with the single white strap around the middle, struggle to pull it over my head, look in the mirror.

Laenan Kite. Dark-haired, blue-eyed mage of maybe five hundred years. Appearance . . . mid-twentyish. Normal height, normal width, normal colouring, normal everything. Except for the magic, that was. The magic that had probably gone a long way to making the name Laenan Kite a legend in Haven, a curse in Nightkeep.

I admit that a smile of pride did cross my face at that thought. Reclusive I may be, but I'm still allowed to be as smug as the next man. And the blue robe did go well with my eyes.

The good thing about owning the Key to one of the many kingdoms – one of the many good things - is that you don't have to be lonely. You want a great conversationalist with tastes like yours, and hey presto, there will be a great conversationalist.

And if you happen to be running a little low on imagination there's always one dreamer or another who may have found their way into your land. It's a way of learning new things, I suppose.

That's where Nightkeep really falls down. Rather than listening to those from Earth who wander into its domain they send them running round the incomprehensible depths of chaos. They leech their lives, and the madder they can make their visitors from another plane, the better. Madness encourages fear, and all necromancers like fear. So they'll have dreamers running round in circles, blind but at the same time aware of their blindness, hollering for what was theirs and cannot be theirs again. But while all this may be fine and pleasant on the draining-of-emotion front, it's rubbish in the area of 'acquiring new and bright ideas'. As a result the privies are old, the rifles often backfire, the word 'microwave' is just a collection of wasted syllables and everyone you meet has the computer literacy of a carrot.

Okay, I admit it – Haven isn't much better. The king is far too traditional. Hell, the whole family is far too bound up in the idea of knights in shining armour. Dreamers know about cars and planes and things for getting power out of the sun and all kinds of stuff – and our average royal family still pisses in the bushes!

My Key-bound senses stirred once again. Someone had just entered Stormpoint. I wandered over to a balcony and looked across my forest kingdom.

A single messenger, I realised. Now he was actually inside my domain I could see him clearly in my mind's eye. He wore blue and white, rode a white horse of Haven and carried the eagle banner of that land. Only horses which are literally summoned, stabled and fed in the emptiness of the Void can safely walk the roads between kingdoms, without fading to a wisp of thought. That worried me – it meant someone thought the journey was important enough to waste magic on.

I watched him with half a mind's eye as I fussed over tidying away the stuff of breakfast. Unless Nightkeep had suddenly learnt cunning, then the man was what he appeared. An envoy from Haven.

Something about that bitter realisation soured my otherwise cheerful mood. Envoys always spelt trouble, and the bad feeling inside me was kicking up a whole ruckus of that. The weather, in due respect to my feelings, provided a low roll of thunder. There was going to be a stinking storm later, the way I was going. I wondered if I should accelerate it, just to get the man soaked. Stormpoint was naturally famous for its storms, and if I got into a really bad mood I could conjure stuff to make meteorologists cry.

No! Stop being childish! snapped the part of me that had long ago put its name down as a father, and I the disobedient child.

An envoy from Haven.

I would really have preferred drooling demons.

'My Lord Kite!'

The voice echoed off the edges of the tower and back again. The grey wolf, sitting companionably by the horse's side, sniffed as I approached, and gave the wolfish equivalent of a grin. Basict was a werewolf. It was for his sake the moon never quite reached full.

What, you might ask, is a werewolf doing in a pleasantly enchanted forest? Well, why the hell not, I'd reply! It's unfair that darkness should get all the really smart, dangerous animals to guard their lands. Fairies are crap at watching the road – you'd never get one on patrol in Nightkeep. They spend their lives giggling and getting messed up with love potions and stuff like that. Dwarves are stubborn and always demanding pay rises or else they strike. Elves are forever busy pampering themselves in mirrors and ordering fashion magazines from far-flung publishers for outrageous prices.

But your average demon doesn't get excited over looks, because let's face it, he doesn't have much to get fussed over. Gargoyles are great at just sitting around watching the road, and ogres would think you were honouring them if you told them to stay put and munch rocks all day.

Even Haven has the odd monstrosity lurking in the cellars for those times when war is really having a ball. And Basict – Basict was good at being a werewolf.

'I represent him,' I announced, standing defensively in the door at the base of the tower. The messenger jumped. He hadn't seen me approach, but then, I hadn't wanted him to.

'I . . . bring a message from Haven.'

'I guessed as much. Any particular message or just the usual demands for tax, magic and time?'

'I bring a summons.'

'You'll learn.'

He licked dry lips. Clearly the name Laenan Kite still carried as many meaningful looks and awed silences as I'd intended. 'The Mage Laenan Kite, Warden of Stormpoint and one-time Master of the Mage's Library and Councillor to Haven, is requested at the Palace in Haven.'

Too many titles have always worried me, and that sentence was packed full of them. I've had enough titles in my time to fill a small book, and know that they bring nothing but trouble. 'For what purpose?'

'For the crowning of King Talsin the Second and the raising of the Wardens for war.'

I admit, it took several seconds to sink in. That's the trouble with being reclusive – it's so hard to keep up on news. But to not have known about Talsin . . . 'When did . . . the king die?'

'Three weeks ago, repelling Nightkeep invaders from the lands around Haven.'

Now I was really surprised. Invaders? Near Haven? I'd noticed an increased number of raids on my lands, but for the nightmare to dig so deeply into the depths of dreaming? It seemed impossible.

That explained the mention of war. Talsin had been close to his dad, to say the least. The death of a king would hardly go unpunished. And who better to have casting spells than your old friend the great mage Kite? I realised the messenger was waiting for an answer. 'Thank you for your service. I will of course relay this to my master, and I expect he will obey the king's wish in this matter. May your dreams be bright.'

'Dreams be bright, sir.'

I drew the traditional blessing in the air, and then, because I was now feeling slightly guilty at giving the man such a hard time, re-wrote it in magical fire. The messenger gulped, not sure whether I'd blessed or cursed him (blessed, dear dreamer, how can you doubt me?), and made as hasty a retreat as he could. I watched him go, and hesitated before calling out again.

'Is . . . Lisana still . . . close to Talsin?'

'Yes, sir. I believe so.'

'I see. Thank you.'

He hurried away.

❊

It was no big thing for me to pack a small bag of Void-made garments, and dress in simple brown travel clothes – all I possessed that could withstand the pressure of possibility outside Stormpoint. Void-made equipment was literally forged in the fires of possibility by talented mages, and were the only things which could pass between kingdoms without undergoing significant changes to their very nature.

'You're going, then.'

I spared Irinda a brief glance. 'No choice. A summons is still a summons, no matter what the reason.'

'You never obeyed summons in the past, and nothing happened.'

I grinned despite myself at her simple statement, which couldn't be more naive. 'They never dared summon me in the past. The old king knew me far too well. He . . . conformed pretty much to the wise-old-man-of-great-intelligence model. He would never have run the risk of a direct summons on a mage like me.'

'Talsin, though, isn't like his father?'

'Oh, he's got wise-old-man material in him,' I replied loftily. 'But he's still a little rusty on the simpler things in life. Tact. Thought. General background knowledge of any kind, to tell the truth. Great man in a fight, though. He's conquered more nightmares than anyone I know.'

'Including yourself?'

'Get your facts straight. I never conquered nightmare, Irinda. I was more the make-a-mess-of-whatever-looked-as-if-it-doesn't-like-me kind of fighter.'

She nodded understandingly. I'd killed men, she knew it. She also knew that the life of running all over the place with a fireball at my fingers was one I was keen to avoid. 'When do you go?'

I shrugged. 'As soon as I can. Can't wait to see some of those court faces when Kite makes his dramatic return. I may make a few detours though.'

'Skypoint?'

'You know me far too well, my dear.' I pulled the bag closed, and swung it onto my back. With the plain brown travel clothes, plain brown boots, bag and hat, I could have passed for utterly anyone. The staff I carried didn't possess any great magic – it was just a stick for hitting people with. The water bottle I carried didn't contain any great potion, I just didn't want to get thirsty.

And incredibly, I was ready.

'You'll look after the dreamers, won't you?'

She snorted. 'We get so few as it is. Nightmare is devouring more and more humans these days. What about the safety of the realm? You going to leave us here to be eaten, I take it?'

I groaned. Yes, there was always that to worry about, sooner or later. I closed my eyes, placed my hands together, and pulled them open slowly. The ceiling creaked. A gust of slightly hot and extremely smelly air brushed my face. In the window in front of me a piece of flapping ribbon twitched in its golden swaying, and caught the light like that, and like that. Scales briefly flashed in the sunlight and dazzled me. A very pointy tail dropped out of my line of sight, down towards the base of the tower. The ceiling creaked again under the massive weight of something pressing down on it. A giant stomach rumbled loud enough to make the floor hum beneath my feet.

I turned very slowly and looked into the shimmering, spinning eyes of a dragon, peering in at the window. Irinda groaned. 'Do you know how big those creatures' crap is? What kind of welcome is that for a human seeking paradise?'

'Brilliant fertiliser,' I retorted. 'The garden needs a little natural oomph.'

And now, there was only the Void.

Have you ever stood at the top of one of those really high boards above a swimming pool, looked down at the tiny waves and heard the very distant voices of the children playing in the shallow end? Well, that's how I feel every time I have to walk through the shimmering purple barrier along the dirt road that somehow, impossibly, is supported on nothing just a few inches away from the end of my toes. All right, the road is wide enough to get two carts side-by-side down it and strong enough to support the weight of infinity – but it still makes my stomach churn to look down and know that somewhere in that silent, dancing light that makes up the Void, is a never-ending fall.

Dreamers are the only ones who can walk through the Void without a road. Well, of course they can – otherwise they'd stand no chance of finding a kingdom to dream in! If they can't find anything in that infinity before the morning rises on Earth, then they sleep a dreamless sleep. Yet still are they called dreamers, forever drifting through the Void as substantial as their namesakes. Perhaps 'sleepers' would be a fairer term, but the court at Haven has always been uncertain of using it. 'Sleepers' implies that they are powerless and cannot think for themselves, and that is far from the case.

Some mages have nets set up all around their little kingdoms to trap dreamers and pull them into either nightmare or dream. I do not understand why. Whether they are, as some mages believe, walking walls of power or nothing more than shadows created by I know not what, I have yet to see a dreamer heal a wound or teach a child or give a mage his lost strength.

I stepped out, into the Void. Nothing. No cold, no hot, no loud, no quiet, no wind, no still. All I could see for about two hundred yards in front of me was a dazzling blanket of light. I began to walk. After maybe five minutes Stormpoint was gone from sight, and I was alone.

So I walked, and walked, and walked.

A dreamer passed by me briefly. I remember his face – a young boy, hardly more than five. Children are always better at finding the kingdoms furthest from home. They are freer to travel further and faster. The adult mind has not the same capacity for dreams.

'Are you going to fly with me?' he asked plaintively.

I hesitated for a second. True, the boy wasn't actually a responsibility of mine. Mages have only a duty towards those inside their kingdom, to see that they are happy. But then, if I didn't give the boy a push in the right direction, he could well take the road that leads back toward Nightkeep, and I didn't like the thought of those demons getting their claws on anyone.

'Fly over there,' I said, pointing back the way he'd come, to Skypoint. I tried to give the boy an image of that kingdom, imprint on his mind. Instantly, the dreamer was gone.

Humans can do that everywhere save Earth, I discovered. They travel at the speed of thought, and thought isn't above jumping from one place to another if given the proper stimulus. I set out walking. Again. It seemed stupid that the human mind should have the capacity to jump while asleep, and not while awake. Somewhere, I decided, the creator had got his numbers jumbled up.

The boy was the only one who'd got this far from Haven. That made me seriously worried. If dreamers didn't find the roads, then that meant either empty sleep without a chance of the paradise we offered, or nightmare. Somehow, I had a feeling one was more likely than the other. To coin a phrase, the tide already seemed to be turning against Haven.

And I hadn't even gone more than a few miles outside Stormpoint. If you can call it miles, in the Void.

TWO

Spectrum of the Void

The Void varies in colour immensely. Sometimes a pleasant pink, sometimes a blinding orange, sometimes a shining green. Ahead, pushing through the murky blue fog of maybe, the Void shimmered around a crossroads. I looked carefully at the three choices open to me. The trouble is you can never tell which road is which – they all look exactly the same. But I knew this part of infinity well enough to realise that the road straight ahead led to Haven, the road to the right to Skypoint and the road to the left was probably a pretty fast way of wandering into some nightmare or another.

I took the right-hand road and quickened my pace.

There was only one kingdom between me and Skypoint. Westpoint is one of those strange kingdoms where the nomad tribes who move through the Void all year round, looking for places to camp before moving on to yet

another kingdom, like to spend their summers. The rule
of Westpoint has always been a bit of a double-edged
sword, because people are in and out in such large
numbers. As a result, the latest lord of that land has built
up one of the strangest armies in the world of dreams,
who are often hired as mercenaries. They are utterly
strict about who goes through their kingdom and how,
and even I wasn't about to argue with them.

When you enter Westpoint it's surprisingly empty and
barren. The first thing that greets you is a pine forest,
dense and full of, not surprisingly, wolves. Changelings.
Nature elementals. Anyone fool enough to go into that
forest would not expect to come out in a hurry. The long
shadows and the pine needles that crunch under your
boots are almost as freaky as the silence of the Void – but
at least in the Void there's nothing more between you and
an enemy than closely-packed maybe. In Westpoint,
where the roads wind around huge boulders, and cliffs
block the view on either side, there could be an enemy a
few feet away and you'd be none the wiser.

I knew this, but since Westpoint is so big I just kept on
walking down the road, sending out a steady signal to
the mages who I *knew* were watching. Cliffs began to rise
above me, dust from the road puffed up around my feet,
clouds scudded across the blue sky, dead leaves were
blown across my path. All the while I listened to the
distant minds of the mages, waiting for them to address
me.

They didn't move in on me though, for several
reasons. Firstly, by advertising my presence so openly I
suggested I was friendly. This is always confusing to
armies, probably because they're not trained to cope

with niceness. Secondly I was making it clear that here
was a mage, bearing a Key, whose magic was not
insignificant. The tight shields I kept raised were proof
enough of that; it would have taken a lot of magic to get
past the wards I had ready.

As I passed through the shadow of one cliff-face after
another, forded trickling streams and marvelled at the
several new species of bush that had evolved while I'd
been away, the road began to loop and climb. Soon I'd
emerged from the lowlands and was panting up a steep
hill. Dreams, did I need more exercise!

Just when I'd decided that the warden of Westpoint
was deliberately adding more land ahead of me for fun, I
came out from a stand of prickly green bushes, and
beheld the plateau of Westpoint in its entirety.

A tribe of nomadic horsemen wheeled across the plain
below, spears raised as they pursued a herd of
Westpoint's equivalent of bison. Tents clustered beside a
silver snaking river and farther off a little town of houses
with mud walls and carved wooden roofs rose from an
otherwise treeless landscape. Why anyone wanted to live
there came down to one thing: space.

The nomads, whose tents those were in that strange
land, moved through the kingdoms because they loved
change. Because they didn't want to be dependent.
Because they loved nature, and sought it in every way.
Here in this barren land the fools could get closer than
ever before to their pagan gods of nature, hunting and
foraging – and forgetting that they were still dependent
for their sustenance on a mage.

'If you are armed, lower your weapons now.'

The voice was the heavily accented sound of a

Westpoint guard. I turned slowly, careful to keep my hands visible and my magic to its lowest. The soldiers of Westpoint look a lot like your American Indians. I guess the lord of Westpoint made them like that because the Indians could live so well in conditions similar to those he tried to recreate. Throw in order, magic, unity, a few classes in policing and crowd control and you have, very simply, the soldiers facing me now.

They wore animal leathers of some kind or another that I didn't dare speculate about and carried those small swords that look pathetic but are still perfectly good at killing. The rifles they all had were innocently slung over a shoulder, but I knew better than to test their owners' reflexes. Their dark skin was tanned by long hours beneath the hot sun, and they were healthy to such an extreme that I suddenly found myself contemplating jogs in the morning.

'I am not armed. I am going to Skypoint, and then to Haven.'

'You are a mage. A warden of a kingdom too.' It was not a question.

'I mean no harm. If my presence is not acceptable I will go another way.'

'All who visit Westpoint do so because they are called by the spirits.'

Oh yes. Here, it always boils down to that. 'I am not called by the spirits, but by the king. I go to Haven,' I repeated.

'All who are not called by the spirits must pay tax.'

I hesitated. Somehow I could see that tax being a good deal heavier than what I had to offer. 'I am just a mage of a small kingdom. I can offer blessings, curses, wards or potions. The travellers who go through my kingdom are not taxed, therefore I have little tax to give myself. I am trying to see the king!'

'Our master has already left for the city of dreams. He said no one must be allowed in who is not called by the spirits.'

'Called by the spirits? What the hell is that supposed to mean?'

The guards shifted meaningfully, and I tried to control my mounting annoyance. 'Called by the spirits. Called by freedom and love of the chase.'

'What, like the nomads? Why are you people so stubborn?' I was losing my temper, and I knew it. I never liked to be mucked around by people who had no idea what they were dealing with. It wasn't so much the inconvenience, it was the fact that they assumed so much. Sloppy thinking. Mess. Things which annoyed me, both of them.

I raised a hand and drew my symbol – the symbol of Stormpoint – in the air, shoving it towards the leader's face in a blaze of light. 'See? This is my kingdom! I have fought beside kings and bloody well slain the lord of Nightkeep in passing! I have killed more Key owners than you could imagine, seen more gloomy dungeons and lost more dreamers than you can count on the legs of a centipede, and have just been summoned by a man whom I despise, to kneel at his feet! A man who shut me away in the darkness and betrayed everything I held dear! I am not in the mood to be summoned by spirits!'

I stopped myself, aware that I'd just gone too far. Did I really feel so strongly about kneeling once again in

Haven that it could break down my barriers of self-control? All that knowledge of my own heart that I had been building up for centuries suddenly seemed very uncertain.

The leader of the guards hesitated, his eyes growing darker yet. A pony whinnied somewhere in the bracken, the faint wind stirred up the dust and turned the silence to a roar. 'You ... say you do not wish to travel to Haven.'

I stood a deep steadying breath and forced my voice back down to its normal tones. 'No.'

'You do not wish to kneel.'

'No.'

Suddenly he gave a great laugh, which was more unsettling than rifles, believe me. 'Maybe the spirits are in you after all! A man who burns with fire and curses serving another who is not of his blood should be one of the nomads!'

I glanced down at my hands. They were indeed surrounded by a halo of ruddy red fire. Embarrassed at my own magical failure I slammed every shield I had back up in front of my bubbling magic, and tried to calm myself down.

But still the image wouldn't go away of having to bend my knee before those who had laughed at my falling and cursed the day I walked away free from that laughter.

'Do you hear the spirits, mage?' demanded a guard.

'No. Never.'

'Do you hear the call of the hunt?'

'No.'

'Do you run with the wind and dance in the flame?'

'No.'

'Then why do the spirits surround you?'

'I don't know! What's wrong with this place? Why is everyone obsessed with spirits?'

The guard seemed happy, despite my outburst, which was making my face burn and my heart turn away from me in disgust. 'You may pass through this kingdom, blindfold and unarmed.'

'Blindfold?' I squeaked indignantly.

'You would rather we turned you out now? You are a strong mage, Warden of Stormpoint. My master forbade that anyone should enter his kingdom while he was away, and we are bending the rules greatly for you as it is.'

I thought about arguing, and decided against it. I was in a bit of a hurry, considering all the things I had planned for. And to refuse a gift of the nomads or their guardians – even a gift which involved practically throwing myself on their mercy – was never a sensible move.

But being blindfolded would bring back memories.

'Kneel!'

I didn't kneel. A pike butt rammed into my knees, and I slid to the floor with a grunt. A cloud of foul breath brushed by my face. I could feel the claws of my captors digging deep into my arms, drawing blood.

'Finally. You took far too long to capture him.' The voice was a sneer, close to me and just as foul as the nightmares which held me. I couldn't see the face through the blindfold, couldn't feel my legs either. All in all, a worrying situation.

A hand, blessedly human but with long fingernails which might just as well have been claws, curled round my face, tilted my chin up so that the unseen mage could study every feature and flaw. 'Yes, it is him. I knew you'd return sooner or later to finish your handiwork, Kite.'

I began to reply but a mailed fist curled around my throat choking off words before they could begin to form. Clearly they were taking no chances. This is it then, you're going to die . . . began the manic voice of dread.

'I never did expect you to last so long, I must admit. Your shielding is remarkable. So tell me, my dear Laenan, how did you manage to block my scry?'

The hand fell from my throat, but this time I wasn't about to reveal anything. A claw drove suddenly across my face, and I was thankful for the blindfold which probably prevented me from losing my eyes.

'How did you block my scry?' repeated the hateful voice.

What could I say? That I'd been watching humans on Earth, that I'd copied their scientific techniques into a spell and it'd worked? Could I even begin to explain about the nature of photons and fluorescent paint in the context of the shield which had kept me invisible and safe in the hellish kingdom for so long?

'We're waiting, Kite.'

I decided to aim for a quick, unexpected death rather than the long trial which faced me. 'You never were good at this kind of thing, B'rtac. You should have stayed at the bottom of the class in Haven instead of trying to pretend how good you are at nightmares. Your scrying, your warding, your shielding all sucks . . .'

The clawed guards struck again and I spent several minutes curled up wondering if the blindfold was keeping me in darkness or if something major had just been damaged.

When finally I could think in more or less straight lines, hands pulled me back onto my knees and the sneering voice spoke again. 'You think I am not a lord of nightmare? Even when you threw the fire at me and saw me burn you thought I was not a *lord of the dark? You're wrong, Kite. You're wrong about so many things. Remove the blindfold.'*

Light flooded back in, painful and blurred. I blinked several times and raised my head in search of something to focus on. The mage, my tormentor, leant forward and I looked into the face of a monster . . .

The pony stopped abruptly. Hands helped me swing down onto the dry road. I felt slightly woozy and very disoriented. Someone turned me around, and I saw something *through* the blindfold.

It's in these circumstances that it really helps to be a mage. If I were not what I am there is no doubt in my mind that I would have jumped up and down screaming and waving my arms in the air. But no, being hardened to weirdness, all I did was keep on staring without eyes, listening to a buzz that might have been magic without using my ears, and wondering. It seemed to be a person, whether man or woman I couldn't tell – the bright power it gave off made it hard to judge any form beyond the reassuring thought that it was human. Or at least human-shaped.

Someone undid the blindfold. The Void swam into focus, just a few feet away. The cold night had settled and my breath steamed, illuminated by the light of the Void. A guard handed me my pack and staff, and saluted me sharply.

'You have the spirits in you, mage,' prophesied the lead guard.

I hesitated, not really sure what to say in response. I'd never had much truck with nomads and knew nothing of the rituals of this place. I could have dealt with the

Warden of Westpoint easily, thanks to years at court, but these soldiers were a different matter entirely. Also, the more I looked, and cast about with every magely sense at my call, the more I now felt no sign of the burning figure who had stood before my eyes. 'Was . . . someone there?' I asked nervously, waving a hand at where I imagined the creature to have stood.

'No one.' The soldier sounded *very* confident of this, almost proud. 'Not unless you see spirits.'

I stared at his sincere face for a long while. Sincerity, I often find, is more unsettling than doubt. There was an awkward silence, in which the soldier's beam only seemed to widen.

'Dreams go with you,' I finally mumbled.

'Farewell, Laenan Kite.'

I stepped out into the Void and onto the road to Skypoint. It was only about ten minutes later when I stopped dead and looked over my shoulder. The Void filled my view all around, like a brightly coloured fog.

Never, at any point, had I told the man my name.

Skypoint leapt out of the Void at me so suddenly I swear I jumped for at least a foot. No matter how often you travel these roads, kingdoms always have a habit of appearing from nowhere and it scares me stiff. I hung around for a few nervous minutes at the edge of the kingdom, just so any over-zealous guards could see I wasn't an assault party, before stepping inside the purple shimmering shield that defined the start of one reality or another.

Skypoint is an amazing place to visit, unlike Westpoint in every respect. I recommend it, dear dreamer, if you ever find yourself wanting a break from the slog and routine of worried dreams and vague memories of some road leading from one dull place to another.

The single stone block I stepped onto was about ten square feet, and supported by nothing. Down, say, a mile, was a vast blue sea, dazzling me as it reflected the sunlight. Up, say, another mile, were circling dragons, wyverns, flying horses. The soldiers of Skypoint. And ahead . . .

Towers rose from the sea, miles high, thin and white, all built of the same stone, each with landing platforms at every opportunity so that the effect was that of a very spiky stone stick. They weren't connected, but each was at least a hundred floors tall. As I watched the nearest, a woman stepped onto a landing platform from her room, hefted a pair of wings and leapt without even a thought. Soon she was lost amid a whirling mass of fliers. As they went about their business they were mingled with dreamers of every shape and kind, riding the thermals which gusted melodiously up from the sea.

Skypoint was the dream of flying. In my opinion, it's the most glorious dream to which anyone can find their way, maybe with the honourable exception of Stormpoint. Why at least one person hadn't found their paradise here I don't know. Dreamers who in other places were insubstantial here took on a life of their own and existed inside the clouds to the constant tune of uncontrolled laughter and mirth.

Sad that their memories should fade so soon on awakening, that they shouldn't remember the happy times we gave.

'Declare yourself!'

I looked up carefully, squinting against the bright sky. Two winged men in the light blue uniform of Skypoint were hovering several feet above me. Two rifles pointed neatly at my heart. These guards were different from those of Westpoint. They had just been told to stay in this place and make sure everyone got a good yelling at, and then they could go home and clean their boots or whatever it was they did in the evenings.

If it had been Stormpoint I could have just banished them with a thought. But someone else held the Key here. Someone else decided. Fortunately I knew who.

'Laenan Kite, Warden of Stormpoint, to see the Lord Windsight!' I yelled.

There was only a second's hesitation as this information was relayed to Windsight, no doubt lounging in some tower somewhere and watching me with half a sceptical eye, before the guards responded.

'Welcome, Warden Kite. From your name we assume you can fly?' There was a chuckle from the guards that set my teeth on edge.

'Give me a pair of wings and I will fly like you have never seen,' I replied haughtily.

Windsight would have nodded and left it at that. He knew me too well to doubt that I hadn't come across a few dreams of flying in my time. But the guards weren't as bright as I would have thought of the old lord's creations. Rather than get a dragon to give me a ride, as was the custom with most VIPs such as I, they judged the book by its cover and decided that this plain little man was capable of no such feat.

They threw me a set of glider wings. Very well, if that's how you like to play it . . .

I strapped myself in easily, walked with only a little staggering to the edge of the platform, firmly resolved not to look down, and looked down. Fortunately I'd already jumped by this time, which left no room for second thoughts on the matter.

Maybe about a hundred feet down the wings finally did what they were supposed to do and I rocketed back up, everything blurred with speed, into the sky. A pair of dragons busy playing games looked startled as this bullet of mage and wing tore by. The wind was deafening, but it was surprisingly peaceful up in the sky, despite the lurching in my stomach, the racing water which soon became just a white speckled blanket as I followed a beam of sunlight across the sea, the towers that went by at one a second, and the gliders who scattered out of my way with many an obscenity for alleged bad flying. All I had to do was twist occasionally, keeping my eyes focused on dead ahead, and shut out the roar of the wind, the racing water, the passing towers . . .

A wind blew up against me without any warning, and I smiled grimly. Windsight was paying attention, then, if he was ready to try and redeem the honour of his guards. But not for nothing had I been regarded as a strong mage. I wrapped a shield of bright power ahead of me and twisted the air behind me, at once cooling and heating it. The result was a gust of wind so strong and sudden that I doubt Windsight with all the powers of the Skypoint Key behind him could have stopped it.

You see? Science, that's what you Earth people have to offer. That's what I like to use. Just don't tell any other mage, else the great spells of Laenan Kite will lose a lot of credit, okay?

Dreamers laughed to see me race by, and soon I had acquired quite a following of playing minds struggling to run this race and see what it was I was in such a hurry to reach. I could have tried to explain to them that this was nothing compared to the time a demon pushed me off the edge of a cliff with only a spell of air mastery behind me, but they probably wouldn't have heard me. Besides, I like people to believe (foolish though it may be) that I don't like to boast.

I rummaged around the local area, searching out a bright patch of power that might just be the mage I was looking for. Windsight was in the heart of a maze of massive towers, his magic flared up just bright enough to draw my attention. A good sign then – a sign that I was welcome as a friend, even after so long.

I slowed a little as I began to negotiate the towers of Skypoint that led to its lord, but I was still flying fast. Yet someone was beginning to overtake me. I couldn't understand it. In my five hundred years of running, fighting and falling from high places, no one had ever come near to overtaking me. I chanced a glance – always a risky thing at that kind of speed – and saw a single dreamer. She was so close to paradise she was almost solid – more solid than any dreamer I'd ever encountered. She caught my eye for a second before a tower split our path, and her laughter somehow reached my ears over the roar of the wind.

Then Windsight's tower was dead ahead and I was slamming every inch of wind I had at my disposal to slow me down, and raising myself up high in a desperate bid for a steady speed. I don't pretend my landing was graceful – it was more a fall barely postponed.

The grey-haired, square-faced lord of Skypoint caught my arm as I staggered on the landing platform. He helped me out of the faithful wings in a second and to a chair with the simple words, 'You certainly know how to make an entrance.'

I was flattered. Windsight had always outrun me in the sky, and a compliment from him meant a lot. 'Hello, Windsight. Still flying, I take it?' I managed to gasp between breaths.

He grinned and waved vaguely at the expanse of sky that made up his perfect kingdom. 'As if I'd be doing anything else. I'm glad to see retirement hasn't dulled your instinct for the chase either.'

'I'd hardly call daily battles against raiders a retirement,' I said reproachfully.

He laughed heartily — a habit which has always unnerved me. 'You in the old days, Kite, would make that seem like a picnic. Oh, we had some times!'

I winced. Dark cells and cackling nightmares seemed to make up what little I remembered of 'times' in the company of this particular mage. 'I always wanted to spend my days being chased by various fiends, oh yes!' I retorted weakly.

'Where's that fighting Kite spirit?'

'Not Void-proof enough, I'm afraid. Look, Windsight, it's really great to see you, and I appreciate being let into your kingdom without lightning and everything, but the truth is I'm on the way to Haven.'

The cheerful, hearty face darkened slightly. 'Talsin didn't summon you, did he?'

'Sure did.'

'The fool! Doesn't he know . . . well, the court . . .'

'Hates me, yes. Probably that's one of the reasons he's summoned me. Show the court he's so much in charge that he can make such people as Laenan Kite answer his call.'

'Why did you? You could have stayed in Stormpoint and no one would have dared raise a finger against you. Did you go through Westpoint?'

'Of course.'

'And they turned you out?'

'No, as a matter of fact.'

'They've been turning out just about everyone for months. Everybody's afraid, Kite. Why did you come?'

I shrugged. The truth was, I couldn't be sure myself, and had rather hoped the cunning Windsight might have an explanation or two. 'Perhaps retirement is starting to grate a bit. Have you been summoned to the coronation?'

'Of course. And as a humble mage without a record of slaying demon hordes, I must go. You've made incredibly good time, to get here before I leave.'

'I didn't want to miss you.'

His eyes narrowed. 'There's another reason why you're here, isn't there?'

I nodded. 'I couldn't keep anything from you. I needed one or two facts cleared up before I dare go anywhere near Haven.'

'Ask me anything.'

'Okay. The king, that is Talsin's father, fell in battle defending Haven, right?'

'Indeed.'

I let the incredulity show on my face for the first time. 'But how? I don't understand? How is it that I could have turned around to find that Nightkeep has advanced all the way to the gates of Haven and killed a king? Why is Westpoint, which was once the meeting place of man, so afraid? Why do guards challenge wardens at every turn and the Void is so empty of dreamers?'

He sighed patiently. 'You really have been out of touch, haven't you? When did you go to Stormpoint?'

'Shortly after Lisana attempted to get me tried for treason.' Lisana. The name still bought back unpleasant memories. Oh, she had tried every trick to win me over, every seduction had been neatly catalogued A to Z and brought round for my inspection. And when she'd failed to win the mage who suddenly stood by the king's side, she'd tried to bring him down . . .

'That's what? A hundred years ago.'

'Roughly.'

'And you defeated the king of Nightkeep . . . what? A hundred and ten years ago?'

'Single combat in the middle of the Void, you said it.'

'I thought it was with dragons screaming at you from every corner and the hordes of hell rising beneath your feet.'

'Stories always get exaggerated.'

'The king had a son.'

'Most kings do.'

'The name Serein mean anything to you?'

I thought about it. 'Apart from heir to Nightkeep, tall guy, looks a bit like a tiger in black and white, too quiet for anyone's liking, no, I can't say it does.'

'Well, he's a bastard.'

'As in . . .'

Windsight raised his hands defensively. 'Oh, don't get

me wrong. He's perfectly legitimate, and Nightkeep would follow him to the end of the Void and back again. What I meant is that he's a bastard towards Haven. We've already lost maybe fifty kingdoms, and a few weeks ago his troops got right to the edge of Haven itself. They were repulsed, of course, but there are now thousands of nightmares wandering around every road in the Void just looking for another thing to gobble up.'

I let the information sink in. 'So this Serein is a bit good, I take it?'

'You bet. Earth is being dragged more and more into nightmare, and many roads are being blocked too.'

'What Windsight isn't saying,' announced a strange new voice, 'is that without a bright young mage to trek all across nightmare slaying evil kings, Haven is screwed.'

I turned in my chair and craned my neck. The woman bore down on me with easy grace, and offered her hand without a flicker in her serene face. 'Renna.'

I took it, vaguely. 'You're . . . the dreamer I raced.'

'Renna is my prize pupil,' agreed Windsight.

'She is?'

'I am,' she said proudly. 'I've had ten years under the tutorship of Windsight and believe me, I can fly.'

'Ten years?' I squeaked. 'But . . . you're a dreamer!'

'Coma,' explained Windsight.

I looked at her in astonishment. I'd heard of the phenomenon, of course. Of people on Earth who are catapulted into dreams and can never walk the road back to Earth. 'I'm . . . sorry. How did . . .'

'Lorry. I remember screaming brakes, a big metal grill heading towards me, and waking up here.'

'I looked after her,' explained Windsight. 'She still doesn't believe she's not dead.'

'Of course I'm dead,' she retorted. 'And don't try to talk me out of it.'

'I wouldn't dare,' I said, and realised I meant it. There was something in the set of her dark brown eyes and the line of her face.

Windsight stood up in a manner suggesting that I stop staring, and we move on. 'Well, now you're here we can go to Haven together, the three of us.'

'The three of us?'

'You've got a problem?' Renna demanded. 'Then it's settled! Unless you have other places you want to visit?'

I shook my head. 'I think I know what I need to for now, thanks anyway.'

'Excellent!' Windsight said. 'You'll stay the night?'

'I'd be grateful.'

Renna didn't look happy, and Windsight shot her a look. 'Kite is an old friend, Renna, and a bit of a legend. Just because he managed to outfly you doesn't mean he's a bad person.'

'You don't look like a legend.'

I realised she was talking to me. 'Have you ever met one?' My pride had done the unexpected, flaring up at the slap in its usually unseen face.

'Can't say I have. But I have certain expectations. When did you last clean those boots?' She had a point.

Windsight patted me on the arm. 'We think she was a shoe shop assistant. It's the only possible explanation. Come on, I'll see if we can't find you a room.'

He made towards the platform, but I hesitated. 'Windsight?'

'Yes?'

'I don't suppose we could take the stairs, this time?'

One thing I will say for the rooms in Skypoint – they are airy. A pleasant cool breeze blew in from at least four neat little windows dotted at even points around the room. They were various star- and crescent-moon shapes and when I pulled the blinds down over them, golden suns winked at me through the fabric. Even so, light managed to work its way in through every crack, casting a grey glimmer in beams across the room which caught the dust like tiny snowflakes. It was a little cooler than my preferred temperature at Stormpoint, but the breeze that made the blinds swell like sails was a relief after the trudge in sullen Void.

So I lay on the small bed in the middle of the large room, staring at the ceiling (more clouds and suns), and trying to get events back into order. I knew that quite a lot could happen in a mere hundred years, but I hadn't expected it to happen so fast.

Serein was king of Nightkeep. And pretty bloody good at the job, it seemed. Talsin was king of Haven, and trying to be just as good. So . . . he summons me? The two didn't fit. All right, I had accidentally got into a fight against the old lord of nightmares, but it had been whilst we were doing quite well against the dark and I'd only won by use of trickery and deceit being thrown around like bullets from a machine gun. Yes, I know what a machine gun is, too. You think I haven't listened to the dreamers, heard the stories they have to tell?

But now I had other worries than the scratchings of an alternative universe on the world that I inhabited. Did

Talsin want a repeat performance? Did he want me to try and pull the same stunt on Serein as I had on his father? His father had been a little slow, more the big whatcha-looking-at kind of man than any great strategist. Serein didn't sound such a simple prospect.

Then there was Renna. I'd never met anyone in a coma before, and doubted that Renna was her real name. Could she even remember who she was? Oh, Windsight was more damn clever than he appeared. If dreamers could actually remember the dream, or even exist within it, suddenly they became something far more powerful.

They could jump between kingdoms, if they knew how to focus. They could make new universes in a second, just by imagining them, and control the Void around them like a toy, if you taught them how. A dreamer who stayed in dreams long enough, and remembered all you spoke of, could tip the whole balance of war.

But at the same time they were fragile. Everyone knew the mages of Nightkeep drew more power from the fear in their victims, and anyone in a coma would be a rare delight. So Windsight was keeping her safe, holding her back and not revealing her true potential just in case the war between nightmare and dream should knock at the door of his kingdom. Then, she might prove the most important asset he had.

Which left one last, worrying conclusion. If Windsight was taking her with him to Haven, it meant the situation was now so bad he was willing to offer his greatest weapon in the cause of dreaming. It was something the sly lord of Skypoint would never do under normal circumstances.

I found it hard to sleep that night.

THREE

City of Dreams

Haven. City of dreams. No, really, that's exactly what it is. It squats at the centre of a spider's web of dream after dream, and for those who dream, it is the only place to begin their journey.

The bubble of reality which makes up Haven is roughly a hundred square miles. Of these, maybe three square miles make up the capital city of dreams. The rest is a bizarre mixture of farmland, lakes, cliffs, etc. It's been estimated that maybe twenty new nomad races pass through Haven every year, feeding off the land which never runs dry and drinking in the rivers which can carry no ill.

As a result, Haven is extremely busy.

'Void-clothes, sir! Capable of withstanding the pressures of reality at a very reasonable price, sir!'

'Fresh fruit, all the way from Hillpoint, get your fresh fruit here!'

'Divine water from Healpoint, a cure for all diseases, sir!'

'Dreamers – real or not? Come to the lecture at the University!'

'You look nervous.'

I jumped at Windsight's words, despite all my efforts not to. Truth is, I was on edge. I kept on watching the rooftops for dark shadows, kept on checking and re-checking my shielding just to make sure I hadn't left out some vital layer of wards. Haven may be the city of dreams, but even dreams can turn nasty.

I guess you're wondering. But why, Kite, why are there all these traders? Are they real people, dreamers or just produced from the imagination of the guy who rules this place? Now and again kings have been known to invent their own traders selling false goods, just to make the place look busy, but a lot of the traders who come to Haven are real people. Just not mages. You're not a mage, you can't rule a kingdom. You can't rule a kingdom, you have to ask if you want to stay in someone else's kingdom, and keep your nose clean. You stay in another's kingdom, you've got to do them the odd favour.

Hence, traders.

But what about dreamers, I hear the strangled cry? Sorry guys, dreamers are never in the kingdoms long enough – the longest you see any dreamer for is ten or so hours – to set up shop. So, you wanna job? You gotta stick to your own dull little planet.

It's hard to describe the actual appearance of Haven. The place changes too much. A pub on some back street which was the King's Head when you went in, some fine summer's evening, will be the Queen's Arms by the time you come out, and the back street will be some white square gleaming with winter frost.

We'd arrived in winter. A nice, crisp winter that turned the high roofs of Haven to a picture of black and white and filled the air with the cries of children building snowmen on every corner. The king of all those bright clear winters we always hungered for that makes you think it is winter, and will always be so. The red tiles on the roofs of the guilds were thick with snow, the sigh squeaked faintly in the cold winter breeze above the tanner's just round the corner from a fountain that was pouring golden light into the square. Carts bounced across the cobbles and windows were grey with condensation. Lanterns hung at every street corner, casting a pleasant glow on the dreamers as they got into yet another snow fight with children from the high-walled, grey-stoned school whose brass bell in the topmost tower had just stopped swinging.

The guards even gave us woollen cloaks at the gates to keep us warm. 'Compliments of the council,' they said. I took one look at them saw that they were part of Haven and not Void-proof, and tactfully declined. I wasn't about to wear anything on my back that might change to a snake.

So we walked down snow-covered streets, our breath condensing into little clouds that caught the bright sunlight and sparkled as we plodded on. Our hands were chilled and numb, but in every square a mage-fire burned and the happy citizens gathered round it, warming their hands and greeting each other with the smiles that everyone in the city always wore.

It unnerved me. Upset me, even. Talsin could already control the mood of a city, and had worked the weather so that, while cold and damp, it was beautiful enough for the whole city to unite behind him. He'd won the crowd already, and the winter city glowed with its own life.

Thousands of people bustled from street to street, talking merrily, always ready to meet the next man's eye and give a smile. Jugglers and fire-eaters had gathered in some squares despite the cold, and a frost dragon was taking the children for rides. Even through my walls of bitter memory, cynical detachment and sour regret, I felt some of that joy touch me, and a corner returned of the love I once had for this heaving town.

Why does Haven alone support so many people not just of our world but from some other? Why does your kingdom not do the same, Laenan Kite? Because I am on the outer edges of the web. Because I can be invaded by nightmare at any time. Haven wields those outer kingdoms like a shield, protected by depth. It can afford so many thousand souls, so many signatures of life confusing every scryer who listens for a signal given out by any one. But I must have only a few lives in my land, and many of those must be of my design, creatures of my own imagination.

That way I can find the attacker, find the smear of darkness before it can find me. In Haven there are too many souls for any man to find just one.

Unless that one man was looking before the soul arrived.

So it was that, the moment I stepped out of the Void into Haven, I felt him seeking. I could feel the magical touch, just on the edge of my sense, running along my shielding, probing deeper in a vain attempt to establish if I was who I seemed to be. I repulsed it with an easy mental shove, and focused on the long cobbled streets before me, trying not let my worry show.

There was the pub where many a wandering dreamer and I had downed pint after pint and talked of Earth. There was the market where a dreaming technician had told me the principle behind the internal combustion engine, the open green where another dreamer told me of a strange game called football. There was the fountain, its water frozen solid and replaced by magical light which rose hundreds of feet, where a dreamer child had shown me a cat's cradle. There the university, place of long dull lectures and great leaps into new dimensions of magic. There was the guardhouse where I used to hear the gossip of the Void and listen to dreamers telling of their escapes from the nightmare.

Here were dreamers. Swarms of them, delighting in the freedom of Haven, blissfully unaware that in the morning they would wake up in their old beds in their grey and empty world, and remember nothing of the glories we had to offer.

And here? Here was the crossroads between two points in reality. No one has ever been able to walk more than one path before the other reality summons them home. A thousand times I have dreamed of Earth, and had no way of controlling the world around me, just like the dreamers here. The link works both ways. They come here in their sleep, we go there in ours.

But we remember. We are stronger than they are.

'What are you thinking?'

I started to hear Renna's voice. All throughout the journey to Haven she had been unnaturally silent, no doubt remembering when she first journeyed through the Void after the coma. Now we were in Haven, she seemed more settled. Real houses and real people pushed a little warmth back into her tense face.

'I was thinking about dreamers, if you must know.'

'And what conclusions did you reach?'

'That I'm not so sad that I'm me.'

'I should hope not! If I were you I'd be laughing!'

I was genuinely surprised. 'Why?'

'Because of this.' She waved her hand at the city. 'Because you will live for thousands of years in a forever changing paradise. Because you can summon fire, and fly without wings and make plants grow at your feet.'

That was what got me thinking.

'You sure we can't convince you to come with us to the palace?'

I shook my head. The alley where we'd stopped was a few blocks off a square roaring with life, and I kept having to check the sky for eavesdropping dragons. 'Not tonight. There are people I need to see.'

Windsight frowned. 'You think the Silverhand will still be around after all this time?'

Renna frowned. 'What's the Silverhand?'

Windsight and I exchanged glances, casually strengthening our reflective shields which were designed to keep away prying ears. Her eyes narrowed. 'You can't not tell me.'

'I know, I know,' sighed Windsight. 'And I promise that when we get to the palace and I can ward us properly I'll tell you everything.' He gave me a worried glance. 'I can, can't I?'

But would Renna know who else not to tell? As I

caught her eye again, I realised this girl wouldn't blab to anyone, even if red-hot branding irons were involved. 'Sure. Telling seems good.' I shook Windsight's hand gratefully. 'See you at the palace.'

'You coming to the Elemental Ceremonies?'

'Of course.'

I watched them go, waited until their mental signatures had faded to almost nothing, and gently let my shield down.

Talsin's presence rushed in like a storm. He was determined to find me. I held firm, and gently began broadcasting into the heart of that magical presence. <Yes. I'm here, my lord.>

A portal opened up in the wall next to me without a sound, a glimmering black opening into another place. I grinned. <To the palace? No, not yet. Besides, I've been tricked so many times by people with Keys I don't like to walk up blind alleys. No offence. I'll come the old-fashioned way.>

The portal closed slowly, almost reluctantly. Talsin's ability to twist the very fabric of Haven didn't much bother me. Once I found myself a crowd and began throwing shields around left and right he wouldn't be able to track me, nor know where to bend Haven to his will. However, he was a king, or would be very soon. <I still serve you, my lord,> I sent hastily.

Did I? To tell the truth, I'm not sure. But it seemed the right thing to say at the time.

With that happy thought in mind I turned on my heel, and went in search of the Silverhand Consortium. After so many years I needed to do some serious catching up.

❈

Sometimes I envy your technology, dreamer. We've tried to get it right here too, but nothing seems to work unless you wrap a bit of magic round it, and of course that's cheating. There are times when I long for a radio, which you can set at a particular frequency to send a message to just one man. It saves so much trouble.

I guess I tried at least five taverns before a bar-keeper actually sat up and took notice of the coinage I was offering. Most of the coins, copper and silver alike, bear the head of whoever happens to be ruling at the time, or his granddad, or merely some bloke with a suitably regal face. The coin of the Silverhand bears no such thing. There's just one hand, raised palm out to the user, and on the other side a spider-web. It saddened me to see so many bar-keepers frown at the coin and say, 'I'm sorry sir, that's not accepted currency'. In the old days you just needed to flash a glimpse of it in any respectable tavern and the bar-keeper would fall over himself to get you the contacts you wanted.

The man I eventually found with half a memory was behind a long bar in a long street, cleaning mugs. He spared me only a glance, taking in the traveller's clothes, the plain staff and fairly young face (though I was feeling anything but young by then, believe me), and quickly lost interest.

There was something familiar though about his grizzled and bearded face. I searched my memory for a long while, trying to find a name, then pinpointed it, and leant on the bar as casually as I could.

'What's your pleasure, sir?'

'Just water and something to eat, please, Virisin.'

He looked disdainful that I'd come to him for water,

but after five pubs'-worth of ordering beers in search of recognition, I didn't want to risk any more of my mind.

'You new here?'

'I've passed through before.'

He handed me a jug.

'What's it come to, Virisin?'

The fool still didn't catch on. 'Two coppers.'

'Daylight robbery,' I declared. 'I remember a time when Virisin charged that for a pint of ale.'

Finally I saw a flicker in his eyes, a sign of surprise. 'Do I know you?'

'There's a theory, on Earth that is, that everyone is just six people away from knowing everybody else.' I pushed the silver onto the table. 'I suspect the figures would be somewhat different in the real world, but who am I to judge?'

His eyes darted over the coin, saw the hand, and went back to me. And now he knew who I was. For just a second his expression twisted into one of dumb surprise, before professionalism put on the stern bar-keeper look that guided drunks to the door in the small hours of the morning and revealed nothing to anyone.

'I can't accept that coin, sir,' he said sternly. 'Look – it's so old! Come into the back and we'll see if my log books have anything remotely like it for exchange.'

I rose eagerly, aware of the eyes on me and wanting to get away from their stares. Virisin led the way into a small backroom of rough stone walls and barrels of beer, waited until the door was closed and turned to me with a smile.

'I never thought we'd see your face again, Laenan Kite.'

'I know. You missed me. Can't be helped.'

'Missed you? Do you know what's happened while you've been gone? That bastard Jehirer has driven the Consortium into dust! He can't run his own home, let alone us!'

'I noticed how hard it was to make contact. There was a time when every shopkeeper in Haven knew someone who knew someone who knew a Silverhand. I nearly risked a mage-sign after the first three, but the bloody palace has been scrying for me ever since I walked through the gate. What happened to Terime? I gave explicit instructions that he was to take over after I left!'

Virisin shook his head. 'Wandered into one nightmare too many. That was always the problem with Terime – he had to go for the personal touch.'

'And Jehirer took over? What about the elemental network? Surely he hasn't been able to damage that?'

'No, no. The elementals are still in contact. But the web is wearing thin.' He laughed suddenly, relief in his broad face. 'We all wanted you to come back, you know. You're the only guy who really managed to keep things moving. Are you going to take over again?'

'I'm only here for the coronation. After that, I'm gone.'

'Why?'

'A little thing called a kingdom. Believe me, it's nearly as hard to run as a network of spies.'

A network of spies. Well, there you have the crux of it. The Silverhand Consortium is the largest web of mages and non-mages in the universe, always moving through the Void, keeping their leaders informed, looking out for each other, and most important of all, finding out and solving all those little internal problems.

'Why are you looking for them?' Virisin asked as I stepped through his door and back into the street again. It was his parting question, and obviously one that had been on his mind all through our conversation.

'Because . . . because I feel I ought to know. And that's a reason I wouldn't give to anyone.'

'What *is* the reason you'd give to anyone?' he asked with a smile.

'That they know things. They can tell me things. They can see things that no one else sees. That at least is what I tell myself. Truth to tell, I think I just want to be sure.'

'Of what? That the Consortium's well, or that Haven's well?'

'Both.'

That's the trouble with Haven. It thinks that since it's a city of dreams, nothing inside its walls can go wrong. That's crap. You've had dreams, you know how suddenly they can change, how a bright day can become dull night in the blink of an eye. If a weak mage takes a weak kingdom, the Silverhand Consortium is not above slipping a little aid inside his borders and boosting the magic ratings. And if a nightmare takes a kingdom and needs backup? Well, let's say that we're not squeamish about dressing up in the odd black robe, chanting about demons and blood, and setting light to his palace in the process.

So where do I come in? At the centre, to tell the truth. I didn't found the whole thing, of course. But I was the mage who made the elemental network. A web of magical beings from all four spheres of power, who can withstand the Void. That's the interesting thing. Just as clothes and weapons are made in the Void to withstand the Void, so I made life. Fire spirits, will o'wisps, water elementals, earth giants – they all came alive in the Void, and were all nice and co-operative when I said, 'Hi, how'd you like a part-time job in spying?' All loyal and kind, all compassionate and understanding, just like I'd made them to be. They were my greatest success, the great triumph of magic. But like everyone else I'd ever managed to throw together out of spare dreams, they all had minds of their own. So I was pleased indeed when ninety-nine per cent of them took one look at the package on offer, and said yes. The remaining one percent took off by themselves, and are probably working like mad in their various elemental homes.

Many mages have tried to copy, bribe or even black-mail me to find out the spell which can make an ordered being out of nothing. So far they've failed, for reasons something like these:

Copying, trying to make living beings of magic instead of mundane creations out of the Void, has resulted to date in more than a few mortalities. Bribing has come bloody near to working, believe me, but I have yet to find an offer which I think worthy of me. Blackmailing has always been sorted out by the Consortium. They were so pleased to have a network of creatures who could enter kingdoms undetected, make accurate and concise reports and fly home in time for tea, that they'd do anything for the young mage who'd done them such a favour.

That was how I leaped my way up the greasy pole, and sat at the top for several hundred years, in the centre of the largest secret police you'll ever find.

We're the ones who watch God, and ask if he deserves the power he holds. The power behind the throne of all good kings, the power in front of all the bad ones.

But if a man like Jehirer gets in charge, it raises the big question you dreamers have worried over for thousands of years.

Who will guard the guardians?

There's only one answer to that.

I met Virisin's concerned eyes. 'You want me to go up to Jehirer, and tell him to piss off?' I groaned.

Who guards the guardians? Muggins, that's who.

So began my stay in Haven.

FOUR

Silverhands

The hall was in uproar. Silverpoint is such a small kingdom, it's usually missed by most people, who go round it. It lies only a few realms off Haven. But, like Stormpoint, it's refused to have any roads run through it, thus reducing its political power to microscopic levels.

The mage who runs this place is of course brave, noble and wise, and elected by a council of Consortium members to be the owner of that small land's Key. And in that place, so small that all armies take one look and decide it's simply not worth conquering, the Consortium meets.

Members of every shape and size who'd heard the call were now pouring in, talking heatedly with their neighbours and comparing stories of their exploits in far-flung kingdoms. I'd been forced to wait three days for this meeting, and knew that it would have to be the first and last for a long time. Soon the palace would start asking,

'Where's Kite?' and I'd have to go and bow and scrape for a least a few weeks.

Which meant I'd have to get this thing done with now.

A bell pealed over the busy hall. Positioned amid a shoving crowd of spies, from the front of a balcony I had a prime view of the floor below. And I saw Jehirer.

Most people age faster in his job than at anything else – it's surprisingly hard to manage. But Jehirer looked younger. More powerful, too. That worried me.

The padded chair, just one step from a throne, also gave me a touch of concern, as did the red robes he bore with such aplomb. Most former leaders would have been grateful if they got a table to lean on. Also, though the Silverhand Consortium keenly encourages its members to be self-sufficient, I couldn't see Jehirer sewing that robe by hand.

I heard whispering nearby. A group of water elementals – beautiful blue-skinned ladies whose garments glinted through shades of green and purple as they moved – were pointing at me. Some fire elementals, wrapped in sizzling flame, were also muttering and pointing. As my creations, it was hardly surprising that they should recognise me. I was just grateful no one else could. I winked, and turned back to the hall, where Jehirer had sat down with all the self-possession of a king.

'The Consortium is assembled, let the meeting begin,' he declared formally. 'For what are we gathered?'

The usual reports were read out. A lord of some outer kingdom was planning a treaty with Nightkeep. A monarch of some other kingdom had attempted to catch a dreamer and assault her. A mage in some other kingdom was receiving assassination warnings. A nomad tribe from somewhere in the Void had come to this kingdom requesting sanctuary. What action should be taken? . . . What action? . . . What action?

Jehirer listened carefully to every one, and nodded to each speaker. Then he turned back to the first man who had spoken.

'Kill him.'

Before, if I'd said something like that, the hall would have erupted into uproar. The Silverhand Consortium does not kill! I wanted to scream. It violated everything we, as subjects of Haven and thus dreams, stood for.

But instead, there was just a faint murmur, and no one raised their voice in complaint. I glanced towards Virisin, who shook his head. A soft voice by my ear murmured, 'They say he killed Terime. No one stands up to him, sir. Not any more.'

I recognised the air elemental's tone, struggled to find a name, found one. 'It's all right, R'niss. I know.' I turned to the floor, took a deep breath, and stood up.

'I don't think we should kill anyone, sir.'

Jehirer looked up, eyes narrowing in annoyance. 'You question me?'

'That is the purpose of the meeting.'

'Not as far as I am aware.'

'Then I advise that you study your texts more closely. They clearly state that the leader of the Consortium may be questioned, denied, or even deposed if it is felt that he is taking wrong action.'

<He controls the mage of Silverpoint, sir. Chose him, commands him. Beware, sir,> whispered the elemental's voice in my mind.

<Gather your brothers and sisters. Tell them to get as close as possible to the mage nearest Jehirer. Anything starts to change, hit him.>

<We obey, sir.>

God, I love those creatures.

'Are you threatening me?'

'Of course not. I am simply attempting to resolve a few failings in your general knowledge.'

A man standing next to Jehirer leant forward with sudden eagerness, and whispered in his ear. The leader of the Silverhand looked up slowly, a frown on his face. 'My mage informs me that you possess a Key. No Silverhand may rule a kingdom without prior consultation.'

'Unless that Silverhand is a mage and actively involved in the infiltration of Haven. In seeing that those fools at court don't destroy us all. In *doing something useful* rather than sitting on an expanding backside.' Like him, I was quoting from the book – more or less. I added, 'I qualify well enough in that sense.'

Someone in the audience pointed at me, and I felt a change in the mood. Clearly an old employee had just worked out why this strange agent was nonetheless somehow familiar.

I admit that what I did then was a little flashy, but it had to be done. I stepped forward briskly, onto the edge of the balcony and into the air. There was a general *'ooooh'* as I drifted into the crowd below, my fall controlled by more magic than I usually like to expend. Show-off spells like that require too much energy to be safely used in battle, but if it's just a little audience-impressing you're after, you can loll on the magic thermals all you like.

However, by the time my feet touched the floor I wasn't feeling the least like God. Jehirer was glowering at me, though I knew I'd shaken him by my easy show of air mastery. 'Was there any point to that display?'

'The point is that you're a corrupt bastard and I have the power to stay alive long enough to prove it.' I pulled myself onto the platform and turned to face the audience. 'Let's see what a hundred years have done for your memories. Who made the elementals' network?'

The cry was taken up by only a few older agents, but they said it with a passion and conviction that carried across the room. 'Kite!'

'Who prevented the Seven-Kingdom revolt?'

'Kite!' More voices now, as more memories clicked.

'Who introduced the canteen in the lower halls?'

'Kite!'

'Whose soup gave everyone food poisoning for a week?'

'Kite!' I doubt there wasn't a single voice which didn't yell out.

'Who's standing on stage now, saying that you,' I pointed a dramatic finger at Jehirer, 'are no good at the job?'

The cry shook the ceiling and echoed across the hall, growing in strength as the chant rose to a fevered pitch. I was grateful – for several terrifying moments I thought they wouldn't actually recognise me and just shuffle their feet and go 'erm . . .'

'Kite! Kite! Kite! Kite!'

I turned to Jehirer with an easy smile. 'I call for a vote of no confidence in Jehirer. To be held as soon as every-one's calmed down and can think clearly. You,' I told him, 'have the right, as it is written, to one speech defending your rule, as do I.'

The mage standing next to the livid Silverhand raised his hands suddenly in a gesture of magic. There was a roar from a throng of elementals. An air elemental, sweeping out of nowhere, rammed into him. An earth elemental rose through the floor, wrapping his arms round the man's legs. A water elemental held his nose and mouth in her liquid grasp until he slid to the floor, unconscious and gasping hoarsely for breath.

I turned back to Jehirer. His eyes burned. 'You have no right!' he spat.

'I have every right.'

'You think you can come back here and take your old job? After a hundred years?'

'I don't want my old job.'

The yelling died away abruptly. I turned to the rows of staring faces. 'No. I can't face returning to that life. Always on the go, always having to think my way round and round plot after plot. Let someone else have a turn. I am done.'

The hall muttered its reluctant agreement. I raised a warning finger. 'Someone who I get to meet first, just in case.'

As one man, the Silverhand Consortium erupted into applause, and I knew in that long minute of uproar that I was home.

This is the happy part of every story. The part where you walk through familiar corridors and hear familiar voices yell out your name with genuine delight in every tone. Where you sit down with people you never thought

you'd see again and catch up on a hundred years' worth
of gossip. Where you see something which once you
loved, cherished and nurtured, fall, then pick itself up
with a smile.

'But why won't you be leader?' Virisin demanded.
'Everyone would vote for you.'

'I can't. There are too many problems, too many trials
and troubles.'

'Nightkeep?'

I nodded grimly. 'Serein. God knows what he's up to,
but I don't dare turn away from him now.'

'We might be able to find out what he's up to. You
know we've got infiltrators everywhere.'

'I know. And I'm grateful that you offer. But I can't be
leader.'

Virisin knew better than to argue.

And then there were the elementals. I'd no idea they
could be so pleased to see me. They kept on calling me
'Father', which in a way I was.

I spent that night at Silverpoint, in my bed in my old
room, and dreamed.

*I opened my eyes in a white room, brightly lit. A nurse walked
through me, obviously in a hurry. Nurses equalled hospital. Or
something medical at least. I hadn't dreamt of many hospitals in
my time, I admit — it's a strange mind that sends itself to such
places. Still, since I happened to be there, I decided to take a look
around. See if there was anything scientific I might use.*

*Hospitals are dull, I soon discovered. My ideal dream is to
wake up in one of your university things. Then I can have a few
blissful hours sitting in a big hall with all your young men and
women, listening to a guy talking about technical stuff. I love to*

learn, especially about things which you take for granted and which I might find handy later on. So your teacher people are very useful, and I often wish they'd come visit Stormpoint more often. But why some of them talk about maths, I don't know, and half the time I don't understand them anyway. What are formulas, for one thing? Why is it 'm' over 'a'? What's 'm'? What's 'a'? Why does one go over the other and not the other way round? But you young dreamers just nod and sigh and eventually get up to ask questions like 'If "v" wasn't an integer variable, would "z" have to be divided by the square?' Or words to that effect.

Now, hospitals may be dull, but at least I can understand them. I've even used some of your techniques myself. The hypodermic needle, for one thing. Sterilisation. Defibrillation. All useful, practical stuff.

But this hospital not only had nothing interesting to learn, there were no busy people to look at! Just the occasional nurse moving between long lines of beds.

Since I had nothing better to do, I wandered over to the nearest bed, and looked at the label on a wrist. Mr Thomas Oakly. At the bottom of the bed was a chart which let down my usual image of charts, which are supposed to be zigzagging lines steadily going up. This was just a near-straight line.

I looked at the next bed. Mrs Sophie Peterson. Another near-straight line. The nurse passed back through me again, damn the woman. She reached the end of the long room, sighed, and went out.

Well, I thought, this is going to be just the best dream I've had in a long time. It certainly wasn't as interesting as the one with the president getting shot a few years ago. The gunman kept on walking through me in that, too. Nor was it as much fun as the time a woman with second sight kept on telling me I was the spirit of her ancestors. Did I really look like her Dad?

Since it seemed like a long night in store and I didn't sense any readiness to wake up, I drifted along the line of beds. A man was snoring in a chair. Now he does look a little like me, I thought proudly.

In fact, he looked bloody well just like me. And I'm not kidding. He had the same blue eyes, the dark hair, the same ordinary nose, chin, face . . . All that was between us was maybe a bit of grey in the hair and the odd extra line around the eyes.

I don't know how long I stood there in shocked silence, watching his chest slowly rise and fall as he twitched in the chair. One hand was dangling over the edge, clutching the hand of a woman with the same dead-straight chart, the same blank expression, the same steady breaths and unmoving eyes.

Numbly, not sure why, I looked at the tag on her wrist. Mrs Jane Kiteler.

I looked back at her face, and saw Renna sleeping before me. Then she opened her eyes, and stared straight at me. I backed away in horrified silence. The woman was staring straight at me with unseeing eyes. But I knew she was studying every line in my face. Fear gripped my heart, seized it tightly. I couldn't breathe. My legs wouldn't move. I couldn't feel them. The lorry bore down on me as in a dream, the horn a mournful scream through the sky, the face of the driver pale and gaunt in the windscreen, staring straight at me, yelling something, trying to slam the brakes on harder . . .

'Kite. Kite, wake up.'

I groaned, and pulled the pillow over my head. 'Go away, Virisin.'

'Kite, Jehirer's gone. The guards saw him leave about an hour ago.'

I sat bolt upright, suddenly aware of the real world

once again. The night gave a sigh, aware that the party was over, and slipped into the back of my mind. 'Gone? And they just let him walk out like that?'

'They couldn't stop him. The elementals are out looking now, but we thought you ought to be informed.'

'How did an idiot like Jehirer get into the Consortium?' I muttered, staggering upright. 'We got any idea where he's gone?'

'Somewhere towards Nightkeep. Probably through Waterpoint. We've alerted all our agents on every road we can, but he's got a good head-start.'

'Waterpoint. That's . . . Lisana's domain, isn't it?'

'Yes.'

'This day just gets better and better,' I muttered. 'He took a horse?'

'And let the rest out of the stable.'

'Dammit! Okay, we have a problem.'

And what are you going to do about it?

I'm going to . . . to use my fine magical skills to solve it, that's what. 'Where's R'niss? I need a hand with this one.'

Okay, so I exaggerated when I said how wonderful my elementals are. Sure, they're brilliant in the Void. Sure, they're the only creatures in the universe who can enter kingdoms undetected and without following a road. Sure, they're great company, and really smart when it comes to figuring things out in a hurry.

But they draw their power from the raw possibility in which they were forged. Take them into an ordered place like a kingdom for too long, and that possibility becomes less and less likely, making them even weaker. That's why Silverpoint's meetings traditionally have five-minute breaks every ten minutes – it's not just that we're incredibly lazy, honest.

For spies, who are in and out like a fiddler's elbow, that draining of reality is no problem. But elementals would make a crap army – all the enemy would need to do is lead them round and round in circles until they're as substantial as mist. And as an occupying force – never!

However, if you want someone to get you through the Void from A to B really fast, there is no one quite like an air elemental.

I'm generally against maps with movable symbols and the like – flags on sticks manoeuvring together usually mean people are going to get killed. But I discovered in the Consortium that having even a vague map was useful, and little flags could be more helpful than they first appeared.

So I unrolled a map of the universe (not to scale, obviously). It looked like two spider's webs, dotted with water droplets between huge crossroads and joined to each other by more roads than I was prepared to count.

Jehirer had been sensible enough to keep the map up to date. Black dots indicated nightmare, spanning all the first web and a worrying amount of the second. Red dots indicated dreaming kingdoms where dissent was brewing or some great plot was about to be hatched or something needed to be watched. (I was insulted to find Stormpoint in red too.)

Blue was the colour of kingdoms still totally loyal to dreams. There were worryingly few.

Then there were the flags. Green for earth, red for fire and so on in the elemental series, all dotted along roads.

Brown for real people, all inside kingdoms in groups of three or four. Yellow for mages, every crossroad or so and one or two inside the red kingdoms.

I remember a time when the map was packed with flags. Now there were very few indeed. I found Silverpoint, and traced the nearest route to nightmare. It wasn't very far.

Two elementals, earth and fire, were on the road. I met R'niss's eye. 'Do they know about Jehirer?'

She shook her head. 'The messengers headed towards Haven and dreams first. We didn't expect him to head into nightmare.'

'You're slipping. Always expect the worst in this job, and then be delighted when it doesn't happen.'

'That's cynical,' said a Silverhand, also watching the map. I gave him a sharp look. Young – probably no more than two hundred or so – he was nevertheless eyeing the map like a general about to command his troops. You command me, young man, and I'll be . . . surprised. Impressed, but very surprised.

'Cynical but accurate.'

'I'll keep it in mind. You realise that of course Jehirer will never go that way.'

'I thought he might go through Waterpoint,' I agreed. 'But then, that's because I know him, and other gits who think like him and who might lend him a hand in exchange for info.'

'Waterpoint is likely,' agreed the young man. 'Especially since the road is relatively empty. Jehirer must have looked at the map before he left. He's no fool.'

'Does he think he can out-run an elemental?' I asked incredulously.

'He has a head start, knowledge of the road and a hundred years in the Consortium to help him.'

I glanced at R'niss. <Who is this kid?>

<Some newish Silverhand, that's all I know. You'd better decide what to do soon, I need to get back into the Void. Reality is really starting to wear me down.>

<I'm sorry. Just hang on a few more minutes.> 'What do you think we should do?' I asked calmly.

The young Silverhand drummed his fingers for several seconds, then pointed. 'You've got a water elemental positioned here. Move her through Waterpoint onto the road between him and nightmare. She'll slow him, if not stop him entirely. The delay caused by that should give you enough time to bring the air elementals up from behind, and take him home.'

I studied the map. The man was right, there could be no other solution. 'R'niss?'

She shrugged. 'No one can beat an air elemental,' she agreed, and headed for the door. It drifted shut in a breeze behind her, and the massed ranks of air elementals rose, into the Void.

I turned to the young man, who was watching me with a steady eye. 'I don't believe we've met. Laenan Kite,' I said, offering my hand.

'T'omar.'

T'omar, T'omar . . . I searched my memory, but hit on nothing. 'You must be new.'

'About seventy years in the Consortium, yes. I was a general of Mountpoint, before it was taken over by nightmare.'

That went a long way to explaining things. 'I see. And you decided the spying game might be more to your taste?'

'You decided a hiding game might be more to your taste,' he replied easily.

I blushed. 'Sorry. I didn't mean it like that.'

'Good. To tell the truth,' he continued, as if nothing had happened, 'I was fascinated by the Consortium, when I first heard of it. You guys were the ones who got me and my men out of Mountpoint, you know. We were due to be executed, when, "bang", the doors are open, there's a fire raging in the castle, the Key holder is mortally wounded by an assassin no one can catch and air elementals are bombarding the place from above. I was very impressed at the time. A shame you guys couldn't come along before most of my men were wiped out, that's all.'

I remembered the operation clearly. I'd been the one who'd planned it after all, and the Key holder's mortal wound was one of my proudest achievements. But still, the man made guilt stir in me like fire. If we'd got there sooner … 'We only got news of the attack after it came. I was in Haven, people were watching me every second of the day. It was hard to get any contact with the Consortium at that time, and very hard to get news and arrange for operations to be carried out.'

'At the decline of your power, yes.' God, the man didn't know how to soften things, did he? Every word was a punch in my face. 'How long do you think it'll take them to catch Jehirer?'

There it was again, that sudden change from one place to another, without a second of hesitation. This man could think his way from past to future, and back, without ever losing his train of thought. I shrugged, not sure what to say. 'If all goes well, they should be back here in a few hours.'

'And in a few hours you're leaving for Haven. I admire you, I must say. It probably isn't the safest place for you.'

'Nowhere seems safe these days.'

'True. Dreams are falling apart everywhere.'

Mrs Jane Kiteler. And the man sitting next to her who couldn't be me but at the same time was. 'Oh yes,' I agreed softly, trying to force the image from my mind. 'Dreams are getting very weird.'

I tell you, by the time the elementals did get back with a furious Jehirer in their arms, I was nearly frantic. Haven would be expecting me, I'd be missed, what would I tell Windsight . . .

'You bastard,' spat Jehirer.

'Silverhand Jehirer,' I said emotionlessly, 'it is my duty to inform you that a vote of no confidence has been passed against you. You are now stripped of your rank, and must answer to a court of law.'

'Your false court! I am the power of the Consortium! I am the one who will make us great! You just want power for yourself!'

'Sir, you are getting nowhere by this.'

'No, sir, you are getting nowhere! *He* has vowed revenge, you cannot go unpunished for your crimes!'

Unpunished? 'What do you mean?' It's not the kind of question a determined interrogator ought to ask, but in the back of my head little alarm bells were sounding.

'You can't move fast enough. You travel at the speed of magic, they move at the speed of thought! The worlds are too close to break away now!'

It sounded like the ranting of a madman, but a madman who was too near to reality for my taste.

'What worlds? What do you mean?'

'They'll be dragged down with us, darkness here will bring darkness there, you can't stop him now . . .'

Every alarm on the sixth sense was blaring now. A water elemental standing by my shoulder was looking pale, her face twisted into a mask of something near sympathy. I felt the movement, before it actually happened, and lunged forward. 'Poison!'

Not poison . . . 'Get a doctor! Someone's got a breakage ward inside him!' I yelled. Grabbing the staggering man, I slammed the full force of my magic in the face of a wave of destructive power that centred on a single shining ward, designed to break when a certain point was reached.

'Who did this?' I demanded, as the scene erupted into confusion and Jehirer turned into a dead weight in my arms.

His eyes blearily met mine, then slid past, to where a pair of elementals stood in shocked silence, unable to move. He smiled, mind slipping to a place where I didn't dare follow, and whispered, 'She travels at the speed of thought. She proves . . .'

'She proves what? Who is she? Tell me!'

'Proves . . . that the worlds . . . are too close . . . for the first time . . .' I felt the life slip out of him, and let go. Jehirer hit the floor with the faintest thump, and lay there. The first corpse in what I felt was going to be a long line of blood.

A pair of elementals stepped forward without a word, and picked up the body. 'We will take him to the Void,' one whispered.

'That shouldn't have happened,' I muttered, feeling

dread creep through my veins. Damn. Damn and damn again. Now you're going to get messed up in more than you can cope with . . .

I looked up, to where the Void shone outside the bubble of reality. It was as red as blood, and clung to the elementals as they passed into it. First blood had been drawn, and it was murder. Not politics, not elaborate plots coming to fruition, but murder.

The Void had felt things that I couldn't, and was readying for war.

FIVE

Readying for War

'What have you got?'

T'omar slammed the book shut. 'Nothing. At least, nothing too helpful.'

'Even slightly helpful?'

'Well . . .' He looked uncomfortable. 'I looked up everything to do with the Void turning crimson . . .'

'Blood red, yes,' I snapped, nerves on edge.

'It's not good, according to this author.'

'Tell me.'

'Portent of destruction, wars, the usual things. But something also ties in with what Jehirer was saying. Blood red is generally thought of as an emanation from Earth. When reality changes to that colour, it's because Earth is changing towards wars and blood, and the closeness of our universe is kind of . . . running over into each other. Whatever happens there, affects what happens here. Things have to balance.'

'Thank you,' I lied. 'You've been most helpful.'

We were saved further portents of doom by the library door opening, and a Silverhand poking his head in. 'Excuse me, sirs. But the votes are being cast for a new leader.'

So soon. The last one is hardly cold, and already we're moving on. The past is nothing, the future is every-thing . . . The morbid part of my mind was having a field-day, I decided. The rest of me didn't feel cheerful enough to prevent it.

The hush in the hall was stifling. The three candidates and their nominees wound to the end of their inter-minable speeches, and I felt my heart sink. None was exactly the passionate leader of inspired wisdom I was looking for. By the frowns in the hall, the ranks of Silverhands didn't think so either. Several were giving me those looks which suggested they know that Mister Kite is going to do something remarkable. It wasn't a pleasant feeling. Everyone expects a legend to have some great scheme up his sleeve, instead of being just another footnote in the back of the hall.

On the other hand, what could I do? In a few hours I'd be on the road to Haven, where a host of other prob-lems would be stewing in their own heat.

'Nominations are about to close. Are any more to be made?' asked the prim spy on the stage. I twiddled my thumbs, and decided to drop the bombshell. What did I have to lose? I'd already insulted the king-to-be, killed a man (albeit accidentally) who knew a lot more than I did, and seen the Void turn blood red. The guy had come out well when I'd slipped one or two probes inside his head to have a quick gander at the general colour of his soul. I stood up. The hall let out a sigh of relief – they'd all been waiting for me to do that.

'I would like to make a nomination.'

The brightest of them caught on immediately. The rest of the hall waited impatiently for me to volunteer my services as mage and old-time leader.

'I'd like to nominate T'omar.'

A surprised murmur ran through the hall. My eyes wandered over to where T'omar was openly gaping. Aha, I thought, somewhat smugly. You didn't expect that one, did you?

'Is the candidate willing to stand?'

The silence seemed to go on forever. I surreptitiously began praying to any listening gods. Then, the words that I had longed to hear.

'I . . . guess I am.' I wanted to hug the man.

The hall began to murmur, uncontrollably. T'omar was relatively new to the ranks of Silverhands. Few people knew him as anything more than the silent figure staring at maps in dark rooms and occasionally coming outside to teach one man or another how to hold a sword and where to point a rifle.

But if Laenan Kite, the honoured, the respected, was willing to nominate . . .

It was at this point that I began to hate myself. Here I was, coming out of the blue after a hundred years in hiding, and with just a word, riding on the power of a name, I was shaking up a society that I had long ago forsaken and left to fend for itself. Did I have the right?

I looked into a sea of faces watching for my next move, waiting to hear what I had to say.

'Would the candidate and nominator please come onto the platform.'

I moved through a mass of people all clearing a path before me as if I were a great king rather then the man who ran out on his job because of just one setback, and felt the revulsion rise anew. How dare I think that because I'd once been great, I could butt in and change a world?

But my legs went on moving, and my mind kept throwing up new things to say, new arguments to sway the now silent crowd. Then I was on the platform, and there was no room to think about what I was doing, no time to turn back. The other candidates watched me with doubt on their faces, and again I saw that look that made my stomach turn. They'd thought they were doing the right thing in standing for election. But if Laenan Kite said this man was going to be good, then who were they to argue?

'Well,' I said, with a half-hearted shrug. 'Doesn't this seem familiar?' I can't begin to describe how I felt at that point. All those eyes, all that attention pressing down on me, and the knowledge that whatever I said here and now didn't matter. Even if I just stood there like a fool and muttered about change in a hushed voice, they'd still follow me. Only it wouldn't be me, it would be the memory of a great, fiery leader who walked every road in the Void and raised magic into the sky and life from emptiness. That was who they listened to. That was who they cared so greatly for, loved and respected.

I couldn't hold a candle to him.

T'omar was watching me, probably the only man in the hall who could see clearly the conflict flickering across my face, and it was that look that resolved me.

This wasn't about me. This was about the Consortium, and a strong leader. T'omar would be a strong leader, I knew it in my bones, felt it fill me and give me new strength. My voice came back, my eyes regained their fire and suddenly I felt the leader I had been return to my heart, and it was right after all.

'You probably all know me. Laenan Kite, good mage, crap cook. I would like to give you the big long speech, only there probably isn't much to say that hasn't already been said. T'omar . . . well, I just think he'd be a good leader, that's all. Hell, I've hardly met the man, but already he's proved me a dunce in the classroom. I think he'd fight for you. I think he'd probably die for you lot, not that he'd ever admit it. I can't guarantee that his soup'll be any better than mine, but I can guarantee that the Silverhand will survive.' I shuffled my feet. 'To think I used to be good at this kind of thing. See what a hundred years have done for me? Where's that inspired speech, where's the dramatic fireworks and heralding of a new era?' Seas of faces, watching, waiting. Hanging on the words of a memory and turning them into something other than they were. Something great.

'I'll tell you where – it's out there,' I said, struggling to focus on my own mind. 'In other kingdoms, in the dreams. Someone needs but dream of fireworks and it'll happen, in some time or place. And out there, not the empty Void nor the busy walls of Haven, out there is a dream which may turn into someone's paradise. If just one person, one child or one old lady on her deathbed can find that place then the whole universe will change, and all those deaths, all those tears and all those dark nights in nightmare, will be worthwhile. The nightmare digs into the dream, and it turns paradise to dust. It drives shadows into every corner and mocks the man who dares to welcome the sunlight. We have to welcome the sunlight for all those places that can't. That's what the Silverhand stands against, a thousand times better than Haven or Skypoint or Stormpoint or any other self-contained kingdom ever will. We're probably the only democracy in the universe, and even Earth took a few thousand years to come up with that idea. And as a democracy, we can work against the darker side of dreamers' minds and know – *know* – that if we fail we can pick ourselves back up again, and pity the man who stands in the way of our wills!'

I tried to get control of my words, listen to what I was saying, bring my voice back down to normal. 'I once met a man, a dreamer, from Earth. He wandered into my kingdom one bright summer's day and asked for a white Christmas, just like he used to have at home. I obliged, and we spent all day snowboarding with the frostings. And when we finally stopped for food, he told me about Earth, about his job and what he did. And I remember he told me that in the machines he repaired – tape machines, I think they were called – the speakers were only as good as the amplifier. And vice versa. If you have brilliant speakers, but a crap amplifier, then the sound you make is going to be crap.

'The same is true here. We are only as strong as the man who leads us. Okay, I haven't actually proved that T'omar is strong and great, but proof is hard to come by these days and probably a little suspect after our last dousing of unpleasantness. You cannot prove the colour of a man's soul.

'But I say this: if I'm wrong in this then you can send me a message, and I'll come running back to Silverpoint, and by all the dreams in the universe I'll keep on getting up on this stage and making speech after speech until we finally find someone who can lead us.'

I saw their faces, and smiled grimly. 'Oh yes, I can prove this one. Knife, anyone?'

Wordlessly T'omar chucked me a knife. I slashed the palm of my hand, raised it so they could all see the blood mingle with the magic, knelt down on the edge of the platform, and pressed my hand into the woodwork. The explosion of bright power ran through every timber and stone in the hall, and back again into me in the blink of an eye. When I rose, there was a single handmark imprinted into the floor, glowing faintly with its own light.

'There,' I said, relieved beyond words. 'Now if this guy turns out to be a creep, I'll come back and see if we can't do anything about it. And if the guy after that is also a git, I'll return again, and again, and again. I hope you're satisfied with this arrangement?' I didn't really expect an answer, my mind was racing down alleys too dark for the rest of me to follow. Things always move too fast for me to cope with when they need to be understood. Sometimes I just want to bang my head against a wall.

For the second time, the hall went wild.

I didn't stay to hear the result. I knew, as did everyone else, that T'omar had won. The single handmark in the wood would stay there as an eternal reminder of mistakes made, but somehow it lent strength to the entire gathering. With this reminder of the hero who had once led them, with this pledge to return, they were happy.

So I stood once again on the edge of the road, the elementals waiting eagerly in the Void outside reality, waiting for their father to return to them. They didn't seem to mind that the radiant world of possibility was predicting death and bloodshed. They were imbued with a confidence in their creator that gave me the creeps worse than any corpse ever could.

T'omar was staring at his feet. 'You are completely unlike what I expected, mage,' he said finally.

'We do attempt to surprise,' I replied with a smile.

'You realise that you've tied yourself into the Consortium for ever, don't you? That handmark isn't going to fade overnight. Nor if it was written in blood.'

I shrugged. 'You sound concerned. I thought you, of all people, would see what I've done.'

He laughed. 'Oh, I see all too clearly. You think you need never return, because I'm going to be a good leader, because I'm going to return the Silverhand Consortium to its former strength. You only cast that spell to convince people that you had utter faith, and so should they. A clever way of killing two birds with one stone.'

'But?' I asked, knowing that a 'but' was bound to follow.

T'omar leant forward urgently. 'What if I can't lead? What if I destroy everything in one careless move? What if I make a single mistake that shatters everything? Then you will go down too, and when Laenan Kite goes, so does the Consortium which depends so greatly on him.'

I shook my head. 'You won't take the Consortium down. You'll be a good leader.'

'How can you be sure?' he demanded.

'Because you're afraid of failing. Because you fear that you won't live up to your responsibilities. In a leader at the start of his reign, that's a very good sign.'

'People who want power shouldn't have it – is that what you're saying?'

I grinned. 'You attended that lecture too!'

He shook his head slowly, like a man trying to sort out the meaning of life and getting stumped at every turn. 'You are an incredible man, Laenan Kite.'

'On behalf of my ego, I thank you.' He saw my extended hand, hesitated, and took it in a firm grasp.

I left Silverpoint with one more friend to my name, and the confident thought that I wouldn't have to return for several hundred years.

How arrogant and how foolish I was that day.

SIX

Diplomacy of War

By now you're probably thinking, this man certainly isn't mucking around. He's getting out there and solving his problems. While your faith (if indeed you are thinking this) is gratifying, let me remind you that so far only about a quarter of the crises I'd encountered had been solved. And it was that easy quarter, what's more. (If you weren't thinking anything of the sort, you should have been!) It's not as nice as people think, to be able to divide problems into tidy bite-sized chunks. There's always something you've overlooked.

Have you ever, say, stopped a fire starting in an ashtray? And someone saw it, who'd never seen either fire or ashtray before? By the next day the story will be that the fire had spread to the papers around the tray, by the next day the whole table will have been alight, by the next a good deal of the room was also burning. Each time you calmly stopped the blaze.

That's the power of gossip. Of rumour. It gave me the name I have these days, and sometimes I wish I'd never begun to acquire it. In Silverpoint they love me for the name, in Nightkeep they hate me.

What of Haven?

That's probably the trickiest question anyone could ask, things being as they were. If the lord of nightmare hates me so, then Haven must be falling over itself to find favour with me, right?

That would be the day.

The palace was now heaving. With the first of the four elemental ceremonies due in one day's time, lords and staff alike were bustling around with the air of a man doing his job and doing it well. Whether they were, I wasn't about to speculate. Speculation is almost as deadly as rumour.

I declared myself, got the usual suspicious glances and blank looks of surprise, waved a couple of official papers around, and got given a small tower room in one of the back reaches of this otherwise fairy-tale castle. And while other lords from other kingdoms went around the palace renewing old ties and laying the ground for newer and better trade routes, I just sat around and watched the streets of Haven from my single window.

I had no intention of looking for trouble by showing my face any earlier than necessary. It generally found me anyway.

Fortunately, the first knock on my door wasn't trouble. Or if it was, it wore a friendly disguise. It was Renna.

Seeing her in the plush ballgown that Windsight had

found in a wardrobe in some palace room, it was easy to forget that still and silent woman in my dreams, lying in that room of unmoving people. She struck a pose, raised an eyebrow as if daring me to say that no, the gown didn't make her look like an angel – which, by the way, it did – and breezed inside.

'Nice room,' she commented, when it became clear that I was too stunned to speak.

I shrugged nervously – small talk with beautiful ladies isn't my strong point. Besides, we both knew that I was probably in the dingiest, dirtiest room in the castle. Never, dear dreamer, piss off royalty. 'Nice dress,' I managed to mumble.

She twirled, obviously pleased with it. 'You like it? I've got to wear it at the dance tonight, Windsight said. And pretend to be his ward, at least for now.' She pulled a face. '*And* I'm well into my twenties!'

'Very sensible of old Windsight,' I said soothingly. 'If everyone knew who you were or what you might be capable of, you too would get the dirtiest room in the palace.'

She raised her eyebrows, looking for an explanation. I shook my head. 'Politics.' It came out like the filthy word it is.

'Ah. The rich man's excuse to sit on his backside and do nothing?'

'You got it. You know, that dress is *very* nice. I've got a sister who'd kill to wear it.'

'A sister?' she asked, genuinely interested. 'What's she called?'

'Saenia.'

'A mage?'

'Oh yes. More powerful, sensible and intelligent than me, I'm afraid. You should meet her.'

'What does she do?'

'Teaches magic in Haven.'

'Oh. So she's not going to be at the dance.' She looked disappointed.

''Fraid not.'

'You coming?'

'Yes.'

'Did you find the Consortium?'

'Yes.'

'Windsight told me about it.' He was a Silverhand too – he'd joined the Consortium at the same time that I had.

'Good.'

'How many people know about it?'

'Everyone from peasant downwards.'

'That's a lot of people.'

'Not nearly as many as you'd think. Remember, the rules are different here.'

She bowed her head, acknowledging the truth in my words with the grace possessed by all ladies who studied under Windsight. 'Of course. After ten years I really ought to be used to this place.'

It was impossible to contain my curiosity. Leaning forward on the edge of the bed, I asked, 'How much can you remember of your life before you came to Skypoint?'

She shrugged and sat down opposite me, gathering up her skirts like the perfect lady so that the fine silk wouldn't get creased. 'Not much. I remember . . . the lorry. A big house, full of books. A church. A tree with a swing. Nothing too explicit.'

'Were you married?' I asked carefully.

'Don't know.'

'Do you have any idea what happened . . . after the accident?'

'No. I've never dreamt of Earth, not once.' She was eager to change the subject, and this she did without the least self-consciousness. 'What about you? Where are you from? What were you before you became the great mage?'

I laughed. Of all the questions she could have asked, these were the easiest. 'Nowhere. Then Haven. All real people come from Haven somewhere in their ancestry. I was an apprentice to a shoemaker.'

She pulled a face. 'Shoes?'

'Oh, yes. He used to take me down to the Void every single day, and tell me to hold my hands out into the light and think very long and hard of shoes. It was frightful exploitation, of course. The law states that any mages capable of Void-manufacture must report to the council and be given proper training, a good salary, and lots of days off so that they don't burn out under the strain. But I didn't know I was a mage. I thought everyone could do it.'

'You master wasn't a mage?'

'No. I never once saw him stick his hand into the Void. He simply measured feet, fussed over account books and beat me if I became too tired to work.'

'Sounds a real bastard.'

'I don't think about it much, to tell the truth.' It was true. For centuries I'd given no thought to those hard youthful years. Amazing that I'd come far enough to have forgotten. Worrying, too.

A gong sounded. The party was about to begin.

Renna leapt to her feet, glowing with excitement. Of course, this was to be her first royal ball. 'Should we go?'

'I'm not dressed,' I pointed out mildly. 'And it's always a good idea to look at the battleground before sending in the cavalry.' I turned to the window, and pulled back the shutters.

I once visited a place on your Earth, while I was dreaming, called China. There was this big, big city within a city. I remember thinking, 'How pretty those roofs are' and 'How tall the wall is' and 'How colourful everything is'. It was clear, looking across not just the palace but the whole of Haven, that Talsin agreed with me.

The entire medieval city, with its churches and thatched roofs, was gone. Enter Chinese curves, twisting gold ornamentation on every door, high towers in which gongs had replaced the city bells, and huge walls of gaily flapping flags, the main colour against the black and white of winter.

Renna's clothes had changed too – Talsin was really mucking around with reality. I looked at her kimono of intricate gold and silver thread on a blue silk background, and thanked the Gods that the clothes I intended to wear were my own, Void-proof, and not about to be changed by any king with a fancy for things Chinese.

Together we strained to look out of the window. Directly below was a courtyard of paper lanterns, and young men courting young women just as they had for the past thousand years and probably would for millennia to come. Servants in silk moved between pillars with their heads bowed respectfully. Some wailing music started up. Supper would be one of those cross-legged, quiet and graceful affairs, I decided, and struggled to recall how to eat with chopsticks.

'Well,' muttered Renna, 'the decorators worked fast today.'

'If it's a Chinese palace we're looking at, the rules have changed. No lewd, dirty jokes, it's going to be music-appreciation night. No dramatic sword-fights between lords, but respect and manners all the way through.' I frowned. It had taken at least twenty years to get used to what each court implied, the subtleties of every scene the king could write. Greek or Roman palaces generally meant the king wanted everyone to behave themselves in public, but they could scheme in the background. Every time I woke up in a pillared palace of white marble, I knew that the king was trying to get his spies into every room.

A medieval palace usually meant someone was going to die. A lord who'd gone one step too far, and pissed off the king even more than I ever had, could expect to wake up in a palace of harsh grey stone and echoing corridors. He'd know that his plot had been thwarted and soon there'd be blood on the carpets.

The time when the palace literally began floating in the air was when a dozen conspirators were rounded up trying to escape from the building – which, of course, was inescapable. The time when every wall in the palace was made of water was when the king needed to get one of his many mistresses out of Haven before an angry mob arrived. The time every room found itself without a roof was when a delegation of dragons arrived from some far-flung kingdom to discuss a new treaty, and so on. My point is that after a few hundred years you learn to read the signs.

Personally I thought Talsin was taking a risk with Chinese palaces. They were surprisingly soundproof and in the past all the best plots had been hatched in some form of Oriental palace.

I scanned the high walls. At least he'd been sensible enough to install lines of marching Samurai and musketeers. But it worried me that he'd gone for beauty so early instead of down-to-earth practicality. It implied that he was more than a little blind to the view of the court around him. It also suggested he didn't know there wasn't a single lord in Haven who hadn't at one time glanced at a bribe and looked a little thoughtful . . .

'You're really worried, aren't you?'

I snorted. 'You remember that phrase, "Beauty is truth, truth is beauty"?'

'Yes.'

'It's very, very wrong.'

'You're trying to teach my ward about politics?' asked Windsight from the door.

'She's gotta learn.'

'True. But now she's got to meet the king, before the dance begins.'

I saw Renna's reaction, that little gulp, the nervous glance. 'Did he request her presence?' I asked hoarsely. If anything, I was more worried than she was. *What happened to the council of war? Surely battles with sword and fire would be preferable to the torture of waiting for war in this world of forced smiles.*

'Hers, and the presence of all new arrivals to court.' He gave me a long, stern look. 'I think that includes you, Kite.'

Suddenly I wished I was a very long way from that place.

Talsin had obviously tried to give the whole affair a very informal, relaxed feel. He might just as well have put up a sign saying, 'Hi, I'm your greatest friend.' I was one of the last to reach the hall – deliberately, I assure you – and took my place at the back of the long queue of nobles, with my shields raised in a spell of 'Who? Me?'. Windsight, with more awareness of how it was good to be seen, was waiting five people ahead of me. Renna, on his arm, was standing erect like the perfect lady. I scanned the line of dignitaries, and noticed with a bitter smile how Lisana, the fair and beauteous, stood so close to Talsin's side she might have been his mother.

Lisana. Her strongest element is water, and indeed she has shaped her kingdom on that very principle. However, she is rarely seen outside Haven, and with the old king – who was wise enough to be more than a little wary of her charms – out of the picture, she was likely to spend more than just a few holidays by the new king's side.

She'd been the king's mistress for as long as I could remember, so I supposed there must be a little more to her and Talsin's relationship than just the bedroom. I guessed she'd soon be heading towards queen.

This I will say for Lisana. For all that I despise her, for all that she has done to try and bring me down, she knows how to look. Was there a fold of her dress out of place? Was there a single flash of her incredible smile that couldn't turn legs to jelly? (Human legs, at least. I won't vouch for nightmare's inhabitants.) Was there one shimmer of her mage's aura which didn't go with the lustrous sparkle of her hair, her gleaming jewels and bright eyes?

Yet I despised her still. She was the one who had whispered in the king's ear that I was a traitor, the one who had stood in that small cell in the dark basement of the palace and watched every bating and every interrogation with that little smile. She was the one who had laughed as the once-great mage of Haven was dragged before the court in rags.

She was the one I still blamed. The one on whom, if I ever got round to revenge, the full force of my anger would fall. She'd never been my equal when it came to magic. She barely qualified as mage, and had resented me from the first moment. As my greatest weapon was now my name, so hers was her body. It sickened me, made the core of hate that had festered for so long inside me rise up and scream its denial.

Are you surprised, dreamer? Are you surprised that I could be so much less a man within? Do not be. Sometimes I wish I was a lord of nightmare, in the court of Nightkeep. There I wouldn't have to bow to my enemy and say how fair she seems. There I could summon all the spirits of darkness and tear that false beauty apart. And enjoy it, what's more.

'Stand up straight, boy!'

I looked round. A lord and his son were standing directly ahead of me, dressed in their finest. The father cuffed the slouching boy round the ear. 'Stand up straight! I will not have you shaming me here!'

I studied the man. He glowed with a fiery halo of magic, focused sharply at points but flimsy at others. A battle mage, then. All attack, little defence. His wife, a lady of modest proportions, also possessed that same fierce magic. My eyes darted to the boy. His magic was far weaker, and of a different shade entirely. With normal senses I studied first the father's, then the son's face. Yes, the resemblance was there, but the mother couldn't look less like the boy if she tried. An illegitimate child? Probably. Did that mean the mother was barren, or had the father simply got a little drunk one night and found the nearest available kitchen maid? I couldn't tell.

Whatever the parentage, I pitied the boy. Better by far to be the son of a drunkard with a host of unnoticed illegitimate sons on the far edges of nightmare than a princely boy whom kingdoms watch. Especially a princely boy of dubious heritage.

I'd grown up in a place called Sunpoint. It wasn't really aligned to Haven, but nor had it turned to Nightkeep. It was a desert kingdom, very hot, very dry. I had about eleven brothers and at least as many sisters. How many mothers the family ended up with, I can't even remember. Only my sister, my real sister, had any magical talent, and all our half-siblings resented us immensely.

But oh, how much better to be resented in a desert. Then you can run into the sand storm and hide in its embrace with a sister you love by your side, shielded by a comforting magic. How much better to grow up in a family where everyone's only half related to each other and care little or naught for who you are or where you go. Even the various nightmares which the desert occasionally threw up were no worry to us. We could run faster than they ever could.

But the boy standing in front of me had nowhere to run, no one to comfort him. He'd have to stay where he was until his father died, in hundreds of years' time, and then he'd be the bastard prince, the one who only deserved half the Key of his land. And there'd be plotting, and 'true heirs' and rumours and scandals.

No desert to run to. No world of dreams to watch through the Void.

All right, when eventually I did run away I ended up as apprentice to a son of a bitch, but at least it was a different son of a bitch than had gone before.

'But what if he doesn't approve?' whispered an excited voice behind me.

'He will, love, he will.'

A girly sigh of fear, the shuffling of silk. I'd seen cases like this all too often at court. A young, powerful mage, due to inherit some great kingdom, fallen in love with the girl who milked the cows or some such. Daddy doesn't approve, but they've gone to Haven to get the king's blessing.

My eyes strayed back to Talsin, currently receiving a pair of old, slightly dazed-looking lords. Would he say yes to the couple's plea? If he did he'd win a lot of public support, but at the expense of pissing off Daddy.

Of course, Talsin would know who Daddy was. If he was some mage with a great history and enough magic to fry a small castle, then Talsin would definitely come down against the young couple. However, if he was an old fool on the way out, the king would take one look at the lord-to-be and decide to try and win his support via an impromptu wedding.

Renna had reached the throne. She curtsied prettily, Windsight bowed. Of course, they could get away with that. They were far enough up the social scale not to have to kneel, like I would. My stomach churned as she and Lisana shook hands and exchanged smiles, Windsight looked sombre by the king's side and nodded severely as he listened to Talsin's words.

'Laenan Kite. You have been very busy, I hear.'

I turned. The man who stood by me wore heavy furs and had his dark hair tied back in a plait that went nearly down to his waist. The Warden of Westpoint. I bowed slightly. 'My lord.'

'Did you like my kingdom?'

I hesitated, and, thinking of the blindfold, decided to settle for honesty. 'What little I saw seemed very pleasant.'

'Good. Westpoint is frequently misunderstood.'

'I'm sure it is.' I licked dry lips. 'You do not mind, sir, that I journeyed through your land?'

'Not at all. The guards were impressed with you. They do get the strangest ideas, you know. They seemed to think that the spirits surrounded you. I've tried to explain about mages' auras, but they can be very insistent.'

I managed a non-committal grunt, willing the man to leave. No such luck.

'You caused quite a stir, as a matter of fact.'

Damn. No matter where I go, trouble seems to follow.

'The nomads seemed to think you were a portent or prophet of some kind.'

'All I did was sit on a pony, sir. I wasn't even aware that we passed through any nomad camps.' Damndamndamndamngoawayyouoldfooldamndamn-damn.

'That's what I told them. You don't get many nomads in your kingdom, do you?'

'No, sir. It's quite small, and most of it's forest.'

'Good man. Sensible policy. Nomads cause nothing but trouble. Well, if you wish to return through Westpoint on your way home, feel free. Anyone who can keep those fools content for a few more weeks is welcome in my kingdom.'

Then he breezed away. Just like that, leaving me feeling very unhappy indeed. Etiquette, that was the crux of the matter. I bow to him slightly because he's a kingdom ahead of me, I bow to the man after him a little more, I kneel to the king.

'Laenan Kite, Warden of Stormpoint!' boomed the herald.

Talsin, dark brown eyes bright with thought and expectation, red beard and hair making him look like the lion I always remembered, was watching me. Had I reached the throne already? I wanted to stand there, glowing with the magic that I knew no one had ever bested, daring him to deny that I had served Haven better than he ever had as the prince on the white horse. I wanted to point at him with a burning finger and say, 'It was you who fled, not I!'

I knelt, bowing my head and forcing my eyes to the floor. How many times had I done this? So many times I had been forced to do homage to nightmare, risen up and struck them down even as claws dug at my feet and magic tore at my heart. So many times I had been forced to kneel before a king or a great mage and hear him strike me down with words. Never had it hurt so much as now, though not a single hand held me in place and the only chains were those of the past, as substantial as mist but heavy on my wrists.

'Talsin, Lord of Haven and the Kingdom of Dream, welcomes Laenan Kite,' he replied formally. 'You may rise.'

I stood up quickly, relieved but still keeping my head bowed. I knew that if I looked up now they'd see the hate and regret in my eyes.

'You have been summoned to the royal court of Haven. Speak now of what you bring to the city of dreams and what endeavours you have made against the nightmare.'

I guess he was almost as reluctant to ask that one as I was to answer, but tradition stated that all kings must ask about battles against the dark. He knew that I could have reeled off a great list, and was dreading the fact that my list would probably be longer than his. I waited for a long, succulent moment before answering.

'I have journeyed to the walls of Nightkeep and struck demon mages from the towers with my fire. I have walked every road in the land and see the possibilities dance in the Void. To the city of dreams I bring my magic of fire and life. To the king I bring my blessing, if he will hear it sung.'

Talsin's voice was heavy, and it was clear I'd just hit him where it hurt. Have you ever done something really bad to someone close to you, and then regretted it from the bottom of your heart? Then, if that someone forgives you, it hurts a thousand times more than it did before.

This was forgiveness with intent to wound, but strangely I felt no satisfaction.

'The Lord of Dreams accepts your tribute, and welcomes you to this court. Enjoy the dance.'

And that was it. I was away within seconds, and felt no sadness or joy in departing. But what about the Void? Blood red, the signs of death, the portent of war? You can't nod and say, 'Enjoy the dance' to those!

The dance was danced, songs were sung, gossip was well and truly gossiped, and all the way through I sat behind my spells and watched, and waited.

Renna was dancing on the arm of a minor lord, from some kingdom probably even smaller than mine. She was a far better dancer, and I nearly pitied the young man as he stumbled along beside her. A glinting shield, where Windsight was deflecting all probes in the direction of his ward, was so subtly woven that I had to compliment my friend as we passed each other. He smiled humourlessly. 'Can never be too careful.'

Renna was suddenly at my side. 'Good evening, Kite.'

Returning her greeting, I glanced up at the clock. It was already getting on for midnight. Had so much of the night passed? 'These things usually go on until two in the morning, you know,' I told her as we made our way towards a trestle table piled with food.

'You're never going to stay till then?'

'Not me. I'm the first to leave on these occasions, and everyone will probably be grateful. It'll be a chance to plot, without being overheard by the great mage who might or might not be connected with a possibly non-existent spy-ring. How was the dance?'

'Crap. The bastard kept trying to . . .'

'Not a man intent on marriage, then.'

'I hope not, because I'd have to break his heart.'

'You'll have to break several hearts tonight,' I murmured, jerking my head to the right. The illegitimate child

I'd so pitied was stumbling blindly towards her, no doubt propelled by her looks and the nagging of his parents.

'Damn,' she whispered.

'Be nice. He's a very unhappy child.'

'You serious?'

'Truly.'

She sighed as he shambled nearer. 'For a serious Kite, I'll be nice.'

I watched her spin away into the dance hall with the boy on her arm, and smiled to myself. Picking up a strange honeyed thing from a plate of pastries, I ate while watching her. She was everything Windsight must have wanted, I decided. Graceful, clever, sympathetic . . .

Next you're going to be calling her the most beautiful girl you've ever met. I laughed inwardly. I'm a mage. She's a dreamer. I'm five hundred years old. She isn't. Don't even indulge that fantasy.

Turning in quest of more food, I noticed a subtle but definite change in the conversation around me. A faint rising in pitch as people stopped paying real attention to each other and started talking on automatic, with nods and smiles to show their interest now and again. Which meant . . .

'Lady Lisana. I'm glad to find you in health,' I said, not turning to face her.

There it was, the faint hiss of breath. 'You never change, Kite.'

'Oh, the hurt! Mages are supposed to grow wiser every day, aren't they?'

'Have you grown wise?'

'Have you grown a beard?' Deciding this was a strategic moment, I turned, and met her eyes squarely. One nil.

'How is Stormpoint?'

'Stormy.'

'With forests, no doubt.'

'And rivers.'

'And people?'

'Imagination can create all kinds of things.'

'I'm glad to see your mind is as flexible as ever, despite the hardships of a treason charge.'

I winced. One all. 'A small charge is just more stimulus to work.'

'And a large charge boosts the mind into summoning storms, forests, rivers and people of the imagination,' she agreed smoothly.

Two one, I conceded. 'Perhaps you should try it. I'm told the exercise, both mental and physical, can do wonders for your figure.'

'I was told that too, by one whom I trust deeply.'

'Where would the world be without trust?'

'Quite.'

I felt a shimmer of satisfaction. Evasion, bordering on outright hesitation. Two all. Your serve.

'How long do you intend to stay in Haven?'

Oh, pitiful! 'As long as necessary. There are people I have to see, and obligations to fulfil. A good mage's services are often in demand these days. So much to do, you must know how it is.' And it's a brilliant return from Laenan Kite, suggesting spy-rings, magic of a great nature and plots being shattered left and right, at the same time stabbing at Lisana's own feeble magic! Three two!

'Who? Me?' is a wonderful spell, dear dreamer. Low energy output, incredibly hard to detect, so slippery, and covering so many astral planes, it's nearly impossible to shatter. After the little spat with Lisana, I hid behind it for the rest of the evening, and observed. People didn't seem too pleased that the king's mistress had just been annihilated by her old enemy, but I didn't care. I was on a victory high. All right, a small and childish triumph, but a victory nonetheless.

But when I reached my room at the end of the night, with a cotton-wool head and a mass of wards finally able to come down, I collapsed without a sound on the pillows, falling into a deep, dreamless sleep.

SEVEN

Four Elements for the Throne

The first day of the elements began with the cheerful light of every dawn in Haven. I was up and out before the rest of the palace, for I had places to visit. The first was a florist's, where I bought a big bunch of flowers. The second was the high white tower of the mages.

The Key-ward on the gate had been changed since I last visited. But it was simple anyway, designed so that fledgling mages stood at least a chance of finding their way round it. Of course countless alarms and defensive spells would be set off if anyone did get past the ward. But for me this was no problem. With the romanticism of youth and the dramatic instinct of every great mage, I just went round to the back door.

'Yes?' demanded the chef, poking his ruddy face out in a cloud of steam.

'Oh, I'm sorry, sir, but a young man of my

acquaintance asked if I'd deliver these flowers and a . . . personal message to the magess Saenia.'

The man gave the flowers a dirty look. 'Fool. The magess ain't interested in nobody 'cept the mage Zeryan. You tell your friend that.'

The door began to close. I stuck my foot in and forced it back open. 'My friend was very insistent. He said himself, "Kite'll go mad if his sister doesn't get this message".'

Once again, the dreaded power of name swung into play. 'Kite? Laenan Kite?'

'I assume so. Do you know him?'

His manner changed immediately. 'Of course! He's one of my closest friends!'

Sad, isn't it? And such a familiar fib. I put an empty smile on my face. 'Then, perhaps you wouldn't mind letting me in? I gather the message is urgent.'

'Well . . . if it's Laenan Kite we're talking about. The magess is probably with Zeryan. Either her rooms, his, the library or teaching lessons together.'

'Thank you.' I breezed inside. The moral of this particular scene, dear dreamer? Never use a cannon, where a needle might suffice.

As I wandered through the old familiar halls, I tried to place the other name I'd heard. Zeryan. Nope. After hard deliberation, the name still meant nothing to me. I was pleased that after so long alone in the same old tower she'd finally met someone, but if I didn't know his name he was probably only a new mage. New mages were young mages. My sister and I are not so young any more as we'd like to believe. Or it could just be fraternal jealousy or protection or whatever it is brothers feel in such circumstances.

By the time I reached her room I was nervous. What if he's a bastard? What if he's an angel? How do I explain the flowers? What if he recognises me? I solved one problem by finding a handy vase full of slightly withered flowers, turning them to cinders and replacing them with my newer bunch. Throwing the flowers away went against every sense of order, especially in a place that still struck a chord in me and whispered the word 'home'. I went on, my ego turned to full throttle.

My sister's door is on a particularly nice corridor, and has a brass name-plate. I knocked, waited, frowned, sent a few mental probes into the room, detected nothing. Damn. I thought if I got here early enough . . .

Relying more on guesswork now, I headed towards the residential area where I guessed Zeryan's room would be. After several flustered minutes of probes and questions, I found them, and knocked.

The man who answered had blond hair, blue eyes and a halo of earth magic barely held back behind his flimsy shields. He glowered down at me with disdain, as if daring me to speak and doubting that whatever I said could make up for the insolence of my interruption.

'I'm sorry if I've come to the wrong place, but I'm looking for the magess Saenia. I was told she might be here.'

'She's not.'

I didn't need to be as strong as I am to know that he was lying. 'Ah. I see we have a delicate situation here.' I let my aura show, bright, ordered and a good deal stronger than his. 'I'm her brother,' I explained, as tactfully as possible, considering the circumstances.

'I didn't know she had one.'

'I'm the kind of brother she wouldn't mention. I can sense her inside there, so please don't bother to lie.'

He hesitated, the door slammed in my face. I waited patiently, listening with half an ear to the sounds of the tower only just waking up. The door re-opened.

My sister is one of those women who is either incredibly beautiful or strange and twisted. It depends on your point of view. She has the same dark, nearly black hair as I do and the bright blue eyes which shine out in contrast. Her elfin face makes her look fragile as a doll, yet is hardened and tanned by long hours of work and a youth spent in the desert.

Her magic is at least as strong as mine, and when we fought as children – which we often did – I'd always be the one with the bloody nose. It did nothing for my honour among the tougher boys of the house, believe me. The girls worshipped my sister from the day when she first sent me flying. But we were still the closest pair in the family, united by magic.

The only real difference between us are a few betrayals, a few battles, a few spells written in the Void and a few summonings of power. That, and the fact that she despised her gift and all it entailed.

'Hi.'

'Hi.' I shuffled my feet nervously, hands folded as at all those times when my big sister had comforted me as a lonely child. 'I was, erm, wondering if we could talk. Somewhere private?'

She glanced over her shoulder at Zeryan, who was wearing a look of extreme indignation. 'My room?'

'Please.'

My sister despised magic. So what was she doing as a

mage, you might ask? The honest truth is, I don't know. She could have taken any kingdom she desired, could have worked without magic in whatever job she wanted to. She always was the clever one in the family, a good deal brainier than me. But she'd been stuck inside this tower for hundreds of years, keeping herself prisoner for reasons I couldn't begin to guess.

The door slammed, I felt the wards slide into place. Thick wards, which would assure in more ways than one that our conversation remained utterly private. I opened my mouth to speak, but she got there first.

'How dare you?'

It wasn't what I'd expected to hear. As the words knifed into my heart I felt her anger grow.

'What?' I heard myself murmur.

'How dare you come charging in like that?! How dare you come back and think you can just take control again?!'

Her words were worse than any nightmare, each one driving me back a step towards the wall. 'I don't understand,' I wailed. 'Why aren't you pleased to see me?'

'I'm loved now, for the first time in my life! Everyone here admires me, worships me! For the first time I can do whatever I want. And you' – her eyes darkened, fire played on her fingers – 'decide to walk in just as I'm starting to believe in myself.'

'I don't understand!' I repeated, wild, uncontrolled magic flaring from my fingers. 'I only wanted to see you! I just wanted to talk!'

'You'll ruin everything. When they find out you're here, I'll go back to being second best. The plotting, the fighting will start all over again!'

What had I done? 'Saenia . . .'

She just ploughed on. 'I was happy while you were gone, little brother! All you brought was trouble, hatred. You forced me to turn away every friend just so that you could get bigger, better. I did it for you, and then you ran away!'

Realisation, cold and evil. 'Saenia . . .'

She raised her shields. *My own sister raised her shields against me!* The rejection slammed into my face and tore my heart in two. Daring me to deny it, she said, 'Your name means nothing here, Laenan Kite. I know what you really are, I don't listen to the stories. The door is behind you. I advise you to take it now, and leave.'

How long I stood there dumbfounded I don't know. Somehow I reached the door, stepped into the cool corridor and leant against a wall. My head was spinning. I didn't know what to do or where to go.

'Oh God,' I murmured. 'What have I become?'

The ceremony of the elements is one of the oldest traditions in Haven. Any king about to take the crown must pass the four elemental tests, and a fifth spiritual test. I had to do something like it as part of my graduation to mage, but on a far smaller scale. The king – the king has to go at it with ritual and panache on every side.

Picture the temple of earth. It is quite small, with only a few high windows from which light shines directly down on the altar, itself little more than a lump of rock. Vines curl round every pillar and up to the ceiling; the floor is plain stone. The temple's acolytes pad around in bare feet, wearing long green robes and carrying branches of various trees. Low chants echo off the ceiling, seeping into the cracks of beams and columns as the priests whisper their prayers to the elements. These are seen not so much as Gods, but as incarnations of the basic forces which keep the world working.

The courtiers all wait outside, buzzing with tension, as their king, wearing a plain brown robe, steps inside. The door slams with a boom that echoes back and forth for several seconds.

The court waits.

Chanting from inside the temple can be vaguely heard, and the educated ear listens carefully to the archaic words being intoned by a specially chosen mage. Blessed is the soil, grow tall from its might. That meant Talsin was praying. The tallest branch shall touch the sun. Now he was probably pouring magic into the flowers, willing them to grow. And again, to earth we shall return. Now he was lying down in a grave, breathing fast with apprehension but never once wavering in resolve as the acolytes shovelled dirt back over him, supported only by a thin shield of magic.

The king would have to stay down there for three hours, just like I had. If his shield at any time faltered, the soil would sag, air would be lost, he would most likely suffocate. It was a test of endurance and, if you failed, the acolytes would have to help you, and you'd be forever shamed, and barred from the circles of magic.

The court waits.

Renna and Windsight, sitting together opposite the temple doors, are looking bored. They were used to flying, to thrills and laughter. This anxious waiting for a man who they couldn't really care for was wearing on their nerves, and I wasn't surprised. It was wearing on mine too.

The court waits.

Lisana glances up as a gong is struck. The three hours are coming to an end. She hastily moves towards the door, adjusts her already perfect hair and waits for the man to emerge whom she will almost certainly marry. The court, seeing her movement, also rises, heading towards the temple. I draw back, into the shadows.

The court waits.

The gong sounds again, ringing across the courtyard. The temple doors swing open and Talsin, covered in grime, and pale from the strain of the ceremony, emerges, surrounded by sombre priests. He smiles proudly and as one man, the court erupts into applause.

Now only Kite waits.

Lisana, her face a radiant sun, plants a kiss on Talsin's cheek, Renna smiles prettily and curtsies, Windsight congratulates the king from the bottom of his heart, lords and ladies alike slap Talsin on the back and tell him, 'Sire, you are a great mage.' The king, his face lit up by the power of success, turns amid the throng, and for a second his eyes fall on me. The dark shadow, the silent watcher. Once the power behind the throne, now I wait for the smile to falter, for him finally to turn and say, 'I did you wrong.'

His eyes harden, and he turns away without a sound.

The courtyard empties.

I never did get on well with earth, as an element. Sure, I could manipulate it, but all the priests of earth always seemed so dour and never cracked a smile, to the point where I swore never to be like that. Air was always a favourite. Air and fire. Mingled with science, of course.

The doors to the temple were still open. I looked around the empty courtyard, and reached a conclusion.

The temple hadn't changed a bit. A pair of young, watery-eyed boys scampered by me, carrying a pot of steaming incense and whispering furiously. I nearly tripped over the hole where Talsin had lain for the past three hours. I looked closer. Yes, there was the residue of the king's magic, clinging to the soil still. Some kings hadn't been able to support a shield for that long, and many a time another's magic had been detected in the soil, too.

'You do not believe that our king can cast a simple spell?' asked a wry voice.

I jumped. The man moved without a noise – the way priests generally do in these magic temples.

'I know he can,' I replied in a more or less even voice.

'Then you are here to pray?' asked the priest, moving closer.

I recognised him as the same grey-haired man who'd been in charge of the temple when I was just a kid making shoes, but I'd never met him in the flesh. 'I don't know, really. I'm not the religious kind.'

'But you're confused.'

You've got to be ready for priests to say that kind of thing. 'You might say that.'

'You want to make a confession?'

I hesitated only a second. 'No thanks. After all, we've hardly met each other.'

The priest laughed, and held out a hand. 'Then let us get to know each other better! I am the High Priest of this temple. My name is Kassir. You?'

'Lenian Kiret,' I lied. Why did I lie? Ask my sister. Certainly I didn't want my name to drag me any further down.

'Well, Lenian, I am pleased to meet you.'

I took the proffered hand, and risked a smile. 'I . . . was wondering if you might help me with a moral conundrum.'

'But of course. That is what most people ask for when they come here.'

'You see, there's this man who's a bit of a fool, if you must know. Trouble is addicted to him, and he's crap at avoiding it. Now, the problem is this – over the years he's built up something of a name for himself in the kingdom I come from, and when he came back a few months ago after years of absence, he tried digging his nose into things which he thought were wrong. My problem is that we don't want him to do that, but at the same time we don't know how to stop him. He thinks what he's doing is right, and the merest mention of his name makes some more . . . trusting people follow him to the ends of dreams and back again.'

'Tell me, what kind of thing is he changing?'

'Well . . . there's the mage who runs our kingdom. A good king, or at the very least someone who might be a good king. He's respected by just about everyone, and does the kingdom good. Yet this man hates the king, for what reason I don't know. He goes around muttering and plotting, thinking of treason of the highest order, unable to bend his knee to our good lord.'

'I see. Anything else?'

'Well – there's this network of people. Outcasts, misfits. He uses them as spies, and thinks he controls them with a word. And they follow him, because of a name! He can't just barge back and say, "I was once great, and now I want that greatness again for nothing"!'

Kassir then said the word which always comes up sooner or later, and can probably turn lead to gold.

'Why?'

I hesitated. 'Why what?'

'Why can't he do all that? You say he once had great-ness. Surely, however long he spent away from the eyes of men, the years could not diminish his greatness?'

'But . . . but a name can't command men.'

'Of course it can. Names are important.'

'But . . . how can the one with the name judge right and wrong? Who's he to dictate what's good and what's bad?'

'That is the crux of every dictatorship. A name is power, and if used wisely can bring great happiness.'

'And if used poorly will destroy everything.'

'That is the problem.' Kassir sat back, a small smile on his lips.

'What's so funny?'

'You, to tell the truth. You didn't need me to tell you this – you knew it already. You wanted me to tell you that this man using the power of a name was evil. You wanted me to justify you opposing him, give you the courage to fight. I won't, you know. Not until you can prove that he's wrong. A great man doesn't lose that greatness overnight, unless it was ill deserved in the first place, that is. If you wanted comfort, I'm sorry to disappoint you.'

I shook my head, thinking clear thoughts very fast for the first time. 'No. I think you've made things a lot easier to see. Thank you.'

'Any time.'

I rose, and left the temple of earth with a slightly clearer conscience and a firmer idea of what had to be done. This was right. This was good. I began to smile, and didn't feel Kassir's frowning eyes on my back as I walked away with a lighter step.

The city I recognised instantly – Sydney. I'd dreamt of this particular corner of Earth often enough to know the shape of the opera house when I saw it, the burning heat and blinding sunlight. I wandered into the massive building through the nearest wall, listened to the conversations, found nothing that interested me. Then I made my way through the familiar streets, drifted through a few walls, had a bit of fun causing a few freak winds that seriously pissed off a penpusher who'd been droning on in the most obnoxious way, and back out into the streets.

Hospital. It was directly in front of me, all gleaming white. I looked around nervously, half expecting to see a whole host of people staring at me as I floated back and forth. Perhaps . . . just a quick look? To prove to myself that it wasn't the same place?

'The board is nothing but a bunch of incompetent fools!' snapped a voice.

I drifted round, and watched the young doctor. He had a couple of files tucked under one arm and was glowering at a slightly older, slimy-looking man in a white coat.

'They won't like it that you think that of them,' replied Slimy.

'It's true! The rules clearly state that you can't take someone off life-support who shows signs of awareness! Dreaming requires a heightened state of awareness!'

'Then she's been aware for the past ten years, eating up money a thousand times better than she's eaten food!'

'So the board is just going to disregard the rules? And you're going along with this?'

'I intend to get out of this dump and into a proper job!'

'I don't believe I'm hearing this! You know that her husband's coming in today? He'll go spare!'

'He'll survive.'

Around then, I woke up. A pity. If I'd slept longer, later on things might have been a lot simpler.

EIGHT

Sea of Maybe

'Can I join you?'

I smiled to see Renna approach, dressed more sensibly now in plain winter furs than the elaborate gowns which had gone before. I offered my arm. 'I hope you like marketplaces.'

'Love 'em. What are you looking for?'

'Would you believe me if I said the ingredients for a great spell?'

She grinned. 'It doesn't sound so unlikely. You know Windsight's been asked to preside over the air ceremony?'

'Good for him. He's one of the strongest mages, and with a genius for flying. Yes, he sounds ideal. Is that why you're here?'

'What do you mean?' she asked sweetly.

'I mean,' I sighed, 'that you're hanging onto my arm instead of his and probably starting a hundred rumours in the process.'

'Rumours are cheap.'

'Regrettably, yes.' The marketplace came into view, bringing the sounds of a thousand voices trying to sell. I checked my purse, found the few silver coins with the hands on them, and slipped them into a pocket. I wasn't about to flash those about, with the Consortium in the state it was.

'What are those?'

'A way of getting information. Now, if you see a candle store, yell.'

We wandered in silence for a few minutes, listening to the cries of the merchants and the chatter of the buyers. 'Master Storm! Best Void-proof cloth in Haven, sir! Sign of the Moon and Sword on every one, sir!'

I shook my head at the cloth vendor, and walked on without a flicker of expression. Renna frowned. 'What was that about?'

'The Consortium's getting its act back together,' I replied levelly, stopping to examine a herbal store.

'That man was from the Consortium?' she demanded, voice barely above a whisper.

'Uh-huh. Sign of the Moon is my call-signature.'

'Call-signature?'

'Didn't Windsight tell you anything? How much for the witch wort?' I asked the stall-keeper.

'Just tell me,' Renna insisted.

'It's a magical symbol, imprinted into raw magic. Only the very close are allowed to know it, because it's a way even non-magical people can contact others across incredible distances.'

'And the Sign of the Sword?'

'Is another's call-signature.'

'Whose?'

I shrugged, paying the stall-keeper and scooping up my goods even as we talked. 'I'm hardly going to tell you that, am I?'

'You've told me about the Consortium!'

'That's because Windsight trusts you, and I trust Windsight. But a call-signature is like . . . it's like giving your telephone number to a complete stranger, only worse.'

'Can I use your call-signature?'

I laughed. 'If you can find out how to inscribe it in magic, what the Sign of the Moon looks like and the individual pattern of my magic, then sure! Feel free.'

'That's a "no", then.'

'I'm sorry,' I said. 'I've been playing this game for too long. It's hard for me to trust a stranger.'

'Even a dreamer?'

'Even a dreamer,' I agreed.

Suddenly she grabbed my arm and pointed so unexpectedly that I nearly raised fire to my fingers. 'Candles!'

I studied the candles, and bought five which looked more or less suitable for what I had in mind. Nothing too runny, just a plain candle which would withstand the pressure of magic being pumped into it. Runny candles are the kind of thing used by fools with rams' skulls, altars of blood and no sense of proportion.

'How would you like to be a mage's assistant for a few hours?' I asked as we strolled through another passage of stalls.

'Do you need one, or are you just saying that?'

'Theoretically I could do it by myself, but the spell

takes hours to set up, and I could do with someone to help me.'

She smiled broadly, her eyes shining. I got the idea she'd been waiting for me to say something like that. 'Real magic?'

'As real as it gets.'

'Not like the stuff Windsight does, but a big spell?'

I thought about it. 'Yeah, probably one of the biggest.'

'And I can be assistant?' She was nearly shrieking with excitement.

'If you want to be.'

She laughed ecstatically, as if heaven had just opened and announced that she was an archangel incarnate. 'If I want to be? Kite, I love magic! I've always wanted to see a really big spell, be a part of it, even if that part is only drawing chalk lines or holding a candle!'

Strange that a dreamer should love magic so much more than a mage. Reality had definitely got its numbers jumbled up.

'This is witch wort.'

Renna wrinkled her nose in disgust. 'I don't suppose it's all right to open the shutters? That stuff really stinks.'

I folded my arms. 'This spell has to be cast in darkness, or not at all.'

''Cause of the candles?'

'Right.' I dug deeper into my bag of equipment. 'Ah. This is wizard weed.'

'And the next thing you're going to dig out is going to be . . . oh, mage moss or . . . harpy heather?'

'And the next thing I'm going to pull out,' I said, ignoring her, 'comes from Stormpoint. I evolved it specially.'

'You evolved it?'

'Of course. You know all those mages who trek across kingdoms in search of some kind of herb?'

'Yessss . . .' she replied carefully.

'Idiots. If they have a kingdom they can simply tell the ground to create a plant which does this or this. Okay, they may end up with a fifty-foot pink tree to put into their cauldron, but it still saves an awful lot of trouble.'

She frowned at the simple purple flower I pulled out of the bag. 'What is it?'

'Void-proof night bane.'

'Night bane?' she echoed. 'What does it do?'

'Temporary energy boost. Leaves you feeling utterly wrecked after, but useful if you're casting a powerful spell or a series of spells for a short time. I wasn't going to use it, but since the mage I had my eye on for a spot of help can't come . . .'

'We're casting a very powerful spell, aren't we?' she interrupted.

I laughed, not meeting her eyes. 'I'm casting the spell. You're being allowed to tag along.'

'I'm sure the king would have something to say about this.'

'We want the king to have something to say. I want him to see every minute of this.'

'Why?'

'Because it'd make me very smug, prove a point beyond any doubt and may even encourage Talsin to do something sensible for once. The Void burns blood red, he ignores it. Nightkeep hammers at the gates, he holds dances. Not a good sign.'

She folded her arms. 'You are one of the most frustrating men to be with. Windsight always tells me what he's doing in nice simple words. You just drop hints every now and then and let me struggle along by myself. Well, I've had enough. Either you tell me what the hell we're doing, or you lose your assistant right now.'

'It's what all college mages do,' I said defensively. 'They try to be inexplicit all the time.'

'Well, breaking news here! You're not a college mage, and I'm not your pupil!'

I sighed. 'Okay, I'll explain everything, but only once I've attracted Talsin's attention. I want him to hear every word.'

'You promise you'll explain?'

'Promise.'

'Good. How do we attract his attention?'

It is one of the most complicated spells any mage can undertake. It literally summons the Void to the caster, and sorts it into the highest order of reality. Since the Void is naturally chaotic, the sorting part can be danger-ous, and quite often lethal if you haven't taken a few simple precautions.

So, in the darkened room I knelt down on the floor and drew a chalk circle with a cross in the middle, and Renna and I carefully laid four of the five candles at the ends of each line. The witch wort and wizard weed were placed carefully in the centre of the circle, and inciner-ated. The vapours filled the rooms, tickled my lungs. Within seconds I was blissfully unaware of the aches and pains of the day, and thinking in bright, straight lines. Carefully, watching the magic with all the attention of the man taming the lion, I poured a portion of power into each of the four candles. They sprang to life.

'Is he watching yet?' sighed Renna.

I smiled. 'The spell isn't ready yet. It hasn't drawn enough power to distract him. Night bane?'

Wordlessly she handed it to me. I took a deep breath, and sunk my teeth into it. The stuff really did taste foul, and burnt on the way to my stomach, but it had to be done. 'Candle.'

She handed the last candle to me. I reached into the heart of my magic, pulled and twisted. The whole candle, not just the wick but the whole thing, exploded into bright white fire. But it didn't burn.

I felt Talsin's presence, pressing down on me with sudden intensity, as the Key alerted him to the spell going on beneath his very roof. 'Take the candle,' I whispered.

To her credit, Renna didn't hesitate. She took the raw fire in her hand with a confidence that made my heart swell with pride. 'This is called divining,' I explained. 'It . . . kind of looks at the Void, and finds the most likely reality to become . . . well, real. It's like a very short-term prophecy. Questions?'

'Why are you casting it?' she asked in a small, awed voice.

'Several reasons, really. I guess the biggest is that it'd be nice to have at least some idea of the future.' Because if the future looks good I'll stick to the plan I have now, if it looks bad I won't. 'The divining . . . looks at the current intent of everyone who might influence the Void, and draws its conclusions from that. So if one person changes their plans, the whole divining changes.

She nodded. 'So . . . if I suddenly decide to run out of here screaming instead of staying, as I plan to do now . . . the future is changed?'

'Of course.'

'I think I get that.'

'Anything you don't get you'll pick up as you go along. Now stand on the edge of the circle, and just keep holding the candle. If it goes out, come into the circle and see if I'm still breathing.' I saw her horrified face. 'It won't go out,' I assured her.

I stepped into the centre of the circle. Magic stirred beneath my feet and ran along my spine, suddenly aware of the shape of the spell for which I'd laid so much groundwork. I shaped the nearest handful of magic, and sent it flying into the distant Void. It caught a bundle of the raw possibility within moments, and returned to my hands. And now in the centre of the circle I was holding a large yellow sphere of maybe and if.

Talsin was pressing down close now, determined to see whatever vision I was about to draw. That was how I wanted it. If this turned out the way I expected . . .

Renna licked dry lips, staring at the candle which was now flickering faintly as the strain began to draw away at its power. I clamped down on my wandering thoughts and focused on the sphere, pushing information into it in one long stream on intents, observations and ideas.

Observe – Talsin. Observe – Lisana. Intent – no intervention. Intent – leave Haven. I fed all that and more into the sphere, let the possibilities work around the idea that I was going to leave, that Talsin was angry, that Lisana would scheme, that the Consortium would survive . . .

Then I let the Void add its own ideas. Add its own

observations, the highest possibilities and strongest realities.

The candle flickered, began to die. As I began to lose control of the spell I reached deep inside me to the untapped energy of the night bane, and released it. The candle erupted back into life, stars sparkled in front of my eyes and my legs wanted to give way to the sudden weight pressing down on them, which would have sent me to my knees but for drug-induced numbness. Images began to form inside the Void. All the information had been processed, and now the sphere of possibility was returning the greatest likelihood to those who'd created it.

A gallows swings from the highest hill. Another victim, the fifth that day, is cut down. The palace looms in the distance, soldiers pacing every wall. Eagles fill the air, watching for anyone who might breed discontent against the king. The king and his queen are the lords of dreams, no one can speak against them . . .

A single walker staggers down the road through the Void. The side of his face is one massive bruise, his clothes are torn and filthy. The queen has decreed he must die, he has run and run and run . . .

The sun is turning red and sour. Nightkeep hovers at the gate of Haven, the cheers of a thousand monsters fill the air as the king signs the surrender and kneels before the towering lord of nightmares.

This is what will happen, there is no escape, Haven, Stormpoint, Talsin, Kite will fall. This is the truth of the divining, the truth that no man can deny . . .

<Never!>

The fool was inside my circle, his presence tearing at me. At once all four candles burnt out, the fifth flickered and began to fade. The world was spinning as Talsin launched a savage attack at the sphere of Void which had predicted his demise. My legs crumbled beneath me, the candle in Renna's hand died and didn't re-light. The Void exploded in my hands, and faded to nothing, taking the rest of the world with it.

The door closed with only a faint click. The sound of a newscaster drifted in from the room next door, then suddenly fell to silence.

'David? Is that you?'

I watched as my elder doppelganger – David – staggered into the room. His face was white, his eyes glazed.

The woman, who looked a little like Saenia, stood up as he approached. Behind her was a camp bed and a suitcase, clothes strewn across the room. 'My God, David, you look terrible!'

He sat down without a word and stared blankly at the dark television. His hands were clenched into fists, a corner of some paper stuck out between thumb and finger.

His sister sat down next to him, her eyes wide and concerned. 'What happened?'

Then, without any warning he broke down and began to cry, curling up against her and sobbing for what seemed like hours. Startled, she began to draw away, then thought better of it, and pulled his head against her shoulder, murmuring words of comfort. His hand opened, the paper fell unheeded on to the floor. I looked closer.

Deeply regret to inform you . . . tragic loss . . . medical impossibility . . . on 7th August . . . painless death . . . no alternatives remain . . .

❊

I glanced around the room. There was a calendar. It was July 25th. I looked back at the letter, the sobbing man, and felt my heart miss a beat. I began to back away, shaking my head, back through a wall, back onto the street, turn and run.

I ran for hours. Over streets and through houses, out into the harbour and over the sea, never stopping for hours and hours, running faster until I was nearly flying. I wanted to be as far from that place of death as I could. I wanted to run further and faster, never stopping not for anyone . . .

'He's waking up.'

'Thank God.' Windsight's face swam slowly into focus. 'How are you feeling?' he said, loud enough to make stars explode in my eyes.

'Not too good,' I admitted.

'You were forced out of a divining spell. How many fingers am I holding up?'

'Six, and two thumbs,' I answered.

Windsight sat back, a satisfied smile on his face. 'Yup. Kite's going to be fine, though dreams know he doesn't deserve it. What the hell prompted you to do a divining? And alone?'

I tried to sit up, and decided against it. 'Needed to know if it was okay to leave.'

'So you told the Void to work around the idea of you not intervening? What a waste. I would have done it so that you *were* intervening, and then see what happens,' Windsight said disdainfully.

'Are we shielded in here?' I asked nervously.

'Of course. Besides, Talsin isn't going to come nosing around after you for a good while.'

'He isn't?'

'Don't you remember? You blocked him. Sent him flying back into his body with enough force to make him unconscious?'

'I remember . . . I remember passing out. But I never blocked anyone.'

'You must have.'

'I didn't! Renna, you didn't see me do anything, did you?'

She shook her head. 'I guess you must have.'

Windsight clapped his hands together with a bang that did my aching head no good at all. 'This is irrelevant, Kite. The fact remains that you did block his attack, and probably owe your life to it. Talsin wants to see you, as soon as you're fit.'

I slumped back. 'Damn. Is he seriously pissed off?'

'It's hard to tell. The ceremony of air is tonight, and he's been focusing on that. Lisana jumped at it, though. She's serious about getting your blood, Kite.'

'There's a surprise.' My eyes darted past Windsight to where Renna stood silent and unreadable. 'Renna.' Her eyes met mine, and locked. 'Thanks. I owe you one.'

She said nothing, but then, can you blame her? We'd just seen the destruction of the city of dreams.

I was bed-bound for the rest of that day. But by the time the gongs sounded for the end of the ceremony of air, I was feeling a good deal better, if not ready to face the world. The noise of cheering from the court suggested that, despite everything, Talsin had triumphed again.

I just lay there, and thought. Was I surprised? Had the divining shocked me? Not especially, to tell the truth. There'd always been a side of me which had thought Talsin wouldn't be the best king. But Haven falling because of him? Because I was going to leave?

Keep control here. Haven may not fall merely because of you. You're only one man, and don't ever forget it.

But there were a few things that would have to change. For a start I couldn't leave.

Sign of the Sword.

I glanced inside myself, and saw the pool of severely depleted magic. Not long enough for me to sustain a call-signature. But if he sustained it instead . . .

I mustered what little power I had left, and shaped it into the sign with one glowing hand. Then I sent it in search of the man who I knew possessed it.

T'omar felt my touch, responded. <Kite?>

<I've no magic to talk, you'll have to summon me,> I sent, and broke contact. Even that little exertion left me drenched in sweat, and I realised how badly I'd been drained.

Finally T'omar responded. <Kite?>

<Sorry about that,> I sent, relieved that he was now the one supporting the link, not me. <I've got no power left for this.>

<I understand. We know about the divining.>

<Good. You know what we saw?>

<Only vague rumours. Haven's going to be great, Haven's going to be destroyed – nothing we'd put money on.>

<It was the latter of those.>

<Destroyed?>

<You don't sound surprised.>

<I'm not. Nightkeep is planning something big. Our agents have been running home like flies, with various

demons on their tails, reporting massive spells, and
armies that move through the Void faster than any force
has a right to.>

<Talsin saw the divining. I'll try and convince him to
muster the army.>

<He won't do it during a coronation.>

<He will if I yell at him enough. Do we know if
Nightkeep is actually aiming for Haven?>

<No. The Consortium's not functioning perfectly at
the moment.>

I tried to think. <Look, T'omar, I'm going to be tied
down in Haven for a good couple of weeks. The situation
is as bad as I thought, maybe worse. I'll try and talk to
Talsin. We can't be taken by surprise.>

<I know. I've got Silverpoint working overtime at the
moment, and the elementals are sweeping the Void reg-
ularly. There's another problem you should know
about.>'

<Tell me.>

<Dreamers are going missing. Even the inner king-
doms report a massive drop in dreamers. A mage
dreamed of Earth last night, and people are falling into
comas like flies.>

<Comas?> Why?>

<I don't know. They simply won't wake up.>

<Why haven't we seen them in the Void? Surely if
they're all sleeping at the same time the streets of Haven,
of everywhere, should be packed . . .>

<I know.>

<Why hasn't something happened to the Void? Comas
are so rare . . .>

<I know.>

<Where the hell are the dreamers, if they're not on Earth and not here?>

<I've no idea.>

My mind raced, and reached a conclusion which can only be described as magical. 'Oh shit!' <T'omar, get the elementals towards Nightkeep. They've got to find as many dreamers as possible – make it their priority!> *Gather dreamers, don't let Serein pull any more in, don't let him teleport any more soldiers than he already has . . .*

<Very well. I don't suppose you can explain why?>

<Not yet, my friend.>

'Eat up. You need some proper food.'

I was already feeling stuffed, but there was something about Renna which made you do what she said. 'Renna?' I asked carefully.

'Yes?'

'What do you know about . . . well, about dreamers?'

She shrugged. 'Not much.'

'Do you know they can transport themselves in the blink of an eye?'

'No. Can they?'

I nodded. 'Oh yes. Just give them an image.'

'I've never been able to do it.'

'Because of the coma?'

'Windsight always seemed to think so.'

I chewed some potato thoughtfully, eyes never leaving her. 'Renna?'

'Yes?'

'What happens to coma victims?'

She put down her fork with a slow movement, her face serious. 'I never really thought about it. I believe they get put in a hospital somewhere until they wake up.'

'For . . . how long?'

'If they don't recover? Until they either die or the doctors are sure they're never going to wake up.'

'And then?'

'They give them an injection, or stop feeding them or something like that. Why?'

'Renna?'

'Yes?'

'Can I ask a favour?'

'Sure.'

'Will you come to my room tonight, for an experiment. I promise there won't be fireworks or anything. Don't tell Windsight, don't tell anyone.'

'Why?'

I avoided her eye. 'I can't say. Not yet.'

'Can't say, or won't say?' she challenged.

'Can't. Believe me, I can't.' I had a nagging doubt, a feeling deep inside me which kept on growing, screaming that it was right even though the whole world seemed set to defy it.

After what seemed an eternity, she nodded. 'Very well.'

But first there was one more thing to be done. As the sun set I pulled on my grey mage's robes, took a long drink of water, and set out through the palace.

A pair of guards stopped me outside the audience room, looked me over, and stepped aside without a word.

I moved inside the audience room, and pulled the door

shut behind me. Talsin sat on a slightly plainer throne than I'd seen before, surrounded by scrolls and maps galore. I approached, and knelt.

'Laenan,' he acknowledged quietly.

'Sire.'

'You may rise.' I got up quickly, and stood limply before him.

He said, 'They're plotting, you know. Even now they plot, behind their reflective shields, blocking me and daring me to probe further. But I can't arrest them, because I depend on their kingdoms for income, for people, for mages. Without the kingdoms Haven is nothing.'

I said nothing. What the hell could I have said?

'My spies tell me Nightkeep is preparing for battle again. Soldiers are pouring in from all over nightmare, demons and monsters are being summoned and mages assigned to support them.

'What will you do?'

He snorted, folding up a map and throwing it savagely onto a pile of other crumpled papers. 'What can I do? I haven't been crowned yet, and everyone says your divining was fake. That you attempted to drive fear into me at a critical time. But I know – I felt the truth in that spell, recognised every step of it and know that you didn't lie. Haven will fail, unless something is done.'

'Unless many things are done, my lord,' I corrected. 'The vision was strong – so strong the Void nearly thought of it as reality.'

'I can do nothing now, Kite. You must see that. If I step out of line for even a second they'll come.'

'The kingdoms?'

'And the mages. Even Lisana uses me now. I'm a puppet.'

I was amazed. He saw all this? He'd known all along. Talsin began to climb in my estimation. 'What do the kingdoms want?'

He laughed bitterly and pointed at a pile of documents. Cautiously I picked them up, and read. 'Attack Nightkeep? Sign a document empowering them to . . . refuse aid?' I read further. 'Destroy the Silverhand Consortium, put the leaders on trial for high treason? You're never going to agree to this, are you?'

'I can't attack Nightkeep, and I certainly can't survive without kingdom aid. Don't worry, Laenan. Your precious Consortium is safe for the moment too. As are you.'

'My lord, you are king! They can't just make demands.'

'Yes they can! Haven is still weak from my father's death, and they know that I depend on their aid now. Lisana whispers poison in my ear every night, and the court all wonder how best to turn me into a puppet.'

'If Lisana is so poisonous, why do you let her so near to you?'

'You don't understand! The people think of her as their queen, and somehow . . . I depend on her. She serves them, but at the same time she keeps me safe . . .'

'She has seduced you, my lord.'

His eyes flashed angrily to hear me speak so simply, but he couldn't deny the truth, and didn't. 'I love her, for all that she is blind to the good of Haven. Remember that, Warden of Stormpoint.'

I bowed my head. 'Yes, my lord.'

He slumped back in the throne, dejected. I felt very

small, but at the same time as if the world was watching. 'My lord . . . why did you tell me all this? You, who drove me from Haven in the first place, can hardly expect me to aid you.'

'You have aided me, Kite. You cast the divining. Tell me you did that just because you were bored, and I'll believe anything.'

'Sire, I did it because I care about Haven, about my friends in the city and because I do not want to see any more deaths. It was a warning, that is all.'

'A warning which somewhat backfired, I'd say. Did you base the spell on the fact that you'll leave, and that we'll work against each other, as we always have? Don't bother to lie, I felt the pattern of the magic. I felt you pour your hatred for me and mine into that spell.' He leant forwards, eyes burning into me. 'And what is the consequence of your hate and my blindness?'

I couldn't meet his eyes. I felt like a fool, a child who'd dared challenge the teacher. 'Haven will fall, my lord.'

Talsin sat back, a thoughtful look on his face. 'Kite, I won't lie. The court hates you, and you have lied repeatedly when you say that you have no power or influence. You've also let your hate blind you, as I have. So, I suggest a cease-fire. An alliance, even.'

I looked up, eyes flashing as the full force of his proposal sunk home. 'What does this entail?'

'I know you went to Silverpoint. I know that the Consortium is still functioning. You have information, power, influence. I can make that count for something. You give me information, I give you information. We keep no secrets from each other, we listen and co-operate. The Silverhand Consortium used to be

responsible for bringing down plots in the past, so it can
be again.'

I thought for a long while. 'You ask me to commit the
Consortium, as well as myself. That is something I
cannot do.'

'God dammit, Kite! Haven needs this, and you know
it!'

'I will tell you what I know, my lord, and consult the
Consortium. They may well agree to this of their own
volition.'

Talsin hesitated, then offered his hand. 'You are a man
of honour. I trust you to keep your word.'

'And I you, my lord.' We shook hands, and I even
risked a smile. To my relief, he returned it. 'You want to
know what I know? Well, where shall we start . . .'

'You look pleased with yourself,' Renna said as I closed
the door to my room. I hadn't let her in and didn't know
how long she'd been waiting, but the smile on her face
banished any lingering doubts. She was the kind of
person who could barge into anywhere as if she owned
it, and no one would mind.

'Guess who's just reached an agreement with a king,' I
replied with a grin.

'You give him info, he gives you influence.'

'Something like that. There's going to be a lot of plotters who suddenly find there's one fish they can't catch.'

'Kite, if I asked what I'm doing here you'd say . . .?'

'Aiding the war effort.'

'I should have guessed it'd be something like that.'

I sat down on the edge of the bed. 'The leader of the
Consortium said that dreamers are going missing from

the kingdoms, and there are very few coming to Haven. Now, I can dream of Earth, but I can't dream of Nightkeep.'

'And you think I can?'

'Something like that.'

She folded her arms. 'Well, I hate to disappoint you, but I've never dreamt of anything in my entire life.'

'You're dreaming now,' I said quietly.

'I'm awake now.'

'No, you're not. You see, I dreamt of Earth, and I saw you. You were in a coma, and your eyes were moving. Constantly. And the doctors said you were dreaming.'

'Does this mean I'm dreaming of you?' she asked hesitantly.

'Of course not! We are the real people! I guess you're somehow . . . projecting yourself through dreams into the real world, and a constant ten years of it has made that real world real for you too.' I hesitated at the end of my own words. Did I really believe that, or was my sudden and unexpected defence because I suspected something quite different? So often the best defences are born of someone trying to convince themselves, not an audience. But I refused to let my doubt show. Renna did not need doubt at this stage.

'Get to the point.'

I took a deep breath. 'I think you might be able to project yourself into anywhere in the Void, any kingdom you wish. I think you always could in the past. But you simply forgot how to when Windsight found you and this world became your real one.' *Ah. And here we have the nub. I, who have disregarded dreamers all my life as little more than shadows from another place, whether that place is created by us or we are created by them, have suddenly seen a use that can be made of them. And suddenly I have views and opinions and ideas.* I felt almost sick.

She began to laugh, shoulders shaking. I sat sombrely on the bed, utterly unable to see humour of any kind. 'Renna, this is serious.'

'You're screwed, you know that?' she crowed. 'Everyone here is screwed! I'm dreaming of you, not the other way round, and I obey the laws of science! You just think you can shove a wedge of magic in some place or another and hey presto, you're ruler of the universe!'

'Renna, I just want you to try.'

So it was that I became a teacher, and Renna began to learn about dreams.

NINE

Secondary Wards

And still Nightkeep didn't attack.

Have you noticed how, after a surprisingly short time, you get into a routine? I did almost immediately. In the morning I'd have the daily chat with T'omar, keeping up to date on Nightkeep's movements. Then lunch, then time with Renna. Mostly we did meditation, and I would give her image after image to focus on. Did it work? No, never. In the afternoon I'd report anything new to Talsin and get dirty looks from the courtiers, and in the evening I'd attend either the dances or the ceremonies. Windsight never asked what Renna and I did all those hours in my room, and I never once saw Saenia.

And still Nightkeep didn't attack.

After a long time arguing, the Silverhand Consortium consented to a temporary alliance with the king, in exchange for allowing several of its agents into court.

And still Nightkeep didn't attack.

And I dreamt. And watched. And waited.

July 29th. I was surprised that only four days had gone by on Earth — at least a week had passed in Haven. I turned away from the calendar and listened to the sounds of the hospital, now growing familiar. Elder me, David, was there, arguing passionately with a group of nurses who looked more than a little hassled and worn out. Slimy Doctor was watching, saying nothing. Nice Doctor was nodding enthusiastically and giving his partner a series of dirty looks.

I guess it was a bit like waiting for Nightkeep to attack. You knew that someone was going to die, and that there was nothing to be done. It set your teeth on edge and made you want to scream, simply for the satisfaction of hearing one sound break the deathly silence.

David was screaming a lot, I realised. He had a deadline, and he knew what he needed to achieve. Only, no one was listening. No one of any importance, at least.

Sometimes I wonder. Is this world, this Earth, real, or do we just meet some ghostly race of spectres in the real world which we inhabit, and then incorporate them into dreams?

But then, why do our dreams invent so much more so much better than we can? And why do we all share the same dream of a magic-less world?

That raised another question. Assuming Earth is another real world, only on a different plane of existence, don't the inhabitants of this other world think the same about us? That we're just products of their imagination?

If we are just products of their imagination, what happens when the one who dreams of us dies . . .

And still Nightkeep didn't attack.

I guess it had to happen sooner or later – such things do
if you leave them too long. I'd left it for a week, and we
were just approaching the final ceremony of the elements, the fifth and hardest one, when Talsin and I
decided to push the news of our alliance into public sight.
Why? Because the people of Haven were getting rest-
less. Rumour travels fast, especially in a small, densely
populated magical city like Haven, and it wasn't long
before everyone began catching on to the fact that the
increased patrols and constant manning of the gates
weren't as innocent as they seemed.

So Talsin asked me to preside over the final ceremony,
where all elements come together. And the people saw
that a great mage had allied himself with a great king and
was willing to work with him, and were very happy and
confident. (That was the power of a name, again. Dear
dreamer, if you ever get a name you'll find it incredibly
hard to go around doing anything as simple as buying a
potato, at least in Haven. I don't know too much about
Earth. My point is – it ain't worth the trouble.)

The court, on the other hand, went ballistic.

They'd known about my divining, of course they had,
but Lisana and Co. had been convinced that they'd
talked Talsin into thinking nothing of it. They knew
nothing of our meetings behind closed doors – doubly
closed, thanks to the Key my young king held in his
heart.

'Aren't you worried?'

I gave Renna a wry look. 'No, not really.'

'But the court – you said how dangerous it could be to

piss them off.' She was wearing another ballgown for yet *another* dance. A courtier's life, dear dreamer, is one of the most pointless expressions of wealth in the known universe. It's just one dance after another.

'It's a balance. The court is counteracted by the mass of the Consortium spreading nice little rumours, plus the fact that the people are still in love with their legends.'

'Which you . . .'

'Are not above exploiting. Besides, I'm used to this stuff. There've been at least seven assassination attempts on me before, and no one's going after Talsin. Not now.'

'But you think he's less of a balancing power than the people?'

God, she catches on fast. 'Right. He's still infatuated with Lisana. She just needs to take her dress off and he'll do anything. I've often meant to check on her, see if she's using any seduction spells.' I frowned. 'I was about to do that before all hell broke loose. I think she'd caught on to what I planned, so she pushed for a charge of treason.'

Renna gave a cackle of mirth. 'Seduction spells? You don't know how much men have sex on their mind.'

'Only because mine's as pure as can be,' I replied blandly. 'But the point is, her power is strongest in the night, when she's alone with Talsin and he's so drunk on her he'll get down on his knees and beg for more. In the daytime, when he's back in the real world and there's someone to knock sense into him, he can be a great ally indeed.'

'But you can't knock enough sense into him to make him drop Lisana?'

'No.' I frowned. 'Odd, that. I wonder . . .'

'What? What?'

'Has anyone actually tried to get inside her room? To see what equipment she needs for any spells? Check up on her potions and blessings?'

Renna clapped her hands together gleefully. 'Oh, can we? We can slip out of the dance and . . .'

'Aha. First we get a professional opinion.' I rang the bell. Once, strongly. Then twice, weakly.

The Silverhand agent was in my room within minutes.

We pored over the maps of the palace. 'Her ladyship's rooms,' the agent said. 'Tricky. She's got wards written into every wall and door. Even if you could undo them, she'd feel you doing it.'

'Reflection?' I asked hopefully.

'No good. The internal shields are reflective themselves, and would bounce the magic back and forth until your head exploded.'

'Scry-block?'

The dark-haired man, who posed as a cook, laughed. 'I don't even know what kind of magic you've put into that spell, sir, so don't ask me.'

I glanced at Renna, who was frowning thoughtfully. 'Eisirrn is one of our top magical experts, and a real genius when it comes to the court of Haven,' I explained to her.

'And I don't make a bad pudding either, sir,' he added, self-consciously brushing down his cook's apron.

'True.'

'Kite?' asked Renna finally. 'If there's no way to get inside that room without setting off a few small alarms, would it be possible to . . . well, distract her so much that the small alarms can't be registered. Surely there's some potion somewhere which would block that part of her brain?'

I turned to Eisirrn for advice, but he shook his head. 'All courtiers have some charm or another for the detection of poison. Hers is a necklace which she wears for all meals. If she eats poison, she'll know something's wrong and be calling for the guards before you can blink.'

Renna nodded, but her expression didn't change. If anything, it became more eager. 'How about if someone else ate the poison, and then she touched them and got some of it on her? Or if you put the poison where she wouldn't be wearing the necklace when she touched it?'

Eisirrn looked at her, at me, and back at her with wonder in his eyes. 'You thinking of putting this girl up for membership?' he asked. 'It's brilliant! Talsin gets covered in the poison, and the man who laid it in the first place is one of his trusted comrades! Or even better – you lay it before he gets to his rooms all over every surface, and by then he'll be so tired he won't notice anything except her, who's distracting him as much as the poison would.'

My mouth dropped open. 'Oh no. Nonononono. Not in a million years!'

But both Eisirrn and Renna were grinning. The cook reached into his clothes. 'I've got exactly the thing you need. Give it to him in his bath, pour some of it over the bedclothes, you can't go wrong.'

'No!' I saw their grins widen. 'No!'

I'm not exactly used to prowling in the dark. Well, maybe, but not this kind of darkness. I'm used to nice, solid nightmare. Prowling behind a distortion shield in my own city is not my piece of cake.

The tiny bottle of odourless liquid had to go a long
way. Eisirrn had assured me it would. It was something
concocted by the Consortium. During my predecessor's
reign, an alchemists' unit had been set up, and I'd encour-
aged it keenly after dreaming a chemistry lecture on earth
taught by a particularly talented German. I hadn't understood any of the formulas, but the message had stuck.

The sounds of the dance drifted up, but as though
lagging a little. Doubtless the courtiers would soon be
flooding upstairs to their rooms, with, in the case of
Talsin, a certain pretty lady hanging on his arm.

The guards standing by the door were half asleep. But
the gargoyle above it never slept. 'Halt!' it hissed. 'Who
goes there?'

'Shut up, you daft lump of rock, I'm trying to save
dreams,' I snapped, making sure with a quick mental
command that the guards were deeply asleep.

The creature looked at me, then at the bottle and
snarled. 'You are going to poison the king!'

'No! I'm going to poison Lisana!' I opened my shields
to its probing and let it rummage around inside my soul,
searching for the truth in my words. I'm usually against
doing that kind of thing – it's rare indeed for any mage to
let another past his shields – but I'd been assured that,
with this particular gargoyle, it wouldn't matter. It found
the core of intent, peered along my plan both present and
future, sniffed, and looked a good deal happier.
'Silverhand B'aquc,' it whispered. 'Welcome to the king's
quarters, Silverhand Kite.'

I was impressed. The Silverhand had a spy hanging
over the king's door, sustained by the king's imagination?
How much talking had that recruitment taken? Thank

the gods Jehirer hadn't decided to get rid of this particular agent.

I tiptoed to the door, careful to keep the guards unconscious, and smeared a large amount of the liquid on the handle, keeping my fingers clear. The handle turned green, as the liquid settled like a tarnish that had always been there. In the morning it would have dissolved – but then, I didn't need to wait that long. I raised a scry-block and slipped into the room.

A scry-block is a wonderful invention, dear dreamer. My own, and something that I have never taught to any other. Some might call me selfish, some might call me wise. A reflection shield, to the eye of any kingdom's Warden, seems like a silver bubble that cannot be penetrated by the Key. But a scry-block projects an image of what should be there, sending out strands of thought through the magic of the kingdom itself, and making the Warden *believe* he sees all that is. It is beautiful, and I owe my life to it.

Some hasty minutes' work across the sheets of Talsin's bed, a few more in the already run bath, and I was away, my heart pounding in my ears. The gargoyle winked. 'For dreaming!'

'Please God let her come,' I agreed, raising the now empty vial in salute.

We sat in my room, Renna, Windsight, Eisirrn and I, waiting nervously. Every now and again we'd send probes skittering to the door of Talsin's room. No one had come.

'Do you think they've gone somewhere else?' asked Windsight finally.

'Shush!' we all whispered. The palace was dark and silent, the dance had long since faded to nothing.

Eisirrn began drumming his fingers, the most irritating sound he could have made.

I made an attempt at conversation. 'So how did you get a gargoyle on our side?'

'Oh, he's always been smarter than his creator. Ever since the old king gave him power to see into people's souls he's been muttering at anyone who goes by. Kept on saying how everyone was plotting against his creator and how, as a gargoyle, he couldn't do anything about it. The old king was ready to dissolve him back into the Void, he droned on so much.'

'But you showed him . . . the other side of royal protection?' I hazarded.

'Too right. It'll be a great shame if that guy ever gets replaced.'

The conversation lagged again. Then I felt a blue bolt of Windsight's power flash by. 'They're there!' he said.

We all jumped to our feet, creating a pretty daft effect. I sent my own probe after his, focused on the king. Lisana was laughing gaily, Talsin was looking pretty dazed as he threw her onto the bed. I guessed he'd already had a bit to drink.

'You know, if Lisana isn't casting a seduction spell on Talsin,' I muttered, 'I swear my alliance with him is pointless.'

'Shush,' whispered Windsight. 'Wait for the poison.'

It hit Talsin first – he'd got the first and largest dose of it. For a long while he became full of energy. Then he began to tire, and his eyes started to flicker. Lisana too moved with increased energy at first. But the charm which would have warned her was ignored. Discarded on the floor next to her clothes, the necklace turned black as the poison began to wind its way through her system.

It took maybe half an hour before she too collapsed, next to Talsin in a deep sleep. And I knew that her magic was asleep also.

We could do anything we wanted.

'It's time.'

I rose to my feet, nodded thanks at Eisirrn and beckoned Renna and Windsight to follow. Renna would guard the door, and Windsight would watch the corridor and keep us shielded should the worst arise.

I stood outside Lisana's elaborate door and began methodically peeling a hole in her wards. Finally the shimmering blanket of magic was thin enough for me to pass through, and I pushed the door open. It creaked ominously.

Inside was pitch black, as silent as a grave. My breathing seemed loud. I could feel every muscle in my body and had suddenly discovered a host of aches and pains. Every step was across hot coals, every shadow held a nightmare.

I summoned magelight to my fingers, looking around carefully. 'Oh, God.'

The place was filled with magic circles. Not the nice, simple elemental circle I enjoyed using, but the blacker, darker ones. And inside the triple circle in the centre of the floor, silent and sullen, blinking in the light, were three blond infants. Lisana's children.

'Kite? What's in there?' Renna called.

'It's . . . it's a power circle,' I replied. 'There are three kids here, hers. She's been drawing off their power.'

'Go away!' yelled the eldest, a boy.

I didn't want a commotion, so I laid a blanket of magic over him, and he could speak no more. He fought, I give him that. He fought like a wild beast, but his power was untrained, and depleted by his mother's draining off him, so I ignored it.

I looked down at the circle itself. Yes, there was a lock of hair from Talsin, the key to the spell. Cautiously, I reached out with a glowing hand and drew a symbol of breaking over the circle. For a minute it strained, then came free beneath the weight of my magic.

It might have ended there, except that this was the moment a shadow decided to spring forward, and press sharp claws against my throat. I froze – naturally. But my mind was far from stricken. <Windsight! Get in here now!> I sent at the top of my mental lungs.

'No intruders,' whispered the goblin. 'What shall we do with this intruder, little master?'

The children stood up as one, aware that the big, nasty man was suddenly in their power. 'Poke his eyes out!' said the eldest, throwing off my blanket of magic with apparent ease.

'Mummy doesn't want anyone coming in here!' agreed the next eldest, a girl.

'I want my Mummy!' wailed the youngest.

'Your Mummy keeps a goblin as a pet?' I squeaked.

Then Windsight was in the door, glowing with all the force of mages. The goblin whirled, holding me like a shield, but I was ready. I've dealt with a lot worse than goblins in my time. I kicked savagely into his shins and grabbed the clawed arm. Goblins are strong, but I was running on hot magic now. My hands came to life with raw fire and the creature screamed as it burned deep into his hand. Another arm stabbed out more on reflex than anything else and a suddenly burning feeling in my left arm suggested deadly claws digging into flesh.

Even as I yelled with the pain the goblin tensed in my arms. Its eyes bulged and it began to gibber in a hoarse whisper. Then, without another sound it slid to the floor.

The children screamed, and the palace came alive.

Kneeling has never suited me, as I think I've mentioned. Now it was really starting to grate.

Talsin paced back and forth, a furious figure in a red nightgown against a backdrop of hastily lit candles. I'd managed to shield Windsight and Renna before the guards could arrive, and Windsight had quickly taken over the shield. No one saw them. No one needed to see them. I was the wild, foolish mage – everyone knew that.

Finally my king spoke. 'I can't believe you were so stupid!'

I said nothing. Worse was to come.

'You deliberately violated court privacy! You lied and tricked me and even dared to poison my rooms!'

'I did it for you, my lord.' *My arm is bloody well bleeding everywhere, I haven't slept once in this whole stupid night and you dare lecture me . . .*

Talsin was having none of it. 'And what is worse, you refuse to tell me who the second member of your party was, who slew the goblin!'

'A Silverhand, my lord. And you shouldn't be concerned about who killed whom. You should be worrying about who killed what. Dreams above, I came here for

war, because I was told that there were outside threats
and betrayals and fights to be fought! I didn't come here
to watch you prance around like a peacock!'

His slap stung, but I didn't complain. He was within
his rights, after all. 'Don't tell me what my worries
should be! Nor what is or isn't happening! He was my
father who died, it's my kingdom being driven towards
the edge. They are my *subjects*' – the word dripped
scorn, but I got the feeling it wasn't all directed against
me – 'who are no longer backing me, until my great plans
of war, that war in which you seem to revel so' – my head
snapped up, and now I itched to deliver a slap – 'can no
longer be made!' His voice dropped. 'I summoned you
here for a council of war. But how can I wage war
without soldiers, without mages, without men who trust
me and in whom I can trust? How *dared* you presume to
know what I can or cannot do at this moment?'

I hung my head, and waited. Have you noticed how
that seems to be all I do with my life? I wish I could
dream myself into a place where people never have to
wait. It'd be nice just to see it.

'You have disobeyed me, and violated the terms of our
agreement. I could have you tried for treason right now
and no one would think any the worse of me.'

'My lord, will you just hear what I have to say?'

He made an effort to calm down, for which I was
grateful. 'Make it good, Kite.'

'The children who screamed are Lisana's children.
They are mages, like her, and were inside a power circle.
You saw this with your own eyes. Also in the circle was
a lock of your hair. You saw this also. Two were projecting a seduction spell while the third maintained a

reflective shield so no one would be aware of them. You saw all this. Lastly a goblin, from Lisana's kingdom, attacked me. Goblins are violent, savage and blood-thirsty creatures, and this one was no exception.' I paused for dramatic effect, aware that from here it was make or break. 'Lisana used you, tricked you, abused you for her own ends and the purposes of those with whom she plotted. You cannot stand there and tell me that I have done you a great wrong when she waits to enchant you once more!'

'How did you get into my rooms?' He was determined to stay mad.

'A scry-block, my lord.'

'That spell you invented?'

'One of the many I invented.' Yeah, make things better for yourself, why don't you? I heard the sour little voice of reason say.

Talsin was silent again, pacing back and forth, whirling in a wave of silk each time he reached a wall. 'How long did she support the spell?'

'The children say they sustained the spell every night from the moment they could walk. The eldest,' I added, recalling something T'omar had said, 'is ten.'

'Ten years?'

'She's been with you at least a hundred,' I pointed out mildly.

'That was before I was king!'

'Oh yes,' I sighed. 'The crown changes everything. It's like a Key. You hold the crown and suddenly everyone is glowering at you. You've got to control the Key, you've got to take responsibility.'

I guess my words were starting to hit home. Talsin,

pale and puffy-eyed, sank to the floor, hugging his knees and looking exactly like the child I remembered demanding that the young mage, new to court – hardly more than a boy himself – do another trick. 'Ten years,' he repeated. 'And I didn't see it, didn't feel it.'

'Haven has always allowed reflection shields within its walls.'

'What should I do?'

He was the pupil, I was the teacher. A thousand times I'd been somewhere like this, a thousand times I'd fought and won. 'Tomorrow is the final ceremony. And the day after . . .'

'I am crowned king.'

'Okay. If you send Lisana away, you've bought time – a lot of time. But this doesn't solve all our problems – of which Nightkeep is a biggy.'

He snorted. '"Our" problems. I feel reassured.'

'Shut up and be appreciative.'

He opened his mouth to object. Had anyone said 'shut up' to him ever before?

Before he could do anything I said, 'You need to keep the Wardens' armies here, until Nightkeep makes a move. If they are trying to trick their way out of support, you need to play their tricking game too. So . . .' I clapped my hands gleefully. 'I've got it! A ceremony commemorating the soldiers who fought by your father! Soldiers from all kingdoms! They'll certainly refuse to budge when they hear that! Announce it right after the coronation, delay them, keep them on the run, *prove* that you're their king and capable of out-manoeuvring them at every stage!'

The light of realisation crept over his face. 'Kite, I do

believe you're a genius.' He gave a hysterical laugh. 'My God, it'll work. We don't need the lords. With the soldiers and people on our side, the court is nothing!'

'Careful.' I warned. 'Never underestimate the power of money.'

'Oh, sure, they've got money in their kingdoms. But I'm ruler here!'

Watching his face light up and hearing his laughter, it was almost easy to forget what he'd done in the past. His smile was the smile of a man who's just discovered freedom.

In that minute of blissful happiness, I could forget Nightkeep, all those betrayals and even the face of the woman who'd so hurt me. There was nothing in this world I couldn't do. I was king of the magic, and the magic ruled everything.

I guess I deserved what was coming after that.

TEN

Light Inside a Crystal

'To the Consortium!'

The small hall we'd found somewhere in the back of the palace was lit only by a few candles, and they were burning low. A pool of wax surrounded each one. Our escapades at midnight were long over, and in the small hours of the morning the rest of the palace had returned to slumber after the night's excitements.

We were sitting around, generally congratulating each other on a job well done.

'Do you think I should try another divining?' I asked. 'Just to check that we have sorted out the evil influences?'

Windsight sniffed. 'With the ceremony tomorrow and the coronation the day after that? You'd collapse in one or the other.'

'Thanks for the moral support.'

'The pragmatic advice,' he corrected.

'I spoke to a Silverhand today,' Eisirrn said. 'Apparently this new leader T'omar knows what he's about. Do you know, in just a few days he's invented a new way of warfare, for the Silverhands to use in the Void?'

I snorted. 'Battles in the Void are a useless waste of life, nothing more.'

'Not these battles.'

He went on to explain. The principle was very simple, I realised. A group of men would go out into the Void with Void-proof equipment, and literally tie themselves to the bottom of the roads. With their butts hanging out over the Void, they'd be supported by nothing but some complicated mountaineering equipment and a bit of shaped maybe. Then, when an enemy came along, they could literally leap out of nowhere and pull their enemies back into it. I was surprised no one had tried it before.

Then, when I thought about it, I wasn't. You'd need to have one hell of a head for heights, and the preparations would be complicated. Though not too much so for our general, it seemed.

Windsight looked thoughtful. 'Do you think T'omar would mind if I borrowed that?'

'I'm sure he wouldn't. He's also increased pay.'

'Where's he getting the money?' I asked cautiously.

'Nightkeep. There's this new scheme for ambushing the convoys.'

I frowned. It sounded less like intelligence and more like military matters. The old king had said that the two together were a contradiction in terms, and you should stick with what you do better. T'omar clearly didn't agree.

'Windsight,' I added, as an afterthought. 'I still haven't said thank you for saving my life.'

'What?'

'The goblin,' I explained, surprised that he wasn't swelling with pride.

The mage looked bemused. 'I didn't do anything. I thought it was you!'

'No. I thought it was you!'

We exchanged looks. 'I don't like this,' I said. 'First the block spell, now this.'

'Could Saenia have . . . blessed you?' Windsight asked weakly.

'I could feel her magic from Stormpoint,' I snapped.

T'omar, Lisana, the ceremonies – all dropped away to be replaced by the big voice of doubt, rattling around inside my already cotton-wool head and hammering for my attention. This isn't right! We're missing something obvious here!

My eyes raced past Windsight, and settled on the silent shape of Renna. I'd been trying to get her to teleport. But that was influencing herself, not other things. Surely she couldn't have . . . I mean, it was unheard of! A dreamer couldn't influence the real world, just move through it.

'Renna?'

'Yes?'

'When . . . when we were back there, did you feel anything?'

She laughed, a little too easily. 'Of course not! You're the great mage, I'm just a dreamer!'

'But . . . you didn't feel . . . as if something was going twang or anything like that?'

She raised her eyebrows. '"Something going twang"? No, Kite, can't say I did.'

Windsight was giving me a narrow, sceptical look. 'What's this about, Laenan?'

It worried me when he sounded severe. It meant he was concerned. A genuinely concerned Windsight was a double-edged sword.

'I was just wondering if Renna might have done something. You know, like magic.'

The silence could have frozen water. Then, after what felt like an eternity, the mage rose, grabbed me by the arm and said, 'Can I have a word?'

I was dragged outside and faced the man's ghastly stare. It wasn't easy. 'Have you totally lost your mind? I've been protecting her for ten whole years and have kept on protecting her in Haven to the best of my ability. I let her get messed up with you because I thought it may do her a good turn, may help her learn. I do not want you putting strange ideas in her head, okay? She's a dreamer. She's fragile, naive and lacking in any talents which might help keep her alive for more than ten minutes. You will not get her any more involved in this whole affair than she already is.' He was shaking with anger.

I wanted to say, 'But she could have the power to change Haven forever. If she can control reality or twist the Void, she could be the one to make everything better!' Only, I hadn't the guts. There was always the possibility that I was wrong, too.

'It was probably drink speaking,' I muttered.

'Kite, your brain works on too many things at once. One day steam will come out of your ears.'

'Sure.' It's incredible how useful that word can be. But it angered me, that Windsight could just turn round and say 'no' – when so much was at stake. It angered me too that I didn't know more, even though all the clues were hanging in front of my nose!

He's just protecting her. It's dangerous for a dreamer in this world. For anyone who doesn't know the rules.

I said, 'I'm calling it a day.'

Windsight nodded. 'Good idea. You've been under a lot of strain.'

And that was it. He was trying to be kind to me. He thought I was drunk, too tired to think or slightly deranged. Perhaps he was right.

I dragged myself upstairs, the triumph of the evening fading to nothing in the face of guilt at having begun a near-fight with one of my closest friends.

My route took me past Lisana's room. A light shone from beneath the door and angry voices could be heard.

'I can't believe that you'd betray me!'

'My lord, I did it for you!'

'You did it for your own gain – don't lie, woman! For dreams' sake, who else did you do it for?'

'Please! I love you!'

'You despise me, as I despise you!'

I leant against the door, my breath catching in my throat. Talsin was going to banish Lisana, maybe even have her tried for treason. I knew I should move on, but my legs refused to budge.

'Your honoured position in court makes it difficult for me to have you executed, whatever the temptation to do so. Also your heirs are too young to inherit Waterpoint, and I will not have more scandal by installing a protector.

So I'm sending you back to Waterpoint tonight with an armed guard. They'll see to the taxing of half your assets and the installation of a more permanent garrison. You will remain under magically null house arrest, and I shall consult the court as to what must be done with you.'

I didn't listen to any more. Lisana's screams and curses echoed down the corridor behind me as I hurried up to my room with my heart pounding. She'd blame me, naturally. Nor did I put it past the woman to send assassins from within the confines of house arrest.

'Kite?'

With my nerves on edge, I started, fire at my fingers.

'Renna! What are you doing here?'

'Going to bed,' she replied levelly.

Neither of us believed it. Windsight's stare had been formidable, and I knew I was in deep water. I snuffed out the fire at my fingers, smiled nervously and said in a too-fast-voice, 'I'll wish you goodnight, then.'

'Goodnight.'

As I turned to go, the expected question socked me on the back of the head.

'What am I, Kite?'

Oh, God. I probed for Windsight, found him a few corridors away and heading upstairs with brisk strides, senses alert. 'A dreamer,' I said hastily.

'And what's a dreamer?'

'Human.'

'Then what are you?'

'Alien, I guess.'

'I can't influence anything, Kite. You must see that.' The note of pleading in her voice was heart-wrenching, but I had to answer.

'You don't know your own power, because you know the world.'

'Meaning?'

Then Windsight was nearly at the turn, and there wasn't time left to explain. 'Goodnight,' I squeaked, and dived into my room, just as he rounded the corner.

What can I say? Tore off boots, didn't bother with the rest of my clothes, collapsed on bed. I heard faint voices drifting in from outside. 'Did you see Kite?'

'No. He's asleep.'

I toned down my magical emanations to a suitable level, and lowered my shields. Windsight's light probe brushed me a second later, and though every instinct screamed out to retaliate, I held still.

A few minutes later, and they too had gone to bed.

So . . . Windsight really did care about Renna enough to insult an old friend by probing. The breach of protocol was immense, but I didn't blame the man. After all, I was famous for causing trouble wherever I went. Renna was one thing he didn't want me to ruin.

I sighed, as grey light seeped into the room. Dawn was closer than I'd thought. I cast a sleep spell on myself, and fell into a deep, dreamless slumber.

'Another, please.'

'You're eating well this morning,' said Renna, from the other side of the table. The dining hall was heaving with people, and all around us rumours of Lisana's fate bounced back and forth. Renna and I had had some strange looks too.

But where was Windsight in all this? I'd have thought that after last night he'd be zealously keeping me away from his ward. But no. Renna had knocked on the door after three hours of my magically induced sleep, and announced that Windsight had gone to the temple to prepare for some ritual or other. Coronations take a lot of that stuff.

A pair of squires skittered by, craning their necks to look at the small little mage and somewhat more impressive dreamer. Hopefully they wouldn't know which was which, I thought with a wry smile.

Let them stare. I munched another bread roll. 'Need to eat. Ceremonies take a lot out of king and mage alike.'

She nodded, saying nothing. She was looking past me, I realised, watching the whispering squires and minor earls.

'What are they saying?' I asked.

Renna cocked a dreamer's ear.

'That one just said, "Do you think they can cause a Void-rift in the palace?" Whatever that means.'

I laughed. 'A Void-rift. It tears the very fabric of a kingdom. Literally lets in a different reality, which devours everything it touches.'

'Could you summon one?'

'If I was incredibly stupid. Suicidal. Anything else?'

'Well, those two in red by the door have just said "I heard he's cursed her, she'll never be able to speak again".'

'Crap.'

'I know. Oh, the guy in blue sitting next to that guard has just said, "She's been sent back to Waterpoint, lucky she's still got her head."'

I said, 'She'll never cast another spell, without someone knowing.'

'Kite, what did you mean last night when you said, "I didn't know my own power, because I knew the world"?'

'That been bugging you?'

'Have you schooled yourself in vague remarks designed to annoy, or is it just a family trait?'

I laughed. 'You should meet my sister. Compared to her, I'm nothing.'

'Kite, I want an explanation.'

I finished my roll, wiped my mouth with a sleeve, and folded my arms. 'What do you want me to say? You'll tell me it doesn't make sense.'

'Kite, I stood with you while your mind shifted through futures. I watched you shatter a circle that happened to contain a man's sanity. That's something Windsight, or any mage, has never been able to show me. Now that I've seen it, I'm willing to believe almost anything you tell me.'

'Even if it makes you God?'

She gave me a look that could have frozen a fire elemental. 'Tell me!'

'Okay, I'll try. The real world – this world – intersects Earth. And the way from one to the other is through dreaming, right?'

'Right.'

'Now, what if one world starts to affect the other? I mean, what happens if something on Earth, Earth's laws of science, the very people who live on Earth itself, start to affect this world?'

'I don't know.'

'Well, this is all conjecture, but the basic theory goes that our worlds have become . . . entwined, I suppose. This world of magic is a place where humans can escape from their real lives, and over the years it has become like a magnet to them. Sooner or later you people will dream, and when you do you come here.'

'How does this tie in with me?'

'This is the tricky bit. Expansion and dreamers are connected to each other. No dreamers, no expansion. No expansion, no new kingdoms to draw more dreamers. Therefore the kingdoms depend on dreamers. My Stormpoint is being dreamed, somewhere, by someone. They just haven't reached their dream. So Skypoint, Haven, Westpoint – they're the culminating effect of a thousand dreamers, all trying to reach there.'

'I still don't get it.'

I leant forward eagerly. 'Well, what if someone who dreamt of Skypoint actually reached there, and stayed, never forgetting as everyone else does, always in control?'

'I don't know. What would happen?'

'The dream would change! Don't you see? The moment someone reaches a place where they have the control of dreams and the control of themselves, they become like a Key.'

'So . . . I can control things?'

'Just like a mage. The only thing which prevents you from being like a God is the fact that you are too tied up in logic and science to realise your potential.'

'This is stupid. That's like saying you're just a figment of the imagination!"

'Of course I'm not!'

She raised her hands defensively. 'Just assuming you're right, how do you know all this? Windsight never said a word.'

'I . . . I don't know. Some of it is standard theory. Other parts are plain obvious.'

'And some of it comes from inside your head?'

'I guess so.'

She rose. Her face was unreadable. 'Thank you. You've given me a lot to think about.' Without another word she turned and began to walk away.

'Renna! Wait!'

She didn't. Why? What was so bad in what I'd said? I didn't understand her, couldn't see why being the dreamer equivalent of a mage so upset her.

'Kite?' Windsight's quiet voice was possibly the last one I wanted to hear in that soft morning air. How he had moved so silently, I do not know. But I managed not to jump, even as my mind gibbered.

I half turned. 'Renna's . . . got a lot on her mind,' I said weakly.

Her guardian frowned, but didn't ask. 'The ceremony's in two hours. You've got to change, and get ready.'

Changing, as it turned out, involved a grey cowled robe that made me look more like a wraith from nightmare, than the nice friendly man I knew myself to be.

The temple of dreams is the largest, most powerful temple in Haven, for obvious reasons. It dominates the central square, on a massive street leading to the palace. Crowds were already gathering. The crowning of a king was a rare event indeed – the previous old boy had lived to be nine hundred before Nightkeep had messed things up.

Five people presided over this final ceremony – four from the temples, and a fifth whose job was to decide if

Talsin was as wonderful as everyone said he was. And tradition said that this fifth person walked cowled and silent, representing the Void, nightmares, magic, etc.

'I am not carrying that thing!' I exclaimed when the master of ceremonies showed me the heavy staff I had to hold.

'The fifth mage always carries the staff of Void,' said the man primly. 'It is traditional.'

I glared at the vile thing. There was a large blue crystal embedded in the top of the ancient black wood. Up the staff's side curled a thin, carved dragon. The gem was supposed to glow brightly if the fifth judge found the king acceptable before presenting him to the waiting crowds. As far as I was aware, the appointment of the fifth judge was political – and had been from the moment some bright spark realised that the fate of the crown rested on whether some bastard liked the candidate's hair colour.

So why has Talsin got you doing this job? I answered my own question the moment I heard it. Politics. The people will love it if his once arch-enemy and legendary mage says, 'Yup, this guy's nice.'

'Well, I didn't expect to see you here.'

The High Priest Kassir was standing next to me. He was resplendent in his bright green robes, and surrounded by four acolytes, two to carry temple banners, two to bear swords in a suitably regal manner.

'I didn't expect to see me here either,' I admitted. 'Look, about when I came to your temple . . .'

'I was flattered,' he interrupted. 'Laenan Kite, slayer of kings, the fifth and final mage, judge of the lord of dreams and thrice-renowned master of magics, came to me in search of answers.'

'Well, if there's anything I can do to help your temple, a blessing or summoning or anything like that . . .' I mumbled.

'I'll keep it in mind,' he replied with a smile.

The master of ceremonies clapped his hands, to gain the massed attention of four high priests, their assistants, and the small figure standing alone with a daft staff and grey robe. 'When we reach the temple, the king will inscribe the blessings of each element individually into the stones. You will observe these for faults. Then, before the council of mages and lords, you will each ask one question: Is the fifth mage ready?' he asked, in a voice that suggested that he'd be astonished if I was.

'Ready.' I fought down the temptation to turn him into a frog.

'You will ask your question last, then declare him king before the court. You will then proceed next to him onto the steps of the temple, and declare the same before the people.'

'What if I don't think he is king?'

The man looked momentarily flummoxed. 'That . . . is highly unlikely.'

'But what if he's a complete and utter bastard? An incompetent fool who'd be the undoing of Haven?' I was rather enjoying myself.

'If you feel so . . . well, it's unheard of.'

'So I should just make it up there and then?'

'I suppose so.'

'Thank you,' I said, an idiot grin on my face. 'You've been most helpful.'

The man recovered himself, clapping his hands

together. 'Come, gentlemen. We shall proceed to the temple.'

It was a procession of happiness. No doubt about that. The crowds lined every step of the way, and went wild the moment the palace gates opened. The high priests stepped into their elaborate litters, and the bearers lifted them up and disappeared in stately order through the gates. They were preceded by a squad of honoured knights. Then came priests of the fire temple, then the earth, then water, then air. Two squads surrounded Talsin, who rode a white horse and looked quite the fairy-tale prince. A delegation from the council of mages, a delegation of mages from other kingdoms followed. The court were next, resplendent in their various liveries with banners flapping behind them in the hands of some squire or page. I was at the very back – another tradition I was eager to eschew. As the last of the knights disappeared through the gate, I made to follow. A pair of guards stopped me. 'Not yet, sir.'

I turned at a familiar shuffling sound. A dragon, quite small, dark green, was watching me. 'Oh, you have got to be kidding,' I said.

'If you'd just put your foot in my hand, sir, I'll help you up.'

'I'm quite capable of getting on my own dragon.'

The guard barely suppressed a laugh. 'Sir, dragons have the worst tempers of any creatures . . .'

'You've obviously never met dwarves,' I snapped. 'And demons are seriously crap when it comes to restraint.' I softened my expression. 'Look, I'm the fifth mage, right? A figure of legend. So let me get on the dragon, and perhaps we won't have to heal any fractured bones.'

He looked doubtful, but backed down. 'Very well, sir. If you're sure.'

'I am. Would you mind holding this, please?' I handed him the staff, and turned my attention to the dragon.

<I'm seriously going to kill Talsin,> I sent.

<Did not he tell you fly me?> was the slightly disjointed answer. Dragons aren't so much stupid, it's just that they used to be an incredible pest, eating other people's stuff left and right. So most dragons these days are made inside the kingdoms, and controlled by the holder of the Key. And the holder of the Key, with a good understanding of how troublesome dragons can be, always leaves them with just enough understanding of language to get by, and just enough knowledge to know what not to eat. Never more. Yet I've always got on with dragons. They're nice, uncomplicated individuals, who look on stupid things like wars with a disdainful eye.

<No he did not! Do you mind if I ride you? I'm not too heavy, I think.>

<I exist to fly. You ride me.>

<You're very reasonable about this.>

<I exist to fly.>

<What's your name?>

<I . . . was given no name.>

<That's shameful. Can I name you?>

<Do I choose if name good?>

<Of course.>

<Then please, give name.>

I reached the creature's scaly side, found that spot behind the wings where all the dragons of my acquaintance had loved to be scratched, and scratched. The creature crooned pleasure. Carefully avoiding the delicate wings, I curled my fingers around the ridge of its spine, and scrambled up. <What gender are you?>

<I . . . do not understand gender.>

I took the staff off the guard, who was by now looking very impressed. The ground already seemed a long way below me, and we hadn't even taken off.

<Are you a boy or a girl? I forgot to check.>

<I think . . . I bear no child.>

<No child? Then you're a girl.>

<Yes. Girl.>

I glanced up at the gate. A guard was watching the procession, waiting for it to get far enough along so that we could take off with suitably dramatic timing. He shook his head to my questioning glance.

<You look like . . . Saenia.>

<Who Saenia?>

<My sister, if you must know.>

I pulled the cowl over my face and settled the staff into a more comfortable position.

<She look like dragon?> asked the creature with amazement in her voice.

<Oh yes. And she has the spirit of one.>

<And claws?>

<Very sharp.>

<Then I be honoured to be Saenia. What you name?>

<Me? Laenan.>

The guard turned, and gave a thumbs up. Sometimes I long for your aeroplanes, dear dreamer. They just go very fast and then take off smoothly. Dragons take a standing jump, open their wings with a snap that can be heard on the other side of the kingdom, and pull themselves into the air with a series of lurches and wrenches which make the stomach churn. I was grateful for the hood – it meant no one could see how green my face was. At the top of her highest pull, several dozen yards above the houses, the dragon gave a roar, sent a billow of flame into the sky, and levelled out. I leant closely over her neck, fixing my eyes on the temple, where the far end of the procession was just pulling up. 'Fly,' I whispered.

The dragon – Saenia – roared again, and with the crowds cheering below, sped off towards the final ceremony of kings.

The temple was smaller than I remembered. Probably the passing of so much time looking over a whole kingdom. Or the thrill of the wide sky still lingering in my racing heart. Anyway, the hall where we ended up, brightly lit and packed with mages and courtiers alike, was holding its collective breath as Talsin approached the dais where I waited, surrounded with two high priests on either side. I wasn't allowed to take the hood down yet and my nose itched (noses always itch at the worst possible time, dear dreamer).

Like all the other temples I'd visited, there was a lot of light. Unlike them its light was broken into different colours by stained-glass windows depicting earth, air, fire and water. The altar was partly the rough, unworked lump of stone I'd observed in the temple of earth, but blue and red fire moved across the ancient runes carved into it, rushing back and forth like waves breaking on a beach. However beautiful this effect, I doubted that any of the huge court sitting near the back could see. The temple was in fact so big that we were just small figures to them, playing games in the heart of dreams.

Talsin knelt before the altar, then rose to stare levelly at my hidden face.

'Who comes to the temple of dreaming?' intoned the high priest of dreams.

'Talsin, who would be king of the light.'

'Who calls on the gates of magic?'

'Talsin, who would wear the crown of magic.'

'Talsin, who would be king and wear the crown, you have proved yourself before the elements. Now you must inscribe your worth into the dream.'

We moved aside, letting him stand before the altar. The simple stone slab was glowing with magic. A hundred kings had come here before, and written into the stones four blessings a hundred times. This was what Talsin had to do now. He bowed to the north, concentrated, and inscribed a blessing of air. He bowed to the east, inscribed a blessing of water. The south summoned earth, the west summoned fire.

I watched with a curious eye. The blessings were done, and he had put a good deal of magic into the ancient stones. Needless to say he was looking a little pale by the final blessing. Yes, they were good spells, to make any mage proud.

Each high priest then moved forward, and with a small ceremonial knife cut his right arm, just once. The blood dripped onto the altar in utter silence – Talsin did not sway.

The five of us were rearranged behind the now stained and glowing altar, staring at the king-to-be. The staff was cold and heavy in my hand.

'If an army arrived at your gates and you were unarmed and alone, what would you do?' asked the high priest of fire.

Talsin licked dry lips. 'I would stand on the road that leads to Void with fire and ice at my fingers, and send all the forces of my imagination against them until dreams themselves reached up and bore my torn body to heaven.'

I nearly tutted. Textbook answer. However, the court murmured and nodded their approval – clearly textbooks were in fashion. I wondered if there was a standard answer to the question I had in mind.

'If a plague took all in the city, everyone in the streets and palace, what would you do?' asked the water priest.

'I would move among the sick and heal them all with my power until I either collapsed from fatigue or fell foul of the disease myself.'

I had to stop myself from drumming my fingers on the staff. Yeah, yeah. What about quarantine? What about basic hygiene? What about warning the other kingdoms? What about healing those who can then help heal more? You wouldn't just go onto the streets and find any old fool . . .

Air and earth asked their questions. Was anyone doing anything from their own imaginations? My eyes fell on the master of ceremonies. Everything that's being asked has an arranged answer. The king knows what they're going to ask, the court wants him to succeed without even a slight chance of making a fool of himself.

It was my turn. Everyone was staring at me, the mysterious fifth, cowled figure. I was rather flattered that they hadn't dared ask me to give a textbook question –

they probably all knew I'd go ballistic at such a suggestion.

I reached into my magic, took a tiny thread and pushed it into the air. When I spoke, my voice carried all over the temple. 'What gives you the right to rule, where no other may claim it?'

Talsin hesitated. The blood was still dripping onto the altar, I could feel the fatigue pouring out of him. 'No right,' he said in a voice laden with weariness, 'save the study of the world. Save that from the day I was born they said to me, observe this land, for one day you must rule it. So I have striven to observe, watching the people who know so much more of the real world than I ever can. And through this watching I have learnt to love, learnt to care, learnt to understand the lands and the way they work. But you are right – I have no right, and there are many more who have seen greater works and travelled further abroad than I. The only right I can claim is that which I shall strive to earn, that which I hope to gain by serving the land as best I may. That's all I can ever hope to achieve, and you must judge for yourselves whether I shall ever achieve it.'

In the silence that followed I could see him huddled before me, begging advice, the past ten years of his life a fast-fading nightmare, the real world slamming into his face with the full force of a shattered spell. And I knew why he'd asked me to be the fifth mage. Because he needed someone to tell him he would be good. Someone to tell him that everything was all right and he could go on. Was that really so bad? Isn't that why I had turned to Kassir, isn't that why I whispered my woes to Renna and still journeyed to Silverpoint in the arms of friends?

'Talsin, who would be king,' I said, feeling everyone hang on every word. Hang so much, that their weight seemed to pull me down beneath the surface of the sea, and made my heart burn and my lungs tight for want of air. 'You have stood before this court, and declared your just intent. Though you stand here primarily because of the right of birth – a right which can never buy a land – you shall leave here because you have proved yourself more than just a child whose father wielded a great army. Because you have proved with words and blood and magic that you can be something more than a tradition bound by a thousand years of dreaming.' I raised the staff, pouring magic into its ancient wood and letting the crystal shine so bright on my power that it was nearly blinding to look at. 'So we declare that you shall be king!'

The crowds outside the temple went wild. A coronation is a good chance to wave hats and have a bit of a party, and this crowd was really getting into the feel of the festivities. I walked by Talsin's side, holding the staff where all could see, and stood at the top of the steps looking down into a sea of faces and hearing the roar of triumph echo off high walls. Talsin was tired, trembling and pale, but his face was glowing with such joy that it made me want to weep. I lifted the staff again for them all to see, raising such a cheer that the stars themselves must have looked down with a startled cry.

Pushing back the hood so they could all see the figure of legend in a clear light, I knelt before him and that day swore allegiance, as they all did.

Still, it was impressive, from what I could see. Talsin would be king. Maybe a good king, at that.

'Long live the king! Long live King Talsin of Dreams!'

'Well done!'
   'Loved it!'
   'Congratulations!'
We picked our way through a sea of talk and smiles, and out of the hall, which was still celebrating even though the moon was high in the sky. Windsight approached, fairly glowing in his blue mage-robes, and slapped me on the back. 'Well done, Laenan! The fifth mage scored again!' The ceremony seemed to have restored a little vim to him, and his good humour was infectious. All thought of Renna, Nightkeep or the mess I was still in had faded from my mind, and we were laughing and talking just like friends always should. I had the feeling he was being deliberately cheerful, trying to shove the night before into the past by sheer force of character.

I tried to suppress a yawn when shortly afterwards we were outside my room. 'The fifth mage is utterly wrecked,' I announced, leaning against my door.

'Saenia called. She wants to see you tomorrow, before the coronation.'

I groaned. 'Probably wants to tell me off for getting messed up in politics again.'

'And Renna wants to see you.'

I frowned, and gave the answer he was almost certainly longing to hear, and which for once I meant from the heart. 'Does it matter if I see her after the coronation tomorrow? I'm good for nothing tonight.'

'I doubt it. I'll tell her anyway.'

'Thanks.'

'Good night, old friend.'

'Good night, Windsight.'

I fell into bed the moment the door closed, and the second my head hit the pillow I fell into a blissfully deep sleep.

And dreamt.

The hospital was crammed. There was no room to move, on account of the people just lying there, still as statues. The only movement was in their eyes, as they stared at some unseen visage.

'I was bloody grateful to wake up, believe me,' said one doctor, who looked so tired he was about to fall over.

'The scientists say it's a new virus. Attacks the dreaming part of the brain directly.' The nurse was on her fourth cup of coffee, her face pale and her hands trembling.

'You can't keep drinking that stuff! Sooner or later we'll have to sleep – we'll all have to!'

'You think I don't know?' The woman was nearly in tears. 'Two billion people are in a coma! You think I don't know we have to sleep? Of course I bloody know!'

I drifted on, picking my way between people sprawled on the floor, up staircases where nurses had simply collapsed, into the wing where Renna slept.

He was there. Standing over a slumbering nurse. As translucent as I, he was leaning over a woman with a malicious little smile. Renna was in the very next bed.

'No!' I yelled. 'Go away!'

He turned, a furious look in his eyes. He saw me, and a flicker of recognition passed across his face. 'David Kiteler, you can't touch me. You're just a dreamer,' he said with a sneer.

He was Slimy Doc. The same nose like a hawk, the dark eyes, the smug smile. Only now he wore black robes, down to his ankles. Silver embroidery of extraordinary design ran through his silken clothes.

'It's Laenan Kite, you bastard,' I snapped. 'You should have studied your histories more closely.'

I saw his smile falter. 'Laenan . . . the regicide?'

'You're Serein. I'd recognise your smug face anywhere. Look a lot like your dad, don't you?'

'It's too late, Kite. You can't stop it now. I'm already here. There's nothing you can do.'

When I woke up, I knew the invasion was about to begin.

ELEVEN

A Divining Ignored

I'll say this for Serein – he has a sense of timing. During any of the earlier ceremonies there would have been watchful mages, and great gatherings of people ready to defend themselves at any time. Any invading army would have either been struck down by magic, or slaughtered by the mob.

But a coronation is a ceremony of sombre tradition and stately grace, where the crowds are dispersed and there is just the court. The mages sit in their high towers, the guards, with a curious eye, watch the halls where the king sits. No one attacks in a coronation. It'd be like attacking an unarmed man.

I was worried. Well, of *course* I was bloody worried. But I couldn't barge into the middle of a coronation and announce, 'Oh yes, I dreamed there was this guy on Earth, only he wasn't, who's inside Haven, only he isn't and he wasn't, and we're all going to die, only we didn't.'

I rose early, so I could see my sister before attending the crowning of the king. The sun was barely over the horizon as I stood in the gate, watching my breath freeze in the air and feeling a chill wind from the north. Bright mage-lights were strung from every window and criss-crossed up and down the street. Laughter and applause drifted out of the nearest pub, the markets sounded as if they were thronging. Guards were giving out special packages of food in celebration of the new king's coronation.

A bright day brought with it feelings of peace and glory, and everywhere I looked in the palace I saw nothing but good things. My sixth sense twitched nervously, but soon even that fell silent.

The second I was out of the palace gate, the feeling of dread returned tenfold. I found a handy alley, and drew the sign of the sword. T'omar's thoughts were with me instantly.

<Congratulations, Kite. The ceremony was very impressive.>

<Thank you. Any news about Nightkeep?>

<Two-thirds of the force have been sent against three outlying kingdoms. We managed to get warning ahead in time, and anticipate an easy victory for Haven.>

<Only two-thirds? And against three kingdoms? Why?>

<We think it's a feint of some kind. The two-thirds get wiped out, but in the process they cripple three kingdoms. The breach is sealed by the surrounding kingdoms who donate soldiers and food, etc., and the remaining third launches an all-out strike on the fourth, unprepared kingdom.>

\<You've warned the kingdoms, of course.\>

\<Naturally, and the elementals are trying to slow things down for nightmare. If it turns into a kingdom-siege, they'll soon starve.\>

\<So . . . nothing to worry about?\>

\<I wouldn't call it nothing. The Consortium's rushed off its feet as it is.\>

\<Thank you. I won't disturb you again.\>

\<Call any time.\>

I didn't go the back way in to visit my sister, this time. The mage council knew I was back – they'd all seen me. So I walked straight up to the front gate, glowered at the wards on the door, and nullified them in a small, roughly Kite shape. Through a courtyard, up into the tower still full of slumbering mages, and knocked on the door.

Saenia took a long time to answer. And surprise, Zeryan got shooed out as I was fluttered in. 'You're up early,' she said, offering me a chair by her balconied window. From up here, I could see most of the way to the Void. At least Talsin had been sensible enough to leave a few ice-drakes on patrol, flying around the perimeter of Haven.

'Coronation,' I said in a hushed voice. The incident of a few days before still burnt in my mind. 'Can't be late.'

She nodded, uneasy. 'I . . . wanted to apologise. For what I said.'

'Oh . . . it's fine. Really.'

'And . . . I wanted to explain. About Zeryan.'

'You're lonely,' I said with a shrug. 'He's probably very good company.'

'He's a spoilt brat,' she said with a half-hearted smile.

'But somewhere deep down he knows it. And he wants to change.'

'So you . . . ease him along?'

'Something like that. He needs me, I need him. It's as simple as that.'

'Of course. That's fine.' I tried to throw off the image of the arrogant man who'd glowered at me in the corridor. 'Anyway, I intend to go back to Stormpoint when all this mess is sorted out. You can come and visit.'

'Thank you. I've never seen your kingdom.'

'It's wonderful. Rains a lot. No sand, either.'

She laughed. 'You never did like the desert.'

'Not really.' As conversation seemed to be lagging, I glanced out of the window in search of something lighter to chat about. I wanted to talk to Saenia. I hadn't had a chance to do that for so long. 'Nice view.'

She nodded, staring across Haven with a glowing eye. 'An advantage of being powerful, I guess. All the fools in the council think that a big tower is a sign of power. Nothing's changed here for hundreds of years.'

'Still a nice view.' I watched the streets, observing all the tiny figures as they scuttled to and fro. One group moved beneath a reflection shield, and it was interesting to note how the people around just parted blank-faced, not even aware what they were doing as the shield moved in a dead straight line down the road. A dog barked at it, and his owner pulled the creature away with no particular expression on his face. A cat bumped its nose against the shield, and recoiled yowling, not sure what had just hit him.

'Any of your mage colleagues up yet?' I asked, eyeing it carefully. There was a familiar feel to that shield.

'Are you kidding? Most of them don't get up before noon!'

'See that reflection shield, down there?'

She peered into the streets. 'Yes?'

'Together we could slip beneath it. You cloak me, I'll do the probing.'

'Kite. I'm a respected mage. I can't muck around the way you do.'

'No one need ever know. I've just got a feeling, that's all. You know mages are supposed to trust their feelings.'

She groaned. 'I knew asking you here was a mistake. You always get messed up in things which shouldn't bother you!'

'Please, Saenia. I was right in the desert, wasn't I?'

She sighed again, but I felt her magic grow. 'Very well.'

I smiled my thanks and closed my eyes. I was an angel of white shadow, flying on translucent wings. A blanket of warmth, formed of compassion, love and just a little magic covered me, blinding all to my presence.

The reflection shield stood out like a beacon to my magical eyes. I dove towards it, searched it for a crack and, small as a dust mote, swept inside.

The mage felt something, but dismissed it. His probes skittered weakly off Saenia's shielding, and he shrugged and turned away.

But we both faltered when we saw the shape of that probe. Blood red, streaked with black and twisted by chaos, it bore a mark so familiar I could have raised it with my eyes shut. This was no ordinary mage, just as the four soldiers with him were no ordinary soldiers. The black and red livery was the first clue, the necromantic

magic the second, the glowing red eyes the third.
Overwhelming evidence on all fronts.

A dreamer stood next to the guards. His eyes were
shut, he wore rags and trembled all over. Beneath the
protection of my sister's powerful magic, I reached into
his mind.

*Running, the dogs howling on his heels, a never-ending tunnel
of black stone. So tired, desperate to die, longing for the release of
the hounds' deadly claws but unable to stop running . . .*

I drew away, fighting off the fear written into every
part of the spell that covered the man, and turned my
attention to the mage.

*A land of opportunity. We are finally here, the entire Void is
ours . . .* I ignored the thoughts of the fairly typical man,
and looked through his eyes. *Shields on shields, layers of
magic blanketing the entire town, spells of 'Don't Look Now' on
every mage, spells of 'Not My Concern' on every guard, spells of
slumber and spells of peace.*

And now that I had heard his thoughts, I felt the sly
tendrils of magic on me, a spell that made me ignore all
but the most obvious magic. How many mages had been
involved in casting that neat trick, I couldn't say, but my
sister and I threw off the spells with revulsion. We both
despised falling foul of magic other than our own.

So, as the last feelers of necromantic magic fell away,
I looked over Haven and saw hundreds of reflection
shields, each covering their own mage. And over the
palace, one giant shield that would block any signal with
which I might try to pierce it.

My call to T'omar had only worked thanks to my
being outside the palace gates, but what a fool I'd been!
Why hadn't I sensed anything? Why hadn't the mages

sensed anything? Why hadn't my alarm wards gone off, why hadn't I watched my own divining and listened to the feelings inside me . . .

<You did send it. You thought something was wrong.>

I returned to my body with a start. Saenia was already on her feet. She was packing bags, shoving everything into a Void-proof travel pack and swinging it over her shoulder.

'Haven is doomed,' she announced flatly. 'We can never fight off that many soldiers without the Key, and there is no way we can reach Talsin.'

It's incredible how fast she can think. Okay, she was thinking of the destruction of everything and declaring herself coward, but that didn't matter. She'd still reached the obvious conclusion faster than I ever could.

'Not all the shielded soldiers are at the palace, and the shield is so wide it must be fragile.'

'We must warn the town, get everyone out of there. Nightmare is no fool, it'll go straight for the Key. Once that's taken, this whole place will become one big pool of lava.' She snorted, hearing her own words. 'What the hell am I thinking? *We* must get out of here. Fifty thousand people is another thing entirely.'

'You warn them. Get soldiers to the palace, get the mages to assemble in the main square.'

She gave me a long, calculating look. 'You're going to try and warn the palace, aren't you? Get Talsin out? You're really going to walk up to the main gates and say, "Stop the coronation, we're under attack from an invisible enemy"?'

'Yup. And tell the Consortium. They can speed the evacuation and slow down the soldiers.'

'Fifty thousand people through a city of necromancers with nothing but a few panic-stricken mages? What the hell are you thinking?'

'I'm thinking that I saw this coming and didn't do enough to prevent it!'

'Oh, and now you're willing to get your sister killed because you were blind?'

'My sister would be willing to take a few risks so that thousands of innocent people don't die!'

She froze, an argument on her lips. Finally she sagged. 'I'll warn the mages. Kite, you do realise that with that many soldiers we're doomed anyway?'

'Oh, sister,' I said reproachfully. 'And I thought you always looked on the bright side of things!'

She snorted bitterly. 'Brother, there are some things that magic can't blow to pieces. A monstrous army inside the gates comes pretty high on the list.'

I nodded, and advanced to the window. 'Lend me magic, sister.'

Without a word she slid her power, warm and huge, into my hands. I focused on the reflection shield and sent a ball of fire into its depths. The magical barrier exploded into a shower of white sparks. Windows opened as people craned to see. I focused on the mage and touched his heart. The man's distress signal hit Saenia's cool, controlled magic and was frozen. The mage died, before he could warn his comrades, and the city came alive with the commotion.

'There. Now let's see what a monstrous army can do against the power of a mob.'

I passed two more reflection shields on the way to the

palace, and fried them with us much noise as possible. Running as fast as I could I reached the palace gate in under ten minutes, but I could already hear the clang of a gong as the coronation began. I needed to warn Silverpoint. I raised magic to draw the sign of the sword, but froze as my hand suddenly began to glow with a red light. Someone had opened a link to me via the hand mark I'd left in Silverpoint. <T'omar! It is a feint, they're already here!> I sent, too high on fear and self-reproach to care why my spell had been tapped.

<And here!> The voice was strained, the connection weak. <They're using dreamers, trying to knock everything out at once. They just appeared out of nowhere!>

<I know, I know.> I checked my own supplies of magic. Probably I had enough, what with a good night's sleep and those big meals . . . I sent a bolt of energy along the link anyway, renewing the soldier and giving him strength. <You sort out your problems, I'll sort out mine.>

A different link, this time to Saenia. <The Consortium's under attack. They're going to be no help.>

<There's a crowd gathering at the tower. They're confused, they've seen the necromancers. We're lighting the warning beacon, though hardly anyone's old enough to remember what to do once it's lit.>

<Not good enough. Get everyone you can onto the roads. Direct them to . . . oh, Westpoint. Able men to take the rear.>

<Isn't that a little drastic?>

<Saenia, I've already met two shielded groups of necromancers, and I've only just reached the palace. I'm in a drastic mood.>

<Will do.> Behind me, the top of the mage tower suddenly exploded into light, summoning everyone who valued their lives to the gate.

I turned my attention to the palace.

The covering, I realised, wasn't actually a reflection shield. It was just a solid blanket of magic, which projected whatever the viewer wanted to see, while at the same time reflecting any magic.

I reached the gate, and grabbed the nearest guard by the shoulder. 'Do you see me?' I snarled.

'Yes, sir!' he stammered.

'Do you want to see me?'

'No, sir!'

'Good. Now go get all your lazy, blind colleagues and tell them that Laenan Kite has summoned you all to the coronation right now, with full weaponry!'

Somewhere a gong struck again, warning that 'right now' probably wasn't soon enough. I raced from guard to guard, willing them to wake, praying that the hundreds of enemies I'd seen from Saenia's tower had forgotten their town maps and were wandering around looking confused. The military does things like that.

I reached the first of three courtyards leading to the coronation hall, all the while focused on keeping a shield intact and breaking through the magical fog to any receptive mind.

Their attack was perfectly positioned, I give them that. The two assassins from Nightkeep, specially trained by some ghastly institution to kill foolish mages like me who wandered into the wrong corridor, caught me completely by surprise. The one who came from my left I was just about able to deflect with a hasty wind barrier, the second caught me off guard and managed to get in a series of punches that left me torn between rage and admiration.

Anyway, skilled assassins besides, the result of all this was that I ended up on the cold cobbles gasping for breath and with a knife at my throat. 'How did you break the spell?' spat one assassin.

I said nothing. I didn't really feel like co-operating. The one I had sent flying bore down on me, hatred in his eyes. Stars flashed in front of me as he delivered a series of kicks that made the punches which had gone before seem like a child's tickle fight. 'You were going to warn the king. How did you know? Who told you?'

He readied his fist for another punch, and I decided the time had come for talk. 'My name's Laenan Kite. Your spell wasn't strong enough.'

'Then why do you not signal your friends for help?'

I almost wanted to sigh. 'My signals are blocked.'

'We should kill him now.'

The assassins were too well trained to have second thoughts, I decided, and that decision probably saved my life. If people like that think they should kill, they'll do it. Bullets may miss the good guys in fairy-tale stories. But I wasn't about to risk my life on the pretext that Haven was a real city of dreams.

The knife at my throat exploded into burning red iron, the assassin who wielded it was thrown up and over my shoulder by an invisible force, screaming and clutching his scalded hand. Always throw a man with a knife forwards from the blade. Backwards can be messy, and as I've mentioned before, I can't stand mess.

I dived away from the second one through instinct

rather than strategy. Which was probably why he managed to get on top of me, slamming my head against the stones. This time several galaxies exploded behind my eyes. Through my hazy sight a blade gleamed. I ignored my throbbing skull and raised a shield of fire around me. The knife – stubborn thing – arced at me through the flames anyway, and I grabbed the hand which wielded it with a strength born of fear.

No one can stand forever in a torrent of flame, and this assassin was no exception. He screamed and finally caught fire. I pushed him off me and scrambled to my feet, watching with fascinated horror as he turned in moments to a pile of ashes.

The other assassin had changed hands, and knives. This was unwelcome as well as unexpected. My reserves of magic were already suffering and I could feel the inevitable headache coming on.

He cannoned towards me, and I barely avoided him. We became locked in a writhing mass of good-guy, bad-guy, and it soon became clear by a bleeding nose and trapped hands that good-guy wasn't up to the job.

You know how such really unpleasant things seem to last forever, and you'll recall them at the strangest times? For the rest of my life I'm going to be seeing that damned knife heading down towards me with a hiss of steel, and hearing my scream as it embedded itself somewhere around my shoulder and the howl of my attacker, who fell face-first on me, an axe in his back.

Renna backed away, pale and trembling. Blood spattered her beautiful white dress. 'I . . . I listened to what you said . . . and then I tried to believe and . . . and I just knew that you were in trouble,' she mumbled.

I crawled out from beneath my attacker, praying as I did so. She raced forward as I stumbled and fell. 'Let me do that.'

Through a haze of pain I saw her lean forward and pull out the knife. I felt grateful, I suppose, though I was pretty sure you weren't supposed to do that if you could avoid it. 'Hold this,' she said, sternly. She pressed a torn and folded strip of her dress against my shoulder, hard enough to make me want to pass out. Believe it or not, even legendary mages can get queasy when they see enough of their own blood.

'We've . . . got to warn Talsin. Nightkeep is inside the city.'

'I know. I can feel dreamers, just like me, all around. Hundreds of them. All scared.'

I stared at this girl with a new admiration. 'You're listening to yourself, aren't you, rather than science and logic?'

She wrenched another strip of fabric from her dress, pressing it against my shoulder with even more force in an attempt to stop the blood. 'I sat up all night trying to believe. And suddenly it came to me – why am I trying to change the way I think? That's a science too. So I stopped trying, and simply said that it was the truth, that I had seen you summon magic and fly with dragons. It was like a light flicked on in the dark – but until it came on I hadn't known I was in darkness.'

The sentiment was wonderful, the fulfilment of my hopes and dreams, but more pressing matters occupied my attention. 'I've got to get to Talsin. Help me,' I croaked. She pulled me up with surprising strength and together we staggered towards the hall.

'Shouldn't he be able to feel this? This magic? I can almost see it, smothering everything.'

'No. A spell was cast, don't ask me when, which turns the attention away from all but what you want to see. Also he's tired, in the middle of getting the crown and inside a massive bubble of reverse magic.'

'How did you break the spell?'

'I left the palace. Met my sister. Brother and sister mages draw strength from each other without trying. Simply being together was enough to weaken the spell, I guess.'

'You really do come from a powerful family, don't you?'

'Not at all. We were the freaks of the litter.'

We made our way up the steps to the great hall, and Renna pushed the door open.

It was easy, seeing that room so peaceful and the court so resplendent, to believe that I didn't have a gaping tear in my shoulder and Renna wasn't covered in blood.

The priest, in the middle of intoning a speech, froze at the sight of us. Talsin rose to his feet, astonishment on every feature. We reached the bottom of the throne before Renna finally staggered. I slipped from her grip and half walked, half fell into my king's arms.

With that physical contact, I was able to break the spell that blinded him.

'Look,' I whispered. 'We are undone.'

He raised eyes now clear of nightmare's magic, and looked around the room with horror seeping into his face. Reflection shields pressed against every wall and lined the balconies. People behind them were loading guns and preparing to attack, waiting for a simple sign. Talsin lifted a hand to summon four walls of stone around him and the courtiers, shifting reality to shield us, and I heard the first shot. He slumped, now leaning on me as I had leant on him. The courtiers screamed as shot after shot rang out across the room. They fell like puppets, but I was oblivious to them. Talsin raised one blood-soaked hand – his blood, not mine – and stared at it in horror. I slumped to my knees, exhaustion and despair claiming whatever vestige of energy had kept me going.

'I'm so sorry,' I whispered. He stared down at me with unseeing eyes, and vaguely patted me on the head. Then, without a word, he offered his wet hand. Hesitantly, I took it in my own sticky red grasp.

'You are a good man, Kite. The Key is yours.'

Magic flowed between us, amplified by his dying breath and the blood that now poured freely. I felt the tears begin as he slumped back in the throne, staring at nothing, a strange little smile on his face. There was no great operatic song mourning the fact of death, no dignified closing of the eyes. He just stared, and kept on staring, at his court torn to pieces and a palace filled, after so many years, with enemies. It's not pleasant to see a grown man, or even a young child, cry. But I think I had justification in weeping.

As the gunshots died away I just knelt before him, waiting to die. I don't know for how long the battle between mages raged, how many fell. I was surrounded by a shield of shock and despair, which no bullet penetrated.

The court was shoved into the centre of the room, what little survived. I could feel Renna and Windsight among the survivors, and thanked the gods for small and no doubt short-lived miracles.

The Key rose out of Talsin's limp body as the echo of the last shot died away. I saw instantly that something was wrong with it. It glowed as red as blood, and seemed to be trying to tear itself apart. Little bolts of lightning dug from the surface into its heart. I reached out to take it, felt it respond as if it were already mine. Then a hand knocked my own aside, and *someone else took the Key*! The indignation came from a part of me I didn't know I had. It drove hatred and anger into my heart from the place where the primal animal lurks, screaming that it was mine!

Serein grinned as I slumped back, and pulled the Key into himself. 'No, Laenan. Haven is mine. I see you didn't get past my assassins utterly unscathed. Of course it would be you who broke the spell. Do you know it took fifty mages even to establish the basics of that?'

Rough hands grabbed me and shoved me unceremoniously towards a wall where riflemen waited indifferently. *What? Is that it? You're just going to shoot me without even according the dignity of a defiant answer or an heroic speech?*

Get real, of course he is. Outside I could hear more gunshots as the royal guards came into the fray – too late. All our plans, all the careful schemes to keep soldiers and mages alike in Haven, had fallen to dust, torn apart by the element of surprise and my own blindness. I prayed to all the gods that Saenia had been fast enough in mustering the mages. That way at least a few people might survive.

But the image that filled my mind was of the Key, the warped Key, twisted out of shape by a dying man's last wish. 'You're carrying a curse, Serein,' I whispered. 'It's inside you, eating away, burning you. You can't feel it yet, but it'll start to kill.'

He snorted. 'You're a dead man, Laenan.'

I was shoved against the far wall. Rough hands pulled my own together and tied them tightly with rope. 'We got warning,' I said. 'The mages are fled. You attacked too late.'

The lord of nightmare – now lord of dreams – seized a nearby rifleman's gun and took aim. 'All of you take note,' he said in a clear voice. 'This man murdered my father. His death will be an example.'

If it was meant to scare me, it did the opposite. I'd passed through gales of emotion and was out on the calm seas of numb shock. It was probably irrational, but I reckoned I might as well go out with flair. Through what little remained of my control, I took a fistful of power and pulled. The gun cracked as Serein's feet were tugged from beneath him. Windsight leapt forward, and lightning danced from his fingers as he lunged at riflemen with a strength that amazed me. As the hall broke out into chaos once more, I saw Renna dive towards me and grab me roughly by the collar. Then she reached out with an arm which seemed to grow by several inches as she stretched, grabbed Windsight, raised her head to the heavens and closed her eyes.

I looked up to the balconies where soldiers in red and black took aim. I heard the rifles open their salvo, and saw leaden death race towards the three of us. But the bullets seemed to be slowing, running into air that thickened and warped.

Then, with a dread that made my guts twist into knots, I saw Serein stand up, aim his rifle at my face from point-blank range, and close his finger round the trigger. I heard the crack. I saw the sparks.

Saw them fade.

Fade, like him, a ghost. Fade like a ghost, taking the whole world with him until there was just the bright glow of the Void, and the sound of voices . . .

'No one understands what goes on in a comatose mind.'

'Has anybody ever asked?'

'No one seems to remember. Yet they dream.'

'What do they dream of? Do they have nightmares? Years and years of nightmares?'

'Or dreams. Hell, in ten years you could probably dream an entire new universe, with thousands of different people, all acting as individuals yet just part of the dreamer's mind. She might be dreaming that she's some great princess of an Arabian night and there's this strange prince telling her she's not real and that he's the only sentient creature, the only real creature around.'

'She might be thinking she's fighting for a friend who thinks and acts individually, whom she can never predict, when in fact he's just a creature of her mind.'

'Right. Weird way to die, fighting for a dream.'

And the world faded. Like a dream.

TWELVE

Fallen Crown

I woke in a warm bed in a long room, the burning silence of the Void ringing in my ears. Yet neither the bustling of healers nor the hum of low conversation in this strange place interested me – it was that single word 'woke' which had my full, undivided attention.

I was awake. Not playing a harp in heaven, nor drinking cat's piss in hell. I checked for monsters or chains that might suggest a dungeon. The most threatening thing I could find was a nurse wielding a tray of clean implements with horribly sharp bits on them. I checked for sounds of war. A dragon crooned pleasurably some way off as its rider tickled it behind the ears.

Slowly the realisation dawned. Not dead, not imprisoned, not dying, not even hurting as much as I would have expected.

'You're awake, then.'

I turned my head painfully slowly, and stared into the

broad grin of Virisin. He was lying beneath white sheets with one arm in a bandage.

'Virisin? Where am I?'

'Silverpoint. Windsight and his ward appeared out of nowhere a few days ago, you over his shoulder.'

'Out of nowhere?'

'Scared the hell out of us, especially after the last attack.'

The words sunk home, bringing with them a warmth that wasn't feeling at all, but something beyond, warm as the greatest joy. 'She did it, then.'

'The dreamer? She's incredible, isn't she?'

I licked dry lips. 'I think you'd better tell me everything that happened here.'

'Ask him.' Virisin nodded over at a second man, sitting up in his bed with an arm in a sling, his face a mass of bruises and still pale from blood loss.

'T'omar?'

'You should have seen him,' Virisin continued. 'When they began appearing he just ran straight in and laid about them like a demon. I never knew anyone could fight like that!'

T'omar snorted. 'Ignore him. He didn't see anything.' But there was a proud light behind his eyes.

'Nightkeep appeared out of nowhere? Using dreamers as catalysts for teleportation?'

'Exactly.'

'And you fought them off?'

'We had about five minutes' warning. There was an agent in Haven who was near the mages' tower about the same time you fried a necromancer. He sent word of what he'd seen, just as word began to come in from the elementals that all Nightkeep was emptying of troops. So of course we set up defences.'

'Casualties?'

'Of the four hundred agents and elementals in and around Silverpoint at the time of the attack, we lost fifty-eight.'

'Would have lost more, if T'omar hadn't been there . . .' began Virisin again.

'Would have lost more, if our mage hadn't been bright enough to summon a host of dragons to back up the elementals when we counter-attacked.'

'What have you done about defence now?'

'We've expanded Silverpoint by a mile all around, and set up one hell of a sandstorm. Inside we're still raising alarm wards, which should give us warning if anyone else appears out of nowhere.'

'You seem good at bossing people around from a bed.'

'It's a knack,' he retorted.

I steeled myself, and asked the dreaded question. 'What about Haven?'

I saw T'omar wince, and knew it was bad. 'The reports are vague, but we think about half the court was killed in the initial clash. Two more have been executed, the remainder are in the dungeons.'

'How many nobles outside Haven?'

'Seven. And twenty heirs.'

'I suppose that's a start. My sister?'

'The mages led a mob of peasants to the Void. They managed to evacuate ten thousand people before Serein took control of the Key. We don't know what happened to Saenia after that.'

I closed my eyes instinctively, and reached along the

tender link that binds family, probing for her. A small smile crossed my face as I felt her touch, and she pushed energy into me. 'She's outside Haven. Going to Stormpoint. There are ... two thousand? For God's sake! My kingdom's only so large.'

T'omar chuckled. 'Family's always embarrassing, isn't it? You realise that leaves at least fifty thousand still inside Haven?'

'And Haven's now a living nightmare, I know,' I sighed. Incredible how easy it was to accept my defeat. Yet something stirred inside me. *Revenge*, it whispered. *Revenge shall be ours. The Key is ours. We are the ones for whom it was destined* . . .

What's this 'ours'? I turned my eyes inwards, and saw that my magic was somehow different. Almost as if a spell had been cast over me, but so ghostly I doubted there could even be something for me to dispel.

'But Serein is having a hell of a hard time controlling the Key. Something to do with you?'

I felt my mouth drop open. I'd known something was wrong there. The Key's change to the colour of blood, the way it had twisted and torn, the way it had tried to break apart.

Another memory chose that moment to re-surface and start kicking for attention. 'Oh God,' I whispered. 'I held a king's hand in his dying moment, and our blood met. Then he said "the Key is yours", made a bit of magic, and died.'

The silence was as complete as the Void. Then T'omar's laugh filled the room with bitter merriment. 'No wonder Nightkeep is having a hard time controlling the Key! Talsin as good as declared you king of dreams!'

I sat up with a cry of despair. 'No! I've done my bit. I don't want to get messed up again in all that!'

But the general wasn't having any of it. 'You're going to have to save Haven now, it's written into your blood! You've been cursed with duty!'

I couldn't bring myself to see what he found so funny.

'I've got to go to Stormpoint! I've got refugees to feed, sisters to cook meals for, borders to defend!'

'You've got to help Haven! No matter what you think, you'll find yourself going that way.'

Virisin gave me a wry smile.

I looked from face to face. Throughout the infirmary, dozens of Silverhands who knew me well were staring, having somehow tuned into our conversation at the most important moment – the point where I'd been declared heir to a conquered throne.

T'omar smiled, both with pity and respect. 'Long live the king,' he said quietly.

Silverpoint had changed in the short time I'd been away. No more was it an obscure series of halls occupying a kingdom about half a mile across. It had been transformed into a self-contained stone bunker, with one door opening onto massive chambers with few corridors. The rooms were huge so that everyone could keep an eye out for mysterious necromancers.

Outside a sandstorm raged, blocking all sight. I remembered those knife-point torrents of wind from my youth, and felt grateful to be out of it.

'It's in here.'

I was surprised that T'omar was so ready to get up, suffering so badly as he was from a dozen wounds. A kindly healer had put a spell on my shoulder, and a sling had been provided. The pair of us must have looked like a right couple of veterans as T'omar hobbled and I swayed towards the council room.

Windsight was at the head of the table. Not surprising, really, given how many years the man had been so well loved and respected. Next to him was Renna. She looked somehow calmer and more in control than I'd ever seen her. The table rose as we entered.

'T'omar! Perhaps you'd like your seat back? I've had it up to here with this job,' said Windsight, exasperation cracking from his voice like ice.

T'omar sighed his assent, and everyone at the table shuffled round to give us room. I headed for Renna. 'You realise this is the fourth time in a week that you've saved my neck?' I asked as I took the seat next to her.

She grinned proudly, and I added, 'After this meeting, show me what you can do.'

T'omar sat down. 'How is everything holding up? The balance of the universe still intact? Dreams not totally dead, I hope?' he asked with forced cheerfulness.

'Nightkeep appears to be consolidating its position in Haven rather than risking any new attacks. We've sent word to every kingdom in the Void both about the method of attack, and the best means of defence.'

'So we're safe.'

'For the time being.'

I drummed my fingers on the table. 'Okay, I don't believe I'm saying this. But we need to hit Haven now. Hard.'

Virisin explained. 'He's under a blood, death, king and Key spell of duress.'

'What, all four?' exclaimed Windsight.

'There was a lot going on,' I snapped. 'The point is, Talsin said I ought to have the Key. And while I'm not about to go and claim the throne for myself, it is sickening to think of that bastard Serein ruling Haven.'

'The spell's so strong,' continued Virisin, 'that even Laenan can't throw it off.'

'Is it so hard to accept that I might be a good guy?'

T'omar rapped the table at the not quite suppressed merriment that followed. 'We are not here to laugh at Kite. Our purpose is to uphold the dream. Right now it needs a great deal of upholding. Kite, what is your plan?'

I smiled nervously. 'We know a frontal attack on Haven is suicide. And the only person who could get inside undetected would seem to be Renna.'

One or two people turned to look at her. She met their stares with a smile of proud composure.

'So,' I said, 'we need to try a new type of warfare. I read about it in a book. It's named after a kind of monkey, and lets us throw honour and suchlike to the wind.'

They listened as I talked on. It was just a vague plan, more a result of Talsin's farewell gift than of any thought on my own part. But in their eyes I began to see the light of understanding.

So it was that on the third day of Nightkeep's rule of Haven, the counter-attack was set in motion.

But more important than the avenging of dreams, or being nagged by any nurse back to the infirmary, was Renna.

I sat on the battlements, watching her fade in and out

of existence before me. A few yards away the sandstorm raged, behind a shield of Keyed magic. It was oddly peaceful, with just the roar of the sand and the silent shifting of reality.

After a few minutes of vanishing and reappearing, she faded back into existence on the warm stone beside me. 'Well?'

I tried in that second to find words for all the pride and love I felt. 'You are the greatest dreamer of them all,' I said simply.

She blushed. 'It feels so strange. I just want to be somewhere, and I can be. I still haven't mastered the influencing reality bit though, so don't count on it in a tight situation.'

'Maybe you can only do that when in great danger. Fear can knock energy levels up sky-high. If you can break through and tap them – that's a gift indeed.'

'I can take you anywhere. I know I can.'

I looked into the sandstorm with regret. 'I'm getting too old for this kind of thing. Still, a king's dying wish is just that. The elemental network is cutting all the roads to Haven. Silverhands are attempting sabotage and revolution in every local nightmare they can find. Windsight goes to Skypoint to raise an army, T'omar will gather supplies and rally to his cause what few lords survive. They will lay siege to all nightmares on the borders, so that no soldiers or supplies can be sent. Every mage in the Void who survived or was not in Haven has been summoned here. The Consortium is going to lead the greatest army in the world.'

'I thought you said attacking Haven would be suicide.'

'Only because Serein is in there, with limited control

over the Key. However, there's no one controlling Nightkeep.'

Her mouth dropped open. 'Oh, you are kidding!'

'That's the whole point. We pretend to attack Nightkeep with part of the army, while the rest lies low around Haven. Then, while Serein's busy worrying, a small group gets into Haven and tries to hit him.' I saw her expression. 'Yes. As I said, the only way into Haven is through you, Renna.' I sighed. 'But first there are one or two allies who I must call to our cause. I've been assigned two kingdoms to entreat for aid. Westpoint and Waterpoint.'

She raised her eyebrows. 'Isn't Waterpoint . . .?'

'Yes. So let's go to Stormpoint first, and I'll cook supper and get changed into something suitably impressive.'

She reached out without a word, and took my hand. I sent her the image, and waited for her to focus on it. This time, I was ready for the change.

The brown and yellow brightens to whirling orange and red. The battlements are a blanket of purple fire, reaching into the other colours like dyed blue water flowing into its clearer partner. Gradual, thoughtful, fading into just one colour, a mixture of all combined.

Then a river of red possibility changes, twists away into a silver river that races the fire to a distant horizon. The swaying yellow fire of maybe tilts beneath our feet, sways in the wind, mixes like paints on a palette with the blue Void into high green grasses. A pillar of lilac if and perhaps curves into a distant and shadowed tower.

Reality returns, reluctant and slow. Stormpoint builds itself out of fire and magic, and settles around us like a familiar friend.

We were standing on a river bank, maybe half a mile from my tower. The sun had long ago disappeared behind heavy black clouds and a cool wind blew from the north, smelling of rain.

'Should I summon sunlight?' I asked.

She shook her head, watching the heavy clouds above. 'Is this where you live?'

'Yes.'

'It's beautiful.'

I tried again. 'Do you want sunlight?'

Her eyes had the glazed look of someone who's just walked through miracles and come out in magic. 'A good storm. I haven't seen a good storm for years.'

I laughed and raised a hand to the heavens. 'This is Stormpoint! I specialise in thunder!'

On cue, lightning turned the sky white and thunder rolled across the landscape. Flocks of colourful birds rode from the darkened trees that swayed and moaned around the river. It began to rain, a thousand craters pocking the rich soil between the riverbank grass and the clear water on its pebbled bed. We were going to be soaked, but that didn't matter. This was my kingdom, and I could do with it whatever I wanted.

I raised my hand again, and felt my kingdom's Key roar into life at my return to its own patch of reality. Lightning strokes cracked once more, cymbals in the orchestra, heralding the drum-roll of the rain.

'I saw you arrive. Very impressive,' yelled Irinda over the roar of wind and rain. She was carrying a bundle of warm, fluffy towels. Her perfect beauty was barely marred by a pair of old jeans and a shirt covered with dirt from whatever she'd been doing during the day. The whole scene was outlined by the warm lights of home.

We'd bundled inside in a shower of water droplets, and laughed as the door closed. Both of us were soaked to the skin, the sling that held my arm was crinkled and falling off, Renna's hair clung to her face like a spider holding to its prey. But we couldn't stop laughing, all exhaustion burned away by that exhilarating run through the rain with the wolves and elves and fairies to light our path.

'Oh, you poor thing, you're soaked!' exclaimed Irinda. She wrapped the largest towel she could find around Renna's dripping shoulders. 'Really, Kite, you shouldn't have made a storm . . . Oh, and what did you do to your arm?! I turn my back for five minutes and you get involved in war or politics or something equally nasty . . .'

From the kitchen we could see the near-black sky, and the rain against it catching light from the tower. We sat down in the comfortable wooden chairs against the massive table at the centre of the room. 'Irinda, there's a lot of news for you to catch up on,' I said. 'Be a dear and make us something hot to drink.'

'Can't you just summon it?' asked Renna, rubbing her hair dry. She'd been failing to banish a broad grin, ever since we'd raced the wolves along the river.

'No good. The human body is Void-proof, so it has to eat Void-proof stuff.'

'So . . . how do you get food?'

'Either grow it the hard boring way with no magical intervention of any kind, or step outside the kingdom and summon it.'

'The daily shop,' agreed Irinda, bustling round the kitchen and prodding the fire.

'I like the sinks. And the kettle! How did you get that to work? I thought complicated machines couldn't work?'

'Ah.' I looked shame-faced. 'We stick that over the fire, if you must know. The wires and things are just for show.'

'Or summon a fire around it,' agreed Irinda. 'There's nothing to stop us cheating in *preparation* of food.' She handed over two steaming cups. 'Drink up, now.'

She sat down opposite us as we gratefully gulped our drinks. 'So, you're a dreamer?' she asked politely.

'Yes. Coma,' Renna agreed, busy drinking.

'And now a teleporter? I'm impressed.'

Renna looked at me, eyebrows raised. 'How come . . .?'

'Er, Irinda is a product of my imagination,' I explained. 'Anything I know and accept, she accepts too. There's not much you can say which will surprise her.'

'You two look exhausted. What happened?' Irinda asked.

I sent her a second of information, which she absorbed easily. Her expression changed to one of horrified sympathy. In defiance of her creator, she directed this sympathy at Renna. 'You poor dear! Oh, come upstairs to bed. Kite, make a room for Renna to stay in.'

'Next floor up, green door,' I said. 'Wait . . . yes, the bed's made now. Renna, what's your favourite colour?'

Renna looked a little dazed, but not overly so. 'Blue.'

'And do you want pictures, flowers, anything like that?'

'Er . . . no thanks.'

'Next floor up, blue door,' I told Irinda.

'Don't forget to give her an extra toothbrush!'

I raised my hands defensively, summoning the offending item into being in the bathroom. 'It's there!'

Renna was led out by the elven maid, leaving me alone in my kitchen. I was proud of Stormpoint, I realised. It was at least five hundred years ahead of Haven. Earth years, that is. Electricity might not work here, but plumbing need be only mechanical. So too, cookers heated by log fires. Pencils were just pieces of greyish stuff inside a wooden holder, paper just bits of wood pulp, written all over by a compound of coloured stuff. Food storage was easy if you had a nice deep cellar. And there was nothing wrong with lighting that couldn't be sorted out by a few strategically placed spheres of shimmering magic.

It was paradise. For those of us who liked that kind of thing.

I ran a mental finger through the tower one last time, making sure it was clean. No problems there. I rose slowly, stretching what muscles I dared and feeling the aches in every one. A dozen little lights hovering beneath the trees at the bottom of the tower suggested the inhabitants of my kingdom were eager for news. I broadcast a brief burst of information, and turned away satisfied.

A mirror hung at the far end of the kitchen. I'd made it many years ago, and it was profoundly magical. (Can you see me having anything else? We great mages do have standards, dear dreamer.) When a particular phrase was spoken, or a certain symbol inscribed, the mirror could scry most roads in the Void, and in some kingdoms if their defences were weak enough. Or it could show a man the true nature of his soul, heal a grievous wound, summon sleep, or communicate over great distances. All fairly useless stuff for a mage in retirement, as I'd been. So now it was just an ordinary mirror, with a plain dusty frame, reflecting a dark-haired, blue-eyed man with a long shabby robe and one arm in a sling and a strange face that might almost be described as alien.

Lightning struck behind, and for a second the nobody in the kitchen was a great mage. The wet hair, plastered foolishly to the face, now writhed in the gust from the open window like Medusa's snakes. The plain and smeared robe was a garb of power, the eyes were windows to another world. The fact wasn't merely unusual, it was a king's visage as he beheld the battle-ground of his victory. Then the light was gone, and I was blinking in the afterglow.

No. However hard I tried, I still preferred the first figure, the nobody in wet clothes. I felt safer with it, comfortable with the thought that I could hide in a crowd.

'Kite, can we have a wardrobe?' came a voice from upstairs, muffled by the curves of the tower.

I sighed, and summoned a wardrobe in Renna's room.

'Good morning!' I breezed into the room, tray in hand, knowing she was awake and flinging open the windows.

With a snap Renna closed the book she'd been reading. 'I'm not sure I understand this.'

I glanced at the cover and laughed. 'I'm not surprised. That's a book of love stories I picked up from a necromancer's library while I was running away from Nightkeep.'

'Ah. That explains the bit with the vampires.'

I perched on the edge of her bed, enlarged the bedside table to suitable proportions and laid the tray on it. 'We've got fried bacon, fried eggs, fried bread, fried tomatoes, a suspicious-looking vegetable I bought off a man in Treepoint, also fried, and a bowl of orange juice.' A night's sleep in my own bed with the storm raging outside the window had restored something of life to me, and I was feeling insanely cheerful. I didn't have to think about Haven or mourn the dead, although that would come soon and I knew it. But then and there, I could smile.

'Fried,' she echoed flatly.

'Is there a problem?'

'I haven't been to a single kingdom that's got the knack of frying! You people have been so backward!' She nearly snatched though as she took the tray off the table, eyes gleaming. Through a mouthful of bacon she asked, 'How come you're so much more modern?'

I laughed bitterly. 'A hundred years out of politics is a long time. When I got this kingdom I resolved to take a long holiday and sleep a lot. So I dreamt a great deal about Earth. Making a hob that worked was hard, but after hearing of the wonders of frying . . .'

'You decided that what you couldn't make via electrics you'd fudge using magic?'

'Something like that.' I sauntered to her window and looked out across Stormpoint. 'A beautiful day,' I announced. 'With the smell you get after rain and a few fluffy white clouds in the sky. The trees are green, the birds are singing, the river is catching the sunlight as it streaks through long fields of tall green grass.' I glanced at the sky, willing everything to happen as I spoke. 'There's a pair of phoenixes flying today, and the mermaids are in the lakes admiring their reflections and talking about the latest fashions and whether their hairdresser did a good job. The elven court is in full festive swing and the fairies are playing tricks on the slumbering owls.' I turned back to her with a wide grin. 'This is my paradise.'

She smiled back. 'Strange man.'

I summoned a chair next to the large wardrobe, and sat down, watching her carefully. She didn't seem to mind – her new life of dreaming seemed to have brought a new confidence that I hoped wouldn't put her in danger. It's never wise to be over-confident in a war. 'Enjoy it while you can. We go to Westpoint today, to rally the nomads.'

'Who are they?'

'They wander from kingdom to kingdom, looking for a place to hunt and eat and generally have a good time. Full of strange talk about spirits.'

'When do we leave?'

'What with your new-found talents, I thought after lunch. I'm going down to the Void, to see if I can't summon us new clothes.'

'If you see a reflection shield attack it, no matter what. If more than two people appear at the edge of Stormpoint without declaring themselves, close off the borders. I'll leave a pair of rock trolls by the road just in case. There are now three phoenixes as well as the dragon, all with scrying spells written in. So you should be able to see any kind of magic.'

'What if a kingdom spell is cast?' Irinda asked.

I kept on pacing, a gaggle of elves behind me trying to take notes. 'There's a general spell ward on Stormpoint, but it only functions within the kingdom. I've asked the Consortium to send a couple of elementals down this way, so those should be keeping an eye on any nearby activities. Also I'll be in constant contact through the Key, and if I'm outside the kingdom a spell shouldn't affect me. Anything goes wrong, and I'll be back at the speed of thought. Besides, you'll have my sister to keep an eye on things.'

'And two thousand refugees.'

'The Consortium will provide food.'

'They'd better.'

Irinda finished checking her list and stuck the pencil behind her ear. 'That's everything, then.'

I felt more alive than I had for days, even with an arm in a sling. The ministrations of a dryad from the forest, and a bit of work in the Void with a few herbs and a touch of magic, had made regeneration a lot faster than normal, but the wound still twanged when I moved. After only a night at Stormpoint, I knew I was going to miss my old home.

But my blood was crying out to avenge Talsin.

And Renna was waiting.

'Ready?' she asked.

I shouldered my pack. 'As I'll ever be.'

She took my hand, I sent her an image.

The tower dissolves back into lilac flame, the grasses around our feet grow tall, covering us in a shimmering blanket of fire that touches but does not burn. The river is now a red strand of maybe, Irinda's waving hand is no more than a ghostly green blur against the silent orange glory of Void.

But now the Void is re-shaping itself. The red blanket of fire which stretches away beneath us curls back on itself, thickens and deepens into a cliff. The orange wall of the sky turns sour and dark, grey clouds against a darkening sky. The steppe spreads out hundreds of feet below, pinpricked with camp fires and tents. People turn to stare as two grey figures appear above their homes, the silence is replaced with a whispering wind that, somehow, has always been there.

Westpoint has arrived. We haven't moved a muscle.

There was a click of a rifle. I froze in the act of putting another stick on the fire. Renna's eyes met mine over the blaze.

'We've been calling you for more than an hour, friend,' I said. 'You hardly need to come bearing rifles.'

There were soft steps behind me. Renna's eyes travelled up a figure standing directly behind where I crouched.

'Warden of Stormpoint, you return.'

'Afternoon.' I turned, with what I hoped was an innocent-looking smile. 'About us teleporting in here – you don't mind, do you?'

The nomad's eyes darted to Renna. At length he bowed. 'My lady. I thought only Nightkeep appeared out of nowhere.' Addressing both of us, he added, 'I should warn you that our lord has not yet returned.'

'Your lord is most likely imprisoned,' I told him.

'That is what the other man said.'

'The other man?'

'An elemental.'

I nodded. 'Any elementals you see who are acting of their own accord are with me.'

'I would guess you have a story to tell.'

Every nomad from every camp seemed trying to crowd around the camp fire. Beneath a sky of alien stars, Renna and I sat close together as I told the story of Haven.

The leader of the guards, Dactac, nodded thoughtfully at the end of our tale. 'I had heard rumours about the group of which you speak. The Silverhand Consortium. You have led it?'

'Tried,' I said with a regretful little smile.

'Then we were wise to accept the advice of our Warden. But to hear such tidings of Haven is a concern indeed. And you seek to rally an army?'

I flexed my fingers thoughtfully, and went on to outline T'omar's plan.

'Is that all?' Dactac asked.

I glanced at Renna. This was the complicated part. While half the army caused havoc in nightmare, the remainder would try something not totally sane.

We were given a tent to stay the night in – even though by our body-clocks it was barely past supper – and sat down in silence beneath the heavy canvas.

A shadow passed in front of the smelly fabric. The tent flap was pushed aside. Instead of the heavy figure of Dactac, a youngish boy stood there.

'The Bear Clan wonders if you wish to join us.'

I glanced at Renna, who shrugged, as if to say, 'What the hell.' We rose, and followed the boy through a maze of tents, to a much smaller camp fire.

To tell the truth, my memory of that night is hazy. The nomads produced a viscous drink which tasted a lot better than it looked. The trouble was, it also did things to my head that suggested I'd wake next morning with a vile hangover.

One event I can remember with startling clarity. Sometime after the moon was well risen, a tent flap opened, and an old woman came out. I recognised her core of magic, and instantly raised my shields. She smiled knowingly at what I'd done, and beckoned. 'Come, Warden of Stormpoint. I study what the spirits say of you.'

Personally, I don't think you can read the future via cards or suchlike. What you usually need is a good handful of Void and a decent understanding of your own situation. On the other hand my head was already feeling fuzzy, and it's never a good idea to insult a mage by turning down a free offer.

'Back in a minute,' I whispered to Renna, and followed the woman inside the tent.

'Sit.'

I obeyed, sitting cross-legged on the bare ground. There wasn't even a mattress. This woman was obviously serious about the getting-close-to-spirit side of life.

She glanced at the sling supporting my arm. 'Take that off.'

'I'd rather not . . .' I began, and saw her expression. I took it off, provoking more than just twinges.

'Let me see the wound.'

This was absurd! I considered making my excuses, but curiosity, or maybe just manners, prevented me. So I pulled off the grey top, folding it neatly on the ground. Still she said nothing, and with great reluctance I pulled off my shirt too.

The cold poured over me – bitter cold I'd never notice by the fire.

Something in my senses twitched nervously, though. Surely this chill bordered on the unnatural.

'You still have shields raised. Lower them.'

Shivering slightly, I shook my head. 'I always have shields raised somewhere. You have given me no reason to trust you, and I will not be exposed.'

She smiled again, a small smile that utterly unnerved me. Suddenly I could see her magic clearly, as she lowered every shield she had and let me see that her power was small. 'I could not harm you, and would never harm a guest. I serve the spirits, and the spirits would not allow a man with a fire such as yours to be harmed.'

It sounded too good to be true. Something compelled me nonetheless towards co-operation. *Spirits? What if there is something in what she says* . . . Scrying all around in case of trickery, I lowered the barriers of magic that had guarded my soul for hundreds of years. Somehow, I felt lighter without them. It was as if the engine on a boat had stopped, and only in that silence could you be aware of the sound which had gone before.

She leant forward, and examined my shoulder, where it was still puffy and tender. 'You have healed fast.'

'I've been using magic.'

'I see its traces. They cling to you like spider silk. Give me your hands.'

What the hell? I'd already left myself vulnerable to all sorts of nasties. What'd the hands got to lose? I reached out, palms up.

'Put magic in your hands.'

I summoned mage light, two shimmering little flames

that danced between colours in an invisible wind. She too summoned mage light, and lowered her glowing hands over my own, eyes flickering shut.

The coldness intensified. I realised I was shivering uncontrollably now, my teeth chattering. I desperately wanted to raise a shield, but none of my warning wards had gone off. Not one of the little senses that take five hundred years to develop was screaming, 'Betrayed!' So I kept the light up, even though ice was forming on the grass and frost clung to my hair.

I swear it was no illusion, or at least nothing I'd ever encountered. Nor was it a trick in my mind, a twisting of thought or light, for there was no magic with which to twist.

Abruptly, I stood on a long white road that stretched into infinity, like a road in the Void. All around was black, the road was the only reality. Ice still clung to me and when I walked my feet crunched on frost.

I picked my way carefully down that long road, several times sliding and nearly falling over the edge. Then they were in front of me, seven white, ghostly figures standing in a group. I recognised the faint flickering signature instantly – they were dreamers.

But dreamers in this place? Where was this place? What the hell was going on? I asked them as much, and was met with stares that made the ice which had gone before seem almost warm.

'He is stubborn.'

'Blame the parents,' I replied.

'Blind.'

'Erm . . . I don't think I can get family on that one.'

'Arrogant.'

'Look who's talking.' The voices seemed to come from all of them at once, but that didn't bug me. I'd been in kingdoms much like this before. There was always a necromancer somewhere who'd fill his land with blackness and give his voice stereophonic effects to make even the best technician weep. What worried me was that I'd got here at all. That and the fact that I had no idea how to get back.

'We have been asked to counsel you on your quest.'

'You have . . .?' Then a little more of that sentence settled in. 'Quest?'

'We see a great struggle.'

'Congratulations,' I muttered, resenting their sharp tones. Out of curiosity, to see if it worked here, I summoned a quick heating-spell. I reckon I saw stars for a good five minutes, and when I finally got my breath back it was to find myself on a blanket of ice, staring at blackness which only might be a sky.

Did they offer a word of comfort? No! They seemed not to have noticed, and ploughed on, unconcerned.

'If the Wanderer does not complete the Journey, she will die when Earth turns the tide.'

'"She"? You mean Renna? But Renna's safe. We've got it all worked out.'

One of them was standing right behind me. I spun and nearly fell when its cold voice broke into the silence. 'You have done well, for the Journey is half complete. But only when nightmare falls can Earth be isolated.'

'Earth?' I looked to the silent figures for confirmation. 'But you're dreamers? What is this?'

'We suffered the fate of all Wanderers. We were not strong.'

'Wanderers? You mean dreamers? But . . . you're not dreamers. All dreamers wake up, live full and happy lives, die. You don't come back here after death! You die on Earth, not here . . .' My voice trailed off. 'Comas. That's it, isn't it?' I paced round each and ever one, noticing for the first time the tension in every muscle, how empty the eyes were, how pale and dry the skin, how bloodless their ghostly veins. 'You were dreamers, who got into comas and died while dreaming? And you came here?'

'We have no path into a world, save as the spirits.'

The spirits. The beings who held such sway over the nomads' imagination in Westpoint.

'And as the spirits, we can rarely escape. We are trapped here, and do not wish the same fate for the Wanderer. She will join us, if nightmare prevails.' The voices rolled in from all around, suffocating me with their angry roar.

When the echoes and sound of falling ice died away, I risked pulling myself up.

'You're saying . . . that if Serein is still in control of Haven when Renna . . . dies, then she becomes like you?'

'That is correct.'

'And if he's not?'

'If the city of dreams is restored to its former glory, the Wanderer will survive.'

'Wait! I can't find a paradise for her, it's never been done! Besides, you're not thinking logically! They take her off life-support, her body dies, her brain dies! She is just a projection into this world, created by her brain!'

The figures began to fade.

'I can't influence Earth, I can't stop her dying! All I can do is try and give her a happy ending!'

'But this is the world of magic, and you're a great mage. You will remove the challenge of nightmare, place the true ruler in power, whose line has not seen the throne for a thousand years, who is not born of corruption and lesser dreams, and all will be resolved.'

Oh, well, that's nice and simple!

The chill of the ice and the bitter frost rolled in. <We leave our blessing. Free her from nightmare, and all is not lost.>

And I opened my eyes, and looked into the magess's smile. And now she wasn't just a magess, but something more. 'I saw you,' I murmured. 'When I was going to Haven, to meet Talsin. I *saw* you through the blindfold. But how . . .'

She touched my shoulder, silencing me. The wound had healed entirely. 'Sleep a while. Things will be clearer in the morning.' I couldn't argue. I wanted nothing more than to curl up on the cold, frost-bitten grass, and sleep until the sun was high in the sky.

So I did.

THIRTEEN

Overlapping Worlds

*P*eople were waking up. It seemed that Nightkeep had got what it wanted, and was releasing the huge network of spells that held the dreamers asleep. It just wasn't practical any more to waste all that magic on teleportation.

A air of relief had settled over the world. I kept walking past newspaper stands whose headlines declared, 'Virus mutation fails to defeat the human body'. Or, as some papers put it, 'Government experiment goes wrong' and 'Meteorite-borne bacteria will not survive'.

If only they knew.

Strangely enough, for the first time in days I wasn't even on the same continent as Renna's sleeping body. I was in a place called London, where I'd often enjoyed visiting the universities in search of new ideas to steal in my six or so nightly hours of sleep. I wandered vaguely familiar streets until I found a big sign declaring that here was part of the University of London, and went inside.

On first dreaming my way in, I'd soon discovered that the University is huge, with buildings all over the place. This time I'd wound up at a lecture in a grand hall near a long road of shops selling things called 'computers'.

The professor – of whatever he was expert in – tapped the board behind him. The word 'dreams' was scribbled across it.

I resisted the temptation to stay. I had a feeling certain new dead acquaintances were still trying to mess up my life.

Maybe five hundred nomads marched down the long road towards nightmare, a big bustling line of men and women moving with the grim determination of an army with a plan. Worse still, an army with a plan *and* a cause. I wondered how many of them would not return.

The guards of Westpoint had divided themselves roughly in half. One trained and disciplined force was marching towards Silverpoint, to join whatever army had been mustered by the agents of the Consortium. The other half was going to an uncertain fate in nightmare. Strike while Serein is divided, strike where no one expects you . . .

'Waterpoint?' asked Renna softly.

'Waterpoint,' I agreed.

Once again, the world faded.

It's a right shame that Waterpoint should be so good on troops and mages. They have one of the largest outputs of healers and spellcasters of any kingdom but, regrettably, the whole thing was under Lisana's jurisdiction. You want Waterpoint to give you a huge military advantage, you gotta ask nicely.

Regrettably.

'No one may speak with the Lady Lisana! She is under house arrest, pending trial!'

Renna was performing perfectly. All I had to do was sit back and admire.

'So you would turn away the Warden of Stormpoint, the Mage of Haven, the Promised of the Key?'

I nearly laughed. For the best part of an hour I'd been trying to get round the guard the traditional way. I'd fallen back on all sorts of complicated arguments in the hope of convincing him that just because Haven had fallen into enemy hands it didn't take away my own authority. Nor had it been rewarding to try and explain why we'd appeared out of nowhere.

Then Renna had exploded, her impatience overwhelming the man. She'd attracted quite an audience. 'Of course he's the bloody Promised of the Key! The king decreed it in his dying moments, and the hated Lord of Nightkeep struggles to control it against the curse of blood and hate!'

The halls of Waterpoint are made of iridescent blue glass, and filled with running water of perfect beauty. Crystal-clear pools occupy every other room, and the servants are often half-human, half-lizard. Mosaics of pale pink, blue and yellow show fish, whales and heroes, their features distorted by the lapping of the water as it ripples against glass paths that run just above its surface. If I reached my little toe out from the glass square where I stood, I could stir the water, and see if any of the brightly coloured fish would come and play.

Yet I still hadn't felt any touch from a Key. Which probably meant . . .

<You wait here, I'm going to go and talk to our illustrious lady of love.>

Following my instincts, I put up a shield of 'Who, Me?' and headed, suitably casual, towards the likeliest place to find Lisana.

There were two guards on the door, and one was a mage. I shimmered into existence, resulting in a fireball and a rifle pointed at me. The illusion of the captain of the guard whose features I had been studying all the way through our talk seemed to hold against the mage's tentative probe, and I raised my head squarely and met their eyes in defiance. 'Thank you, I'm going to see the prisoner.'

They glanced from one to the other, and finally saluted. I breezed into the cell with not a flicker on my face.

The door clanged (well, clinked is probably a better word to describe the sound of crystal) shut behind me.

I should explain that it was no ordinary cell. Mirrors lined every wall, and it was easy to feel the magic radiating off them. A bed, table and chair had been placed in there, and next door was an equally mirrored room, for toilet and bath. *Well, why not? She is only suspected of treason, after all.* I realised a cell like this was probably the only way to stop her using her Key.

It was easy to remember that when I'd been 'suspected' it had been a beating every night in a grungy basement cell, thanks to the lovely lady now turning towards me with a big 'oh' of surprise on her face. However, the pretty effect of astonishment which warmed me to the bone soon darkened to loathing. 'Laenan Kite,' she said, poison dripping from every word. 'Come to gloat?'

'If only,' I sighed. 'You heard about Haven?'

'Heard, laughed, cried,' she retorted. 'I'm surprised a *great* mage like you couldn't do anything about it.'

'I was busy getting assassinated.'

'You seem a lot better.'

'Oh, I could tell you stories,' I replied. 'It's been one thing after another. Talsin's dead, of course.'

Was that a flicker of reaction, a faint tightening around the eyes? I decided it couldn't be. Not from her.

'I know. You expect me to care?'

'Had to try. Anyway, the crux of the matter is that we're going to get Haven back, and I would rather have the Warden of Waterpoint and her army behind me, than against.'

'I will not send my troops to certain death,' she replied primly.

I was impressed. I'd genuinely thought she'd smile and say, 'Let them die.'

'If it's any consolation they won't die. I might.'

She frowned, her interest raised at the prospect. 'How so?'

'They feint at nightmare, a false attack. The other half of the army we're assembling hides near Haven. It attacks when Serein's dead and the Key is back in my hands.'

'*Your* hands!'

'Temporarily,' I shot back, in a voice whose scorn matched her own. 'In any other hands it won't respond. Talsin laid a curse so that only I could use it. Hell, you think I *want* the crown?'

She considered me with those bright, intelligent eyes which have always managed to win over everyone –

except that young mage whom as an alternative she once tried to get killed.

'I do believe you're telling the truth. You always were a blind fool, Kite.'

'So everyone tells me. Sometimes I just long for a bit of comfort and flattery. Now will you back us?'

'You say us. Who?'

Well, it's out now, everyone's going to be singing its name for a while to come. 'The Silverhand Consortium.'

She didn't seem surprised. 'Whatever that is, I thought you were involved in it. Before you left, Talsin kept saying you were going to turn the Consortium against him.'

'He was wrong. The Consortium was set up to help Haven without having to damage a stupid king's self-regard. We can work round crap monarchs, if it helps the other poor sods in life.'

'And now it's going to take Haven. How convenient.'

'Impossible though this may be for you to believe, not everyone has an ambition like a hammer on the anvil. We just want to see the rightful king enthroned.'

'And who is the rightful king?'

I hesitated. Technically, Talsin's dying wish had made me a serious candidate. But I'd been fortunate in that my suitability was knocked down a few notches by my heritage as a desert low-life. 'I recommend this wonderful thing called "democracy". Maybe we'll give that a try. I haven't thought much beyond the big crunch.'

'Where you might die.'

'Probably. At best, maybe slight headache from shielding spells, severe headache for breaking wards, trembling fingers from frying the guards, and near-death in the process of throwing everything I've got against Serein. Suicide missions are always bad for the health.' I laughed bitterly. 'Or I might get stabbed by the first goblin I meet. Let's not be arrogant.'

She leant forward knowingly. 'You're expecting to die. How can you hope to win, throwing yourself into a battle where you expect to die?'

I couldn't meet her eyes anymore.

'You've got something more planned, haven't you?'

'I'll hardly tell the woman who tried to kill me, and seduced the king.'

'That? That was nothing! You were growing too powerful, you were going to ruin everything.'

'Why? Why was I such a threat?'

She sat back, shaking her head. 'Tell me your real plan.'

'You're in no position to make demands.'

Strangely, she didn't seem too unhappy at my stubbornness. I had a nagging sense that she was keeping score, the way we always did – and winning.

'Very well. Since I plan to back you anyway, I see no problem in being frank. I will answer your question, and hopefully you will deign to answer mine. You saw me for what I was. You looked through my courtly upbringing and saw ambition. I made a mistake, when I tried to win you over to my cause. I'd thought you were ripe for the taking, and would be a powerful asset as a new mage with no bias either way. When I failed, and watched you grow closer to the king and more powerful, I knew you would become an enemy.'

'Of what cause?'

'The cause for which my mother laid down her life,

and her mother before, and her mother before that. That
the crown should rest upon the head of the rightful
queen.'

Lisana was smiling now, as she willed me to back
away before the light of the truth she spoke. 'Talsin and
his kind are mere petty lords, whose plot defeated the
true king long ago. I am the heir of the true House of
Dreams, and for years I have hungered after what is
mine.'

She was opening her shields as she spoke, letting me
delve into her soul. I saw every ounce of truth in her
words, saw how she'd longed to tell someone, how she'd
wanted to whisper it in my ear in the dungeons, when
she was sure I was to die.

At length I forced a shrug. 'What do you want? For
me to turn round, on the grounds of blood-right, and say,
"Sure, take the throne!"? You destroyed me, Lisana. You
are a twisted, evil woman and I'm only here because the
situation is desperate.'

'Am I so twisted? So evil? I would have been a good
queen – a great queen. I was taught the old code of the
courts, the code that only my family has known and
loved. You think I would have executed Talsin, had I
won the crown? You're wrong. You think I would've
ever seen you die? You think you escaped the axe by
your powers of reason alone? I *let* you go. I would have
married Talsin, and my child, a true king, would have sat
on the throne. Haven has always responded better to old
blood, to the old code. It listens to the past, as well as the
future. Talsin's past was one of corruption. Mine is the
golden era of kings.'

Indeed the truth was in her words. With my magic so

much stronger than hers I could read it like a page from a book. 'This complicates the situation, nothing more,' I replied, even though my voice trembled. 'I haven't come to settle past sorrows. As far as I'm concerned they're dead and done. All I want is your co-operation. I'm not here to put anyone on the throne – just to see that the throne is free in time . . .' my voice trailed off. *She's an ambition-filled reptile. She'd turn Haven to dust . . .*

Lisana wasn't stupid, as I've said. Now I could feel her eyes burning into me like a snake hypnotising its prey. 'In time for what, Kite? What are you hiding?'

I couldn't take any more. There swam before my eyes the familiar walls of the cell where I'd been beaten for so long. Suddenly the kindly face of the old king, who'd brought the victorious young mage into court, seemed disfigured with a schemer's eye.

Why had the king been so eager to make me his loyal servant? Was it really because I'd cast one strong spell and was a well-meaning country lad, or because I could curse any of his enemies and they would fall? I'd never thought to ask those questions, blindly accepting what I'd been told like the fool I was.

What if the throne that represented light and dreams combined had been occupied by someone from a kingdom twisted towards corruption? The city had been less corrupt before, and it was said that it responded only to the will of the throne. Was the family which had ruled Haven for so long the cause of that very sickening?

I rose in flustered haste, reached the door and slammed it behind me. Outside, masked again in the illusion of the captain of the guard, I stormed away. I waited until I was well out of sight before letting the magic drop.

Then I leant against the wall, and let the questions roar through my mind.

<T'omar!> The sign of the sword blazed in my hand – I'd hardly noticed that I'd drawn it.

<Kite?>

<T'omar, things have just got more complicated.>

We went to Silverpoint, appearing directly in the room where T'omar sat, his face shuttered and eyes cold. He didn't even look remotely surprised to see us appear so soon out of nowhere, but simply nodded at the two chairs opposite him. 'Sit down. Both of you.'

I sat, my heart pounding in my ears. Renna was looking confused, not sure why we were back so soon in a place we'd left not two days ago but co-operating the way she always did – silently and without question.

T'omar's eyes were burning with anger. I, a Silverhand, had deliberately withheld information about Renna and what I thought was going to come . . . 'You are going to tell us everything, from the first day you set foot in Haven up to the present. You will speak without bias, you will give no feelings, just what you observed.' His eyes darted to Renna and back to me. 'You will also speak of your affairs with Earth, and how they are connected. I want to know how much time we have for this whole thing.'

So I told them everything. From the first second when I entered Haven and graduated as the strongest mage of the year, to the days in the court when Lisana tried to win me over to her group of plotters, to the joining of the Consortium, to the trial, all the way to the present day.

At the end, Renna sat pale and shocked. Yes, I included everything. Even that she was soon to die. All this and more poured out of me in an unstoppable tide.

Then, silence descended and my throat was parched and dry and the feelings of a hundred years were roaring inside me like a still ocean caught in an unexpected hurricane.

'You should have told me. I had a right to know,' Renna said. Her voice wasn't angry. It was just a flat statement that bore burning truth.

I hung my head, shame rising above all the other emotions in the storm like a great wave. 'I know. I'm sorry. Everything happened too fast, too soon.' I turned to T'omar, pleading. 'What now, general? I don't trust my own feelings on this matter. I've had too much time in a corrupt court, too much time fighting and fleeing, too much time suspecting and denying. What do we do?'

He said nothing at first, and just kept on staring at me in that thoughtful way that made my heart race faster. 'You've done so much, Kite. You've made yourself a legend. But you're really just a man, aren't you? So tortured by the deeds you've done that you don't dare do any more, for fear of what you are capable of.'

I leaned forward desperately. Fire was burning round my fingers, and I couldn't bring it back down. 'Please. If you say "crown Lisana" or "let Serein live" I'll do it! There are two thousand refugees in Stormpoint, Nightkeep rules Haven, the woman I despised for all those years was nothing more than a pawn to her family's desire and may well have been the rightful queen. *Help me.*'

There was the smash of a door. I turned, in time to see Renna disappear down the corridor before the door clicked back again. Now that I'd been forced to open up my heart to the flood of history that was Laenan Kite I realised that they'd all been right. Until that day, I had been blind.

'You will not like what I propose.'

T'omar didn't seem to care, his voice was as calm as ever. 'Tell me.'

I still couldn't force the burning fire from my fingers . . . 'We have two things to consider. Firstly, Renna. To save her, the nightmare must be banished, and be banished quickly, from the city of dreams. If these . . . spirits are anything to go by, that means restoring someone to the throne from a line not born of corruption. Technically we could wait to attack. Technically we could muster men for weeks and weeks before we strike at Haven. But if we do . . .' I couldn't meet his eyes.

'Go on.' He sounded almost fatherly, forcing a confession from his errant son. *How many faces do you wear, young T'omar? You are a chameleon, switching from father to son to soldier to spy in the blink of an eye. And dreams help me, I admire you for it.*

'She will die, unless we can restore the dream soon. For all we could wait and be better prepared, she has not the time. One person. That's all it is, T'omar. One person. You are a soldier. One person where the lives of thousands are at stake is usually considered a necessary sacrifice. But she's not, T'omar. She's not our sacrifice. I *cannot* see her sacrificed now. I would rather march into Haven naked and unarmed to die trying for her sake than march in when she is dead with an army of a million invincible warriors at my back.'

He was silent a long while, and I could feel every moment of that silence rushing by like a hot desert wind, burning at my skin and making it tingle from second to second as I waited with a roaring in my ears for his answer.

He was staring at his nails, digging dirt from under them in complete distraction. 'You never married, did you, Kite?'

'No. Came close, more than once, but never got there.'

'You should get married. There's not as many nice people around as women like to believe, and you're going to waste.'

My head snapped up and I stared at him questioningly, trying to read every line in his unreadable face. He smiled uneasily under my gaze. 'For dream's sake, you're the wise old mage. I'm just the kid tagging along and hoping no one will notice. We do what you want.'

I could have hugged him at that moment, but he'd spoken so calmly and with so little emotion that I felt almost embarrassed that the 'wise old mage' should show such emotion where he showed none. So I passed straight on and kept my features as level as his own. I had no desire to be out-done by T'omar. Not now. Not after all that we'd been through in such a short time.

'Thank you. The throne is the second problem. Since you refuse to wear the crown that Talsin promised you, another heir must be found. A line not born of corruption could well mean Lisana. You said yourself she told the truth about her heritage.'

He'd said I wouldn't like it, and I didn't. 'I won't argue,' I said.

'But?'

'But she has been a bitch.'

'Yes.'

'And she may be bad.'

'Yes.'

'I'd like to take her out of Waterpoint. Now. To Stormpoint.'

'Why?'

'Because we don't know what she'd be like when she wears the crown. I want to find out.'

'I'm listening.'

We stood together again, each watching the other like a hawk.

'I'm . . . sorry I didn't tell you,' I said finally.

Renna shrugged. 'I'm just a dreamer. What does another world matter to you?'

'It all matters.'

'But in varying degrees of importance.'

'No. *You* matter.'

'Then why didn't you tell me?'

Honestly, I replied, 'I don't know. Am I going to die, is T'omar going to die? How the hell can I know?'

'And that's it? We just accept these things? What about the spirits? What about dreams and nightmare? Is it all for nothing?'

'Renna . . .' I began weakly. She drew back from me, eyes flashing with fury. 'Renna, I don't know what's going to happen! I wish to all the Gods that you weren't here, because then I wouldn't have to see you get hurt! Windsight protected you from me for good reason. His daughter died by my side!'

'Windsight . . . had a daughter?'

'She was a mage, and a Silverhand,' I said wretchedly. 'We were sent to Firepoint about two hundred years ago, to meet a defector. It was a trap.'

'Why are you telling me this?'

'I don't know.'

Slowly, as if scared that my fingers would scorch her, she took my hand. 'Come on. I'm in too deep to get out now. We might as well finish this thing.'

But she wouldn't meet my eyes, and there was no smile on her face.

Once again, goodbye Silverpoint. Hello Waterpoint.

I must admit that, even with the general overhaul of history I'd gone through, it was pleasing to see the shock on Lisana's face as we appeared out of nowhere.

'Impressive,' she said weakly. 'And I thought this was a magic-null zone.'

'Not magic,' I replied firmly. 'Take Renna's hand, if you please.'

'Why?'

'I said "please", didn't I?'

'I suppose I don't have any choice.' She rose with that old, familiar grace and clasped Renna's hand in her own.

'Stormpoint?' the dreamer asked me.

'Stormpoint. Kitchen.'

A quick in-and-out of Waterpoint, disturbing no one, never once causing alarm. The kind of visit I enjoyed most.

Basict spun, his long canines bared and his nails lengthening into claws as we materialised. Just before his eyes darkened to yellow he saw who we were, and barely got control over his morphic field in time not to spring. 'Oh. Just doing some cooking, sir.'

I went to the window, and looked out across Stormpoint. 'Fifty people playing tug-of-war? And *what* are they doing over there?'

Basict followed my gaze. 'Er, the elves decided to host a concert.'

'And there?'

'The dryads are giving craft lessons.'

I gave the werewolf a suspicious look. 'Dryads are good at one thing only, and it isn't basket-making.'

'But it keeps people busy, sir!'

There was a rattling from the ladder, and Saenia slid into the kitchen. She was wearing one of my dressing gowns, and her hair was dripping wet. 'Kite! When did you get in?'

'About thirty seconds ago. You?'

She laughed. 'About three hours ago. Your people surely know how to make us feel welcome. Oh, and now you're here you can summon everyone a tower of their own!'

I groaned. 'Renna, Saenia. Saenia, Renna. Do you know Lisana? No? Well, Lisana, Saenia. Saenia . . .'

My sister strode past me and took the startled lady's hands in her own. 'Pleased to meet you. My brother been treating you all right?'

For the first time in years Lisana was lost for words. Perhaps she'd just looked into Saenia's magic and seen power greater than mine. Or maybe it was the over-powering effect of my sister in busy-body mode.

'Over supper,' Saenia added, 'you must tell me what you're all doing here.'

'I will, only there's something I need to do first.' I shot a meaningful look at the mirror hanging on the far wall.

Basict took the message instantly, and slunk towards the door. Renna detached herself from our group, and followed with a smile in Saenia's direction. The magess sighed. 'You and politics don't mix, little brother.' But she left too.

That left just Lisana and me.

'Would you care to explain? Why am I here? Where is here? And just how did we get here?'

'Sure.' I ticked each answer off on my fingers as I replied. 'One, because I don't trust you. Two, Stormpoint. Three, via Renna being a dreamer. Now sit down for a few minutes, while I see what can be done about these towers.'

Big stuff always takes a while, even with a Key and an ocean of power to back you. Accommodation for two thousand wasn't like summoning a simple chair. I turned my attention to the far edge of my small kingdom, and pushed. The sky began to expand, the Void to retreat. It would take some time before I'd have the necessary space, but at least it was some hours till sunset.

When I turned, it was to find Lisana giving me the strangest look. 'You really are a good man, aren't you? Always running around doing good things, always trying to keep that goodness in you even when the rest of the world laughs and rejoices in evil.'

'You overestimate me.'

'I never overestimate an opponent. Underestimation has been my most reliable failing.'

Was I missing something? Did she have a plan, a purpose to telling me all this and co-operating with her

enemy? I wasn't ready to take any chance in the hope
that defeat had mellowed her into someone even moder-
ately acceptable.

'Now, will you tell me why I'm here?'

'What?' She'd startled me out of my thought. 'Oh, yes.
The Consortium have been thinking about the succes-
sion. Seeing how you were legally in line for the throne,
we've decided to give you a chance.'

That stopped her. 'No.'

'No, you don't want it?'

'No . . . I mean . . . this is a trick.'

'You think I'd take you to Stormpoint, *my* Stormpoint,
if it wasn't anything but the truth?' I was genuinely
shocked. She'd just been told that her greatest hope, the
one desire that had driven her family for centuries,
might come true, and she was acting as if I'd put a frog in
her drink.

'But . . . you're a powerful member of the Consortium!
And you despise me!'

'I may be powerful,' I sighed, 'but I'm not in charge.
T'omar got everyone together and we talked about it.'

'I still don't understand why you're offering me the
crown.'

'Firstly, I'm not offering anything. The crown is on
Serein's head, and we may not be able to get it back.
Secondly, I still don't trust you, and one of the things the
Consortium agreed was that, in light of your history as a
real cow, we should run a few tests.'

The light of understanding dawned in her eye, and her
face changed to the mask of a court lady. As hard as a
rock, and probably no more absorbent. 'What tests?'

'The Great Mage of Yore tests.'

'Translated as?'

I took her by the shoulders, and gently turned her until she faced the wall and the single, full-length mirror. She gazed, enraptured at her reflection.

'Look in the mirror. Look as deep as you can go.' I'd always wanted to say that.

As she stared, my hands on her shoulders and my head peeking round hers, I let the magic build. I wasn't sure how the spells would respond to a hundred years of neglect on my part, but I wove the old symbols anyway. Magic to scry, magic to summon. Magic to twist the Void, magic to straighten reality. Magic to show a lie for truth, and truth for a lie. Magic to show the soul.

A rainbow of light spread across the mirror, vanishing as soon as it had appeared. Good. It was active and aware. I backed away, not keen to see my own soul for what it was.

The spell of the mirror caught as I pushed more magic into it and, though Lisana struggled to pull free, her own reflection reached out and caught her in a grip like steel. Now there were two Lisana's in the room, one a serene angel, one a twisting, panicky lady of dodgy disposition.

I retreated further, until my back was against the door. Light was swirling out of the mirror, encompassing both the real woman and her reflection in a sheet of power. There was going to be one hell of a magical discharge any sec . . .

The flash of light was so white and so bright that it made the sun look like a candle against noonday. And the crack as magical forces met and expanded was so loud and so powerful it shook the floor. Plates slid off their shelves, smashing to the floor.

I hid my eyes, tried to hide my ears, tried to hide altogether as I cowered away from the power that was, in a sense, my own.

The echoes died away.

Lisana was curled up in front of the mirror, trembling, face buried in her knees. I crept to her side, my head still ringing, and touched her cautiously. She jumped, with a sharp gasp of breath and a trembling retreat.

'Lisana?' I asked softly.

Hesitantly, she raised her head. Her tear-filled eyes met mine, and she gave a cry of despair. She flung herself forward, and I felt her arms encircle me and the tears flow freely as she held close to her worst enemy as if he were her only friend in the world. *I should have tried this hundreds of years ago . . .*

It was a harsh form of treatment, a violent burst of truth that either made or broke the one who beheld it. I'd thought that maybe I'd feel pleased, cheered to see a woman who'd caused me so much grief reduced to a wreck in a matter of seconds. Not so. All I felt was the deep emptiness of a task which had to be done and required more than anyone had in them to give.

I remembered what my sister had done, when I'd gone running to her. Holding Lisana's head in my hands, I made soothing sounds as best I could, rocking her back and forth. After a long while the tears subsided, and an even longer time after that she pulled away, and rose gracefully, her face set.

To this day I don't know what she saw in the mirror, and my magic revealed nothing. Sometimes I think that mirror has a will of its own. Suffice it to say I didn't have the heart to ask, and helped the lady up to her bed in Stormpoint without a word.

She fell asleep, with her back to me, facing the far wall, and I went to find Renna.

She read me without hesitation. 'Something happened.'

'The spell worked. Lisana's lying down.'

'And?'

I shrugged, the way I always do. Shrug at this, shrug at that, shrug at the end of the world. Truth is, there are some things which can't be shrugged off. 'She is the rightful heir, if you can be bothered to check family trees back through a thousand years. She looked in the mirror, and seemed very repentant.'

Renna leant closer, and with her the inhabitants of the whole forest. Everyone wanted to know. Sometimes, I thought, I'm just a messenger, an intermediary between forces over which I've no control. That or paranoid.

Meanwhile I stood before them, to announce news for that once I did control, and that might affect millions of lives. *My God, is this is what kings have to endure every day?*

I ended with, 'If she's no good, the Consortium can still work round her.'

Shouldn't there be a reaction? But the forest of elves and werewolves and refugees just stood there and stared.

I took a deep breath, and forced the words out through clenched teeth.

'Long live the queen!'

Only then did they go, as they say on Earth, ballistic.

FOURTEEN

Greetings and Farewells

The last night. The words that kept on bouncing around my head – I was seriously doubting my own sanity. It was the last night before we were likely to commit suicide. And I was betting on a hope alone. Oh, everyone said I would be a great leader, throwing magic all over the place, with a king's dying wish, a true queen, a thousand spies, a thousand elementals and a thousand soldiers to back me.

But I'd been breaking that down into little, tiddly bits.

What good was magic, if I only had finite power, and a limited control over what it hit? What good was a king's dying wish? Especially now I knew he was descended of the wrong king, and was, as the nature of his influence might suggest, very dead indeed!

Just three days ago, when we'd sat in Stormpoint and talked lightly of 'what we'll do when Haven is free', I'd said how I would like to settle down in Stormpoint and make a map which alters every time a kingdom changed. I'd got it all worked out, too, every twist of every spell.

And here we were, preparing an attack on a city garrisoned by the toughest, fastest, strongest nightmares ever to saunter around the limit of dreams.

My one hope was based on guesswork. On the kind of miracle that happened in dreams, at the last moment. It also involved exposing someone I cared for to breathtaking danger.

Exposing everyone to danger. No doubt about it. Mess loomed.

'Enough,' I said. 'Early start tomorrow.'

The table of Silverhands nodded, but their words were hushed. They knew that what we planned was madness.

Renna touched my arm as I passed. 'T'omar wants to see you.'

I hugged her. After all, it would probably be the last chance I'd get. To my surprise she didn't pull away, but held tight. 'Good night,' I murmured.

'Sleep well.'

We parted without another word, and I went in search of T'omar.

The general was in his study – no surprise there – staring at the double spider's web that is the universe. He didn't even look up as I entered. 'You'd better be bloody good at getting Serein.'

I studied the map. Counters had been laid all across it or, where they ran out, just scraps of paper. Numbers were scrawled on them, and little stars. A star was for an experienced or skilled force, I guessed. Each piece of paper represented where large numbers of people would either stay alive, or die.

I'm not good at tactics, which may be why I messed up with court politics. It is after all just warfare with words. But even I could tell what risks we ran. All along the boundaries where the two spider's webs met were little markers for our forces, scattered over a vast area. They'd be stretched thin, their attacks would be costly and dangerous, we'd lose so many lives . . .

Around Haven were counters of a different colour. And in the spaces between the spider's web were the elementals, close to the walls. They'd strike as we entered the city, distracting Serein. It would be a short-lived, feeble attack, and they'd retreat almost instantly to regenerate in the warm magic of the Void. But a short attack was all that was needed, especially with a massive force bearing down at the same time on Nightkeep . . .

In his place, what would I do if everywhere was being attacked at once? I was almost sorry for Serein – then immediately felt the absurdity of such a thought.

'He'll know you're coming the moment the elementals retreat,' said T'omar. His voice was heavy and resigned. 'He'll start scrying, and the moment he detects you he'll attack with the full force of a Key.' I opened my mouth to speak, but he got there first. 'Oh, I know that you're going alone so that you can keep your precious scry-block working to a maximum. And I know he'll have his hands full worrying himself sick about nightmare. If it wasn't for the limits of that spell of yours we could probably smuggle an army of thousands up to the main gate. But even you can't block him for long.'

'I won't need to,' I replied, with a confidence that I

didn't feel. 'There are still fifty thousand inhabitants in Haven. That's a lot of people to get lost in.'

He snorted. 'It's the size of a army who can die in a day.'

'Once inside the palace, I'll occupy all Serein's attention. Don't overlook the power of a name. To him I'm Daddy-killer, and I'll keep him busy for a very long time.'

'And once you are inside? Give me technical details.'

I sighed – we'd been through this.

'Tell me about your scry-block. Your spell whose secret you've never revealed. Could it shield two?'

I felt the worm of suspicion dig itself into my mind. 'Yes. Why?'

'From the sound of it you'll be shielding all over the place. That could be costly. How much of your power must you use, if you also have to fry the guards?'

'I've always survived.'

'Not this time. You're good at sneaking in to make a mess of small, stupid people with little power, in the remote reaches of nightmare. But this is different. You've never been near Nightkeep as an enemy, and in the Void you fought *only* its king. A great feat, I'll give you, but it was just you against him, no interference.'

'Your point?'

T'omar smiled, but there was no humour. 'You'll need a swordsman. To parry steel while you parry fire. Someone who can watch your back as you unravel ward on ward, totally focused, not able to look for that unseen attacker.'

I shook my head, dread taking root where the worm had dug. 'No. Not a chance.'

'This is not a request, Kite. You made me the leader of the Consortium, and we all know that if you hadn't said "T'omar" I'd have been just another face in the crowd. Now you pay the price for using that legend of yours. I overrule you, and am coming with you.'

FIFTEEN

Return to the City of Dreams

Grey clothes, grey hoods, grey boots. Grey throughout. There were twenty-two of us, and because we couldn't all hold onto Renna we were going in six relays. Four in the first five groups, two in the last. We bustled about the hall in a state of severe nervousness, never meeting the others' eyes as yet another Silverpoint day dawned all too soon.

T'omar checked his rifle. I'd never seen him before as a warrior, with gun and sword. It added a lot to his presence. Suddenly he wasn't the silent tactician sitting in a study with his fingers steepled and eyes locked on a map. Now he was a dragon-slayer in grey, the silent hunter who always gets his lizard. I hadn't properly noticed how he was several inches taller than most of us, a lot broader and carried a massive sword at his hip as if it were a feather blade. The sword had been enchanted for accuracy and power, but looking with a mage's eyes at its faint glow I wasn't willing to bet my life on the magic's abilities in a battle. The rifle was a more reassuring weapon.

The healers had been at work, and like me all he had to show of the all too recent battle were a few fading pink lines. *At least you just had to ask nicely*, I thought. *You didn't have to play at riddles with dead men.*

My staff had also been blessed. It was one of the few times I'd carried one, but they'd been useful in the past when trying to get into nightmare's minor realms, for hitting soft things and, more importantly, for blocking sharp things. The ancient wood was warm to the touch, charged with magical energy for me to tap at will.

But I'd kept my own daggers, and the clothes I wore were mine, scribed with spells of the Void that I knew could work. To my relief Renna also wore the clothes I'd made, which should do her good in moments of trouble.

Windsight stepped forward, armed to the teeth. He was one of five necromancer-mincer-men, as we'd termed our mages, or NMM for short. These were the men T'omar and I were covering by going after Serein. Hopefully they in turn would keep most of the guards occupied.

Which threat was bigger – guards or mages – we weren't sure. But it was a fair certainty that both I and the NMMs would be fighting like hell from the second we stepped inside the walls.

I get nervous at talk of death and destruction. But T'omar seemed to take it all in his stride, which for me made things worse. He was the hero of the tale, all steady eyes and words of encouragement. I was the scared side-kick, drumming my fingers on my staff and trying to remember every trick of magic I'd ever pulled.

I'd just reached trick number forty-two – fire will bounce off a softer magical shield rather than hard – when the call came.

'The elementals are commencing their attack, sir.'

We all have an image of how it must be to go into battle. But standing around in small groups in the hall of Silverpoint, with breakfast plates being cleared away and not an enemy in sight, it was a very civilised order that we'd just received to advance across no man's land.

All eyes turned to Renna. Seeing her stand alone, hands clasped silently in front of her, eyes scanning every face one by one, I had such mixed feelings that I nearly told her what I planned.

But, if I risked imposing order over the chaos on which my scheme depended, without a doubt we would die.

'Group one to the fore!' T'omar called out.

There was a general murmur of goodbye and good luck as Windsight stepped forward. Our eyes met briefly, and then parted. If we'd needed to say anything, we'd left it a bit late anyway.

Renna faded away, taking the group with her.

Seconds drew out to minutes. Long agonising minutes. I felt a rustle inside my magic – the elementals' war leaking back to their creator. Then Renna was back, bringing with her a tide of relief that made my heart skip a beat.

'Group two forward!'

'Group three!' . . .

'Group four!' . . .

'Group five!' . . .

We were the only ones left. Everyone else had vanished to an unknown fate.

Kite, the mage of a thousand spells. T'omar, the warrior of the flashing blades. That was how people saw us. That was what the eyes of the Silverhands said. *If these two fail, no one can succeed. These two are the best we have, together they can win . . .*

And if – when? – we failed?

One consolation I could think of – at least I wouldn't have to watch.

Renna brought us out to about fifteen streets from the palace, in a house that was dark, shadowy and roaring with silence. Haven was seriously changed since I'd last checked.

Through the ruins of a half-collapsed wall I could see the street. It was in near-darkness, and a lot of the houses had shattered and barred windows. Rats raced past, before diving into a sewer from which noxious gases and suspicious sounds emerged. A tavern sign had fallen along with the beams of the house, and lay in the middle of the street as a reminder of what had been there before. Through the black slime that clung to it, I could just make out the name – Dreamer's Rest.

The sun was red and sour in the sky of whirling oranges and browns. From far off came the sounds of battle as the elementals fought against impossible odds on the edge of the Void. Soon they'd be retreating; before then T'omar and I would need to have moved. We'd have to be in those hellish streets where the heat bakes you even while the wind off the haunted ruins tries to freeze your fingers. But worst of all were the flies. They rose

from human corpses left lying in the street, occasionally
with bits missing. A single horse, all skin and bones, was
standing at a water trough so full of green slime and little
blood-sucking insects that it could hardly drink. Rats
swarmed over a shattered cart as they dug their teeth
into a load of mouldy grain. The streets stank of piss,
blood and decay.

But now there were vampires in the streets, or demons
clinging to the sides of buildings, or dark wyverns
hanging in the sky, or black knights laying about an
innocent home with their curved blades.

I turned to Renna, knowing that she was expecting
some kind of comfort. Unfortunately, I had none to give.
'All right, time for you to go.'

'Is that it?'

'You'd rather stay?'

She just kept on staring at me, eyes almost as confused
as the wildly spinning sky.

T'omar came the rescue, bowing before Renna and
kissing her hand. 'My lady,' he said respectfully. 'If it
means anything, we're going to kick nightmare butt as
much for you as for dreams.'

He straightened, and stood by my side. There was a
long silence, which was broken only by the faint scrab-
bling of some monster as it sniffed out fresh meat. 'Go!'
I snapped as the sounds drew nearer.

'Laenan . . .' she began.

'Uh!' I raised a warning finger. 'No time, leave and
don't come back!'

She hesitated, and then faded. It wasn't the most
friendly farewell I could have managed, but something
had switched inside me.

The moment I heard the sound of a nightmare approaching, the other Kite was ready to take over.

I don't believe you've met me. I'm the Laenan Kite from whom legends are sprung. So far my other self, the cheerful, reclusive mage of lazy disposition and a few handy spells, has run the show. Now, with nightmare around me, the memories return. And with the memories, the reflexes to kill.

For the moment, though, the instinct to summon fire and magic to my fingers, and instantly incinerate all enemies, had to be resisted.

The sound came again, a scratching, a faint hissing. A monster of some kind was upstairs, and no doubt saw us as easy targets. Both me's, the fighter and the scholar, shared the sigh. The one thing the legend and the real man can agree on is this – we both hate mess.

The vampire dropped into the room.

You people on Earth get the weirdest ideas. You think you can just wave a cross in front of a vampire and it'll scream and crumble into dust. Why?

This one displayed a set of teeth that bore typical vampire pointiness, and its pale grey face was crinkled into a typical vampire leer. 'Ah. Two fools, one in steel one in magic, think they can take on nightmare.' All in all, an unoriginal creature.

T'omar and I exchanged looks. So, it was *that* kind of imagination running the scene. The sort of mind that hadn't talked to enough dreamers and didn't have ideas of its own. 'Serein has read the wrong kind of books,' I announced.

'Or simply has no sense of style.'

The vampire hissed again, stepping nearer with a movement that was probably meant to be threatening. T'omar hadn't even touched his sword. He just stood there, trying to look as if he wasn't carrying a massive weapon of edged steel. The incredible thing was, he succeeded.

'Look, pal. We know you're just a figment of Serein's imagination, and would vanish the moment you stepped into the Void,' I explained reasonably. 'We're looking for real people to fight, who might still be causing trouble after the bastard who made you is dead.' The vampire hesitated. 'Ah, now you're trying to signal your creator through the Key. No good, I'm afraid. There's an elemental attack going on at the moment and anyway, you're inside the radius of my spell.'

'What spell? You lie!'

'He's a mage,' said T'omar helpfully, still standing like a tourist watching a city scene.

'And pretty good at it,' I agreed.

God, but vampires are stupid. If it had been a sensible, properly balanced monster, by then it would have lunged forward and ripped out our throats. But no, it just hung around looking fazed.

Time to put the poor thing out of its misery. 'This guy is called T'omar,' I explained, pointing at the warrior in shining armour. 'I didn't want him to come, but he's incredibly stubborn and outranks me anyway. He's a knife-juggling general of a thousand battles,' I added when the creature didn't react.

T'omar got the message and acted on it in one swift movement. However stupid vampires may be, they do die neatly. Exploding in a puff of dust is so much more helpful than any alternative. For a start it means you don't have to waste money on a cremation.

There was a hiss of steel as T'omar sheathed his sword. 'That was a very dumb animal.'

'At least we've learnt something about Serein.'

'Yes. He's an unimaginative bastard, isn't he?'

I'd like to say we ran without hindrance through the hot, dry streets, with the sounds of battle fading behind us, avoiding every monster or patrol either by a spell or hasty concealment. Not true. Serein had populated nearly every corner with some demon or another. My guts churned at the screams of the dying, and the roar of reality constantly being shifted where the elementals fought.

But the sounds of war didn't disturb me as much as the new palace. Guards – real guards – patrolled the walls, which had grown back metal spikes, colossal thorns and at some points the mangled body of some dignitary. On the gates flickered massive demons of red flame; in the towers of black stone necromancers watched the battle through telescopes or calmly pulled the life out of a screaming woman from the town.

And behind the walls rose the most practical palace I'd seen in a long while. It was, quite simply, a keep, square but for the towers you might expect on such a building. Gargoyles clung to the walls, spitting acid. A single black dragon was curled around the keep, and if you didn't see it move you wouldn't believe it was there.

'We cannot get over that,' I announced finally. 'We're going another way, or not at all.'

'There'll be monsters in the sewers,' said T'omar quietly.

'But no guards. Monsters don't worry me so much,' I replied. 'Monsters are stupid. Guards have brains.'

'It'll be hot, smelly and full of rats.'

'This was your idea, wasn't it?'

'Actually, I thought you were the one under a death-wish spell . . .'

'This was your *plan*. We need to get inside the palace, so that the troops can stand a chance.'

'We need to kill Serein to give the troops their chance,' he corrected. '*You* need to kill Serein and take the Key.'

I drummed my fingers on the staff. 'Come on Windsight. Blow something up.'

'Is that what you're waiting for? A second distraction?'

I gave T'omar a dirty look. We both knew what I was waiting for. If all went well Serein would think that the elementals had been the distraction to get Windsight into the city, not that Windsight was the decoy to get us into the palace. It was a straightforward plan, but it still had credibility. Only an idiot would attack the palace itself.

'If we wait for Windsight to blow something up, all Serein's attention will go to him. And even your friend can't deflect the full force of Key-bound attention.'

I bit my lip, drummed my fingers, tapped my feet – the lot. The truth was, T'omar was right. If we let Windsight take the full brunt of nightmare's interest I wouldn't have anyone to talk to afterwards. 'Let's see if there's a handy grate nearby.'

It wasn't hard to find an entrance to the sewers. The stench could have attracted an anosmic bat from five miles. The hard thing was finding an entrance away from guards or wyverns or other inconveniences. We eventually found one on a street so full of flies that not even the denizens of nightmare would go there. I solved the problem of flies with a quick ball of magic which I hurled down the street. As it flew, they were pulled towards it like metal fillings to a magnet, and stuck. So when the ball finally incinerated itself at the end of the road, it was black with little bodies. Flashy, but better than the alternative.

T'omar heaved, the grate fell back with a clang. Immediately more flies began to dive into the sewers, attracted by the foul stench. He pulled out a long piece of cloth from his pocket and tied it round his face. 'You'd better have one too,' he warned, voice muffled.

I peered into the darkness, and was nearly sick. 'Just one second,' I muttered, turning my back on him.

Fire flashed at my fingers. I forced it to grow bigger, pumping in more magic, and putting a second layer of untapped power inside, just in case. Even the citizens of Haven go to the toilet, dear dreamer. And, given the right motivation, that stuff burns. At the sight of that ball of flame, T'omar took several steps back. 'When that goes off . . .'

'It'll incinerate everything down there in seconds,' I said with a grim smile. 'There's so much potential magic in this place it'll probably also burn up everything around the grates for at least a few yards.'

'Couldn't we just drop a match?'

I gave him a shocked look. 'Nononono! We want to tap the magical side of fire!'

'Why?'

'I'll show you soon enough.'

'They'll be searching the sewers the second that goes off.'

'They'll be searching the sewers the second it cools down. There is a distinct difference.'

He gave me another look which could have made a lion blush, and I cracked. 'For dream's sake, am I or am I not the great mage of burning magic?' I demanded, seriously pissed off at such a strop over a simple inferno. 'Or are you afraid you'll get hot inside an exclusion-shield?'

He groaned. 'You're just making this up as you go along, aren't you?'

'*No!* Burning everything that squeaks is a time-honoured technique. I can't stand rats. Or spiders, for that matter.'

He folded his arms. 'All right, then. Drop the wretched thing.'

With not a little smugness I edged towards the grate. Trying to stand as far back as possible, I dropped the fireball. Before it even hit the bottom of the shaft I was scampering to a safer distance.

The gout of foul-smelling flame fuelled by things best undescribed erupted in a jet of yellow-red fire that scorched the rooftops. All over Haven similar pillars exploded. Houses began to burn, the roar of flames rising against the backdrop of battle.

'I hope no one was on the toilet when that went off,' murmured T'omar.

I ignored him.

You dreamers have got some things right. Even in Roman times you didn't waste tonnes of stone and mortar in building a huge support for your bridges – you invented the keystone and stuck it in the middle of a much smaller scaffold and simpler support. My point is, never waste big, powerful stuff where a small spell would suffice. Sewage burns very well indeed, if you know how to use it.

T'omar nudged me and pointed skywards. Heavy black clouds were mustering. Less than a minute later, and the first rain hit. 'Serein doesn't want his city to burn down,' murmured the general.

I felt a slight sting, and glanced at my hand. 'It's not just raining water, T'omar.'

He glanced at my hand. A small welt of blood was rising from where an arrowhead of ice had drawn blood. Of course, his monsters would have thick scales. His soldiers would be in armour, his necromancers would raise shields . . .

I looked down at the grate again. It was still illuminated from below by the light of the fires. But then, what was a mage for . . .?

'Give me your hand.'

I drew a symbol on his palm, and a pinkish shield of barely discernible light flashed into existence. I repeated the same procedure with myself, and kicked open the now blackened, smoking grate.

As we clambered down the ladder, the fires beneath my feet seemed to be laughing at their next, willing meal. But the shield held, and every time I reached out to touch a rung on the blackened metal, the pinkish haze bent, curled around my hand, and pushed the heat away. The staff was uncomfortably heavy in my hands, and nearly as cumbersome as T'omar's rifle.

I landed in a field of fire, which rose up around a small

circle of magic, nearly a foot to my knees. T'omar landed behind me, and looked out across a tunnel which could have auditioned for a pathway to hell. We didn't need any light, the orange flame illuminated every crumbling shard of mortar or scorched pipeline.

Then it came – that little tingling sensation that only a mage can feel. 'Look out,' I murmured.

Abruptly, the welcome relief of light from the grate above us was cut off. We glanced upwards, in time to see the shaft down which we'd descended brick itself up, the new/old stones appearing out of nowhere and laying themselves in a blur of speed, down to the ground. All along the tunnel, the same was happening to other shafts. T'omar licked dry lips. 'To keep us out, or in?' he asked.

'Probably out,' I conceded. 'He knows the fires are still raging down here, and probably reasons that only a madman would have gone in.'

'Good reasoning.'

It came again, that tightening of reality. *What now?* The walls buckled. T'omar swore in a way only the military can manage.

'Where's Windsight's distractions when we need them?' I muttered.

The sodden, flame-streaked sewage beneath my feet began to churn as the walls closed in. Either we would drown, or be squashed. *Hopefully squashed*, thought the part of me which had given up from the start and was now sitting over my reason with a righteous look of 'I-told-you-so'. *No, we're going to . . . to . . . to escape*, I thought desperately, struggling to shove the terror away. *How?*

'Kite,' came T'omar's incredibly level voice. 'This would be a good moment to do something magical.'

Okay, change of plan. We're not going to escape, someone else is going to stick their necks out for us. <Windsight! Bloody well cause a distraction now!> I sent at the top of my mental lungs.

<Hold onto something,> came the mild answer. Does no one in this world panic except me?

'Windsight says to hold onto something.'

'Why?'

'Would you rather *not*?'

Unfortunately, all we could hold on to was the walls, which were rapidly turning into a lump of twisted reality. <Windsight, get on with it!> I screamed as the tunnel walls drew so close I could have reached out and touched both sides. The flames were rising, forced together. They were now up to my waist, and the shield I had raised was barely forcing them back as the sheer weight of fire pressed closer. No, we wouldn't drown in shit, my magic would see to that. We'd simply get every bone in our bodies crushed to a thousand tiny bits . . .

There was a flash of light that burnt brighter than any fire and turned the wall beneath my hands to liquid possibility. Then came the noise, sluggishly trying to catch up with its partner in destruction. And trailing behind both, came the *pressure*.

I ended face-down in a sea of fire and ash, mortar crumbling around me, every magical sense I had ringing with the shock of the spell. T'omar crawled to my side through the flames on hands and knees. The walls had frozen in place. 'What the hell was that?'

'Void-rift,' I murmured hoarsely.

'Here?'

I nodded, too shocked to say more. 'Windsight . . .

must have opened a Void-rift to . . . to force Serein to stop fiddling with reality down here and repair the hole in his kingdom instead. Void-rifts destroy miles of reality, turn it all to . . .' I couldn't go on.

T'omar helped pull me upright, but I hardly felt a thing. 'I'm . . . I'm sure Windsight got out,' he said. 'Shielded himself.'

I wiped my forehead with the back of my hand, leaving a black stain. 'You can't shield against the Void.'

<Windsight?> I sent. Was that a stirring of consciousness? A faint gleam of thought? Or was my imagination playing tricks on me? Even Saenia couldn't summon a Void-rift without draining herself down to a gibbering wreck.

<He'll live,> whispered a voice.

<Saenia? Where are you?>

<Stormpoint. I've been with you for several hours. The staff you've got – it's mine. Just in case, you understand.>

<What the hell are you playing at?>

<Just keeping an eye on you, little brother.>

<Why didn't you say something?>

<I'm just observing. And . . . possibly giving you a hand. It's too far for me to give you a shield or anything useful like that.>

I love my sister. There is seriously no one like her. How much greater she is than I in simple compassion and wisdom.

The weariness drained from me, leaving me standing straight, and glowing with magical energy from my sister's own reserves. It filled and renewed me and made me feel confident beyond all measure.

<Good luck.> My sister's link flickered, and failed.

I would have preferred that she said nothing at all. That way I wouldn't have felt so lost for words. Some feelings are hard to express without getting soppy, so I won't try here. Suffice it to say, if you ever find yourselves wandering in dreams and you bump into my sister, give her a big kiss from me.

'Come on,' I murmured.

'Where?' T'omar asked, looking pointedly at the place where the shaft had been.

I sighed. I've tried so often to explain my philosophy of magic on the go, and so few people have ever got it. There's no point having a plan where magic is concerned – the very nature of the beast is so chaotic you simply can't impose the order of sanity on it. 'You'd rather stay down here, I take it?'

'I was just wondering how you intend to get us out.'

'I'm going to bash a hole in the first brick that looks a little unsteady,' I replied. And meant it, more's the thing. On Earth you have a thing called gunpowder, which our alchemists long ago adapted to rifles. Why they weren't used as explosives though, is simple. Nothing beats good, old-fashioned earthbomb spells or a pillar of acid-charms.

He shrugged. 'Very well.'

We made our way in silence through the flames.

It's surprisingly easy to get lost in sewers illuminated only by wildfires and the glow from mage-light. It didn't help that reality was constantly changing as Serein fought to heal a Void-rift (thank you Windsight and Necromancer-mincers 1), then to summon a squad of dragons as replacements for those incinerated by NMM 2, then to repulse a plague of half-illusion, half-real fairies (thank you NMM 3), *then* to replace the spells lost when a tower of necromancers collapsed (NMM 4's proudest achievement) before finally repairing the damage caused by the gouts of flame erupting from the city's plumbing.

T'omar began turning the map over and over in his hands, frowning at the tracery of fine lines and muttering to himself. We stopped in a patch of flame, to consider our next move. There was little sewage left, thanks to the fires which still gnawed away in dark corners. I wiped my watering eyes, leaving a foul-smelling mark across my already filthy face. 'We're lost, aren't we?' I asked, squinting to see T'omar clearly against the flames.

'No! I think we're somewhere near the palace!'

'How near? Are we talking guardhouses filled with soldiers?'

'I think we're about here.' He pointed with a smudged finger.

'You sure?'

'No. But Serein can't keep the sewers closed off all day.'

Further down the passage there was a crackling of flames. That in itself wasn't remarkable, considering the persistent magic I'd let loose. But it was the suddenness, the unexpected roar of fire where it should be dying. Our eyes met.

'Or he might just summon a host of fire elementals to scour the tunnels and devour everything,' I replied easily.

Don't get me wrong – I like elementals and, as I've said,

my greatest trick was to summon such self-sustaining, self-aware creatures from the Void. But they were another matter here, in the sewers leaping with fire and with the eagle eye of Serein scouring the city for anyone who so much as lit a candle with magic. The creatures we were about to face weren't as handy as my beloved creations, being as they were bound to Haven and a little on the slow side. But in a kingdom where reality was controlled by our enemy, they were still enough to keep me very worried indeed.

Besides, Serein could use the Key to summon more of them for his own purpose, faster than we could kill them. And rifles are famously ineffective against any creature made of raw magic.

I tugged T'omar against a wall. 'Listen.'

He put his ear to the wall. 'Fire elementals,' he murmured. 'Possibly the odd salamander too. Can't you smell them?'

I sniffed. There *was* a scent of sulphur in the air. A stench fierce enough to overwhelm the other, methane-based, smells that had assailed us. Strong enough indeed to penetrate the masks and shields we wore.

'Simulacra time?' he asked quietly.

'Definitely.' I leant back against the wall, and sent my mind outwards. Up through the sewers, into the streets. Two guardsmen were patrolling near a deserted square. They wore protective wards, but these were weak, cast by images already drained from too many battles against the citizens of Haven.

I didn't hesitate, but raised a blanket of magic around the two guards, shaping their features and signatures into something vaguely resembling T'omar's and mine. Then I drew light into the illusion, and it was complete.

'Hurry,' whispered T'omar.

Throughout the city I raced from man to man, creating a web of illusion in the form of our two likenesses that spanned them all. Five times I felt the presence of Serein pass me by as he darted among our simulacra, desperate to find the real T'omar and Kite. Each time, I hid. I wasn't about to take on a Key-bound consciousness. Not yet.

I wish I'd seen Serein's face though, as he rushed from one beacon of magic to another, probing area after area, unable to find anything, losing control to the point where madness took over.

'Kite!'

T'omar already had his back against the wall and was swinging his sword in huge arcs, trying to fend off a pair of burning salamanders, who hissed and spat venom. I staggered out of the magical trace I'd used, and was barely in time to raise a reflection shield, cutting the creatures off from their masters.

That enchanted sword of the general's was probably the only thing which stopped him being burnt up then and there. It's hard to make mincemeat of creatures fashioned from raw fire.

I fumbled open my flask of water, and tipped the contents over the nearer salamander. It shrieked and recoiled, the fires along its back going out, to leave charred flesh that smoked and steamed. A few seconds later T'omar's sword swung down on the creature, and it shrieked no more. That left one salamander, lunging forward with bared fangs. The general didn't even grunt as it dug its teeth into his leg, but swung the steel under and upwards, lifting the creature off its feet and slamming it hard into the opposite wall. As the salamander fought to regain its footing and attack again, T'omar wrenched open his flask and threw water in its face. It screamed, so high and loud that my ears popped.

'Come on!' he yelled, dragging me by the sleeve. I dropped my shield, and ran.

We didn't stop until our pursuers were a long way behind. I'm usually against saying things like that, because you might demand, 'How did they get a long way behind?' Please don't ask. Or compare it to the stunt where people hold their breath underwater, several times longer than you'd think possible. Shields were thrown left and right, and tunnels that weaved and divided blended into one as we ran, and ran and ran, desperate to escape. Desperation overruled control, and somehow, through panic and chaos, we got clear.

At the end of our flight, gasping for breath and dripping sewage, we hid for several minutes in a side-passage, alert for sounds of pursuit as we tried to find out the extent of our injuries. T'omar's left leg was a mess of bite marks, some already swelling with poison. We had no water, to clean it, and when I offered to try magic he shook his head with a smile. 'You focus on your scry-block.'

'How long do you think we've been down here?' I asked as we turned the corner into a tunnel that T'omar was *sure* would lead to the palace. The flames were burning lower, but I hadn't risked mage light. Not with the occasional roar of a fire elemental down the long passages.

'An hour,' he said, limping slightly. 'Maybe more.'

'An hour? We've got to hurry!'

He shrugged. Sometimes I can't stand people who are bold in the face of death. 'An hour of hard work for us and the NMMs is an hour in which Serein can be going ballistic with frustration.'

'This isn't psychological warfare!' I exclaimed.

Suddenly he raised a hand. 'Shush!'

I listened. There was the sound of ashes being stirred, a faint crackling growing louder. Then voices, operating on the spectrum only open to magic ears.

<Left.>

<Hurry.>

<Right.>

<Look.>

<Hunt.>

<Find.>

<Kill.>

A series of basic commands, I realised. The creatures had little or no intelligence of their own, and had been thrown together by Serein in such a hurry that he hadn't bothered to give them independent thought. That might be an advantage, though I was damned if I could see how.

We pressed ourselves against the walls, hoods pulled over our faces, masks up to our eyes, and watched as a pair of fiery elementals drifted past. I swear I thought the beating of my heart would give me away.

Minutes went by, in which I could hear T'omar's breath like a gale, my own the hurricane out to sea.

T'omar moved, very carefully. He hastened to the edge of the tunnel without a sound, peered down the long stone corridor of fire, nodded at me. I crept to his side, my footfalls sounding like a drum roll after his cat's tread. 'This way,' he whispered, pointing directly ahead.

I followed, senses alert for any sign of pursuit. Nothing. Maybe the subterranean defenders were as lost as we were.

After what felt like another hour of running, but was probably little more than ten minutes, the fires were fading, and I had to peer into darkness to discern the vague shape of T'omar as he led the way. The smell had become just another background sensation, as was the sucking noise we made with each step.

Abruptly he stopped, and raised a finger to his lips. I strained to detect what he had heard. Voices. Laughter. Not coming from inside the tunnels, I realised, but from *above*.

'Barracks?' I asked.

He nodded, and pointed further up the tunnel. I followed, and we stopped to listen again. 'Don't hear anything.'

T'omar grinned, a flash of white teeth in the near-total blackness. He tapped the wall.

'Here?'

He tapped again.

'Don't be wrong about this.'

He shrugged, and slung the rifle into a more convenient position. After the places we'd taken it I couldn't believe it would do more than go squelch.

I began to draw power from my staff.

Cautiously I sent my mind upwards, to just above floor height. A stable full of the black knights' massive black horses. They whinnied uncomfortably. Horses are

better than most humans at sensing magic. I returned to
the sewers and set to work.

The mortar in the sewer wall was old, and there were
only a few feet of stone between me and the stable floor.
I scooped up a handful of ashy burned sewage, since that
was all there was to hand, and drew a large circle on the
stonework. Large enough, at least, to admit a man. I
tried to tell the circle of scorched human crap that it
wasn't what it thought it was. That it was hot and powerful and could devour anything in minutes.

It began to sizzle faintly.

I told it that, with patience, it could beat back these
stones, which dared to stop it reaching lots of oxygen,
and if it did reach oxygen, it could become a new and
wondrous substance.

A greenish smoke began rising off the stones. I backed
away, breathing through the cloth around my face.

I told it that it was acid, which existed to eat alkali, its
enemy, down to nothing. I told it that here was my
magic, with which it could destroy everything.

The circle glowed faintly, then erupted into white
foam which dug into the stonework in a blur, giving off
bursts of blue-red magic as it encountered any area of
resistance.

'That's one of yours, isn't it?' whispered T'omar.

'Uhuh. The Accelerated Acid Spell,' I replied. 'You
can climb, can't you?'

He gave me a look which could have penetrated the
darkness by its reproachful force alone.

'Sorry,' I murmured.

'Only you would think of turning shit into acid.'

'It works with anything. Just add hydrogen, give it a

little magical aid and that stuff'll eat faster than any fire-tunnel spell.'

'I always meant to ask – how do you get these ideas? I mean, for spells with instructions like "Add hydrogen and give a little magical aid"?'

I grinned, and employed a useful phrase you dreamers have come up with. 'It came to me in a dream.'

Dull light suddenly entered the shaft, accompanied by an avalanche of dissolved mortar and the whinnying of horses. Scrambling to the edge of the hole, I peered up into daylight and straw. 'Give us a leg-up,' I hissed. 'When I'm up, I'll drop you a rope.'

T'omar glanced around to check for elementals, then cupped his hands and boosted me up into the small shaft. I hauled my way to the top, the staff wedged into the back of my belt, and emerged filthy and sweating into blissfully clean air. The horses whinnied loudly, so I hurried to the nearest one and stroked it into submission, sending soothing waves into its mind. Seeing one of their number calm, the rest of the stable were quietened.

'Hurry up!' T'omar's voice came out of the tunnel, more urgently than I'd expected.

I fumbled in my filthy clothes, to find the rope I'd tied round my waist. After struggling with the knot, I got the dratted thing untied and slung one end down to him.

There were sounds in the tunnel. Odd noises. Bad noises.

He caught the rope with a grip that suggested he wouldn't forgive me if I let go. As he started to pull himself upwards the noises drew nearer, bringing with them a sense of magic and heat.

I hauled on the rope, even faster as the elementals

drew near. They'd see T'omar's feet dangling out of the shaft, they'd see the sunlight, hear the sounds of our escape, smell the sulphur and methane that clung to our garb . . .

T'omar's face appeared over the edge of the shaft. I tugged desperately and he popped out like a cork from the bottle, sprawling on the ground. I looked around for something to cover the gap, obscuring the light. A shelf of shields provided the answer, and we dragged a pair of them over it just as a group of elementals, burning brightly, passed by.

The shield came to rest with a scrape of metal on stone, the horses watched us curiously, our eyes met. T'omar began to laugh, I began to laugh.

It was the hysterical laughter of two men who, against all expectation, have survived. We smelt of burnt-out sewers and were covered in black ashes, and brown gunge.

T'omar pulled the slime-covered mask off his face and breathed the clean, open air deeply. I picked my way to the nearest window. We were in the central courtyard, right on target! The laughter welled up again – but I fought it down as a squad of guards hurried by. Soldiers were shouting orders, I knew that necromancers were eyeing the city, and a host of junior mages with scrying glasses were scurrying towards the keep.

I crept back to T'omar. 'We're still in trouble,' I murmured. 'Serein's doubling the guard, by the look of things.'

'Can we call the groups?'

Risky . . . 'Probably, yes.'

'Do it. As quietly as possible.'

<NMM 1, report.>

<NMM 1, Windsight has been injured, we are taking over. Void-rift opened centre town, still raging strong.>

<NMM 2, report.>

<NMM 2, mid-town guardhouse. Two successful strikes, none lost.>

So I went through group after group, listening to the sounds of triumphs and the laments of loss until, <NMM 5, report.>

<NMM 5, we are under attack! Attempting to flee, three necromancers and two squads bearing down on us . . .>

Contact was lost. 'Well?'

I looked at T'omar, assessing what I'd heard. 'They all report that they're doing well. Three squads have seen lifelike replicas of us walking around the streets, and what with the elementals and Windsight's Void-rift, Serein's too busy to catch them all. NMM 4 reports seeing citizens of Haven attack a patrol.' I shook my head. 'It's incredible. You get just five groups of four men, and if they stir up enough trouble, the people think it's a revolution, and join them.'

The general looked pleased. 'That's what I planned.'

A pair of black knights clanked into the stableyard. We froze, crouching lower. Passing the entrance to the stables, they went on to the armoury.

I turned to T'omar again and said in a frantic whisper, 'We still need to get to Serein. What's been destroyed is minor stuff. Two necromancer towers, four patrols, three groups of mages who just weren't paying enough attention. Sure, it'll distract Serein, but it won't take out the palace.'

'Remember, he's still got a force here,' hissed T'omar.

'We need to wear something that isn't covered with . . . *anything*,' I muttered.

'Leave that to me.'

I stared at him in silent horror. 'What are you going to do? Go up to the armoury and say, "I'm sorry sir, there's been an accident, can I have a set of clean clothes for me and my friend?"'

'Something like that. Look, I'm the soldier. I know how soldiers think, and they're never as suspicious or as knowing as you mages. Just wait here, okay?'

It was one of the longest waits of my life. I guess with all that magic in the sewers and all those spells I'd been throwing around the place, I'd come to accept that we were going to do everything with magic. The thought of not using it, leaving us exposed to any mage who happened to be suspicious, made me tighten my grip on my staff and glance around nervously. At any moment I expected to see a looming necromancer whose fist of magic held T'omar's dead body.

'You! Come and help me up!'

It was fortunate I'd taken off my grey top. The shirt underneath was less filthy, so that the man didn't immediately see I was coated in crap. He was a black knight, no doubt a murderous bastard. But his sword and gun, and his elaborate armour, suggested his absence would be felt. I put on a suitably humble expression, and went up to where he was waiting inside the doorway by a saddled horse.

He wrinkled his nose in disgust. 'You stink.'

'I'm sorry, sir. There was an accident.'

He snorted. 'You people of Haven are animals.'

'Yes, sir.'

'Well? Help me up! For nightmare's sake, are you stupid?'

Give us a chance! I cupped my hands, and took the full weight of a knight in armour as he levered himself up. I could hear him muttering. 'Bloody fool . . .'

Then came an explosion whose aftershock made the stones hum and the tack jingle.

'What the hell was that?' he yelled.

I hurried to the stable door, and peered out. 'The necromancers' tower is on fire, sir,' I replied. It was hard not to sound as pleased as I felt.

The mounted knight shoved me aside as he galloped out into the now crowded courtyard.

And I saw *him*.

SIXTEEN

A Curse of Kings

Serein was standing amid a throng of guards, rigid with effort as he summoned forces to aid him. Three dragons who breathed water rather than fire erupted from somewhere into the air, and took off towards the tower. Rain was falling, and intensified, bringing thunder and lightning.

'Why can't anyone find them? I've seen twenty images wearing his face!' screamed Serein. 'Nineteen are dead and still he's here! He moves from place to place across the town, destroying my mages and driving the kingdom into the Void! I want him caught!'

I grinned to myself, and slunk back into the relative safety of the stables. Good. He was confused, and not a little scared. I began to ready the spell that would end the Lord of Nightkeep for ever, when the latest messenger appeared.

'Sir! The citizens of Haven are rising! They're

attacking the guards everywhere, spurred on by agents of the Consortium! They're coming towards the palace!'

Serein's face was a mask of rage – red and bloated. *He can't deal with it all, there are too many problems for him to handle* ... 'Deploy my knights! They'll deal with this rabble!'

He turned, and stalked back into the keep. As he disappeared from sight, so I banished my spell.

'You heard all that?' T'omar, carrying a bundle of clean clothes, had appeared out of nowhere next to me. He'd been watching the scene with a smile.

'Yes. The people will die, if the knights get involved. I'm going to call for the attack. Now. While he's distracted.'

'Sounds good.'

I drew the Sign of the Silverhand, felt contact. <Attack.>

<Dream's blessing, sir.>

'They're coming.' And that was it. A few brisk words, and we'd condemned thousands to die. All those soldiers gathered from all those lands in a matter of days, about to go and be killed because they thought Haven was a cause worth dying for. All those nomads from Westpoint about to draw swords, all those soldiers from Waterpoint readying their guns, ready to kill, and fight and die.

Worse – I didn't feel a thing. Just a big empty space where emotion should have been.

T'omar nodded, calculating. 'The first wave ought to be at the gate in five minutes, the elementals will be with the mob in half that time, the second wave will breach the walls in another ten. By that time, Serein must be either dead, or ... otherwise engaged.'

I gave the manic grin of a scared man hoping he can see the good side of things. 'Don't worry. What with Saenia taking an interest and all the work of your mages, I think I'll be able to keep Serein occupied.'

'Long enough for me to get behind and shoot the guts out of him?'

'I'm glad we both think honour is a piece of crap.'

He gave me a shocked look. 'I'm a soldier! It's only when you know you can survive that honour starts to count. Now get into these.' He shoved a bundle of clothes into my hands. I unfolded the garments, and looked at death's own robe.

Well, not *exactly* that. But a necromancer's robe, which is plain black, with a hood that turns the face into shadow and sleeves that flop around the wrists and hide the hands. All that anyone else can see coming is a big robe supported on nothing and holding a staff with nothing. T'omar unwrapped his own new clothes, to reveal the black and red livery of an ordinary soldier. 'Stop looking like it'll bite you,' he said, stripping off his slime-encrusted grey and pulling the livery over his head.

With a sigh I followed suit, washing myself in the horse trough to remove the worst of the sewer stench.

T'omar slung the rifle over one shoulder, checked his sword in his sheath, and nodded at me. 'Good. You look very . . . deathly.'

'I feel like an idiot.'

'You *look* like a necromancer.' He reached forward and tugged the hood up. 'Now no one will know the difference.'

Resigned to saving the world dressed as a prat, I

straightened up, took a grip on my staff, and stepped out into the courtyard. No one even noticed us. I noted with interest that T'omar had acquired the stone-eyed, empty expression of all guardsmen, and likewise I tried to move with necromantic dignity.

We walked straight up to the keep, mounted the steps to the heavy enchanted door, and knocked. The door swung open, and two armed guards and a necromancer glowered at us. 'Who seeks admittance?' rasped the necromancer.

'Shut up, and let us in now, you fool!' I snarled. 'Or I swear it'll be your blood on the altars!'

He looked panicked. 'Please, sir, I must have identification.'

'You bloody idiots, do you deny everyone who enters?' I raised a hand glowing with fire and swiped it towards the nearest soldier's face. 'Your insolence will be reported to Serein.'

'Oh . . . of course, sir.' He bowed and backed away. I nearly laughed, but managed to strut into the keep without another word or gesture. The secret was to say as little as possible. And not to run.

In a fortress full of haste and noise we got lost, argued, and bluffed our way round the keep. Finally, T'omar seized my sleeve and pulled me into a small room on one of the higher corridors. There was a bed, a wardrobe full of courtly clothes and a table stacked with weapons and armour.

Darkly he said, 'Just how do you plan this?'

I gave a big, false smile. 'I was thinking we should find wherever Serein is hiding, and I'll throw fire and you'll throw bullets.'

'How and where?'

'I just work things out as I go along. There's no point getting stressed out over . . .' My voice trailed off. T'omar was staring at something over my shoulder. His hands, hidden from whatever stood behind me, were moving towards a small dagger on his belt.

I turned slowly, careful to keep T'omar's movements shielded by my own. A man holding a rifle, the end of which pointed at my face, stood in the doorway. You've got to be prepared for things like this in nightmare towns. I hadn't been.

'I'm sorry, would you prefer if we went somewhere else?' I blurted.

'I'd prefer if you'd raise your hands. Both of you.'

I wondered if a combustion spell was in order, then thought better of it. Bullets travel faster than magic, and it might cause more attention than it was worth. If T'omar could settle the issue without too much noise . . .

I chucked the staff aside, and raised my hands. T'omar moved out from behind me, saw the face of the man who held the rifle, and froze.

I've never been sure what happened next. The moment the two saw each other, something seemed to flip. T'omar gave a snarl of anger and leapt forward, the dagger gleaming in his hand. His rival took aim, and pulled the trigger in the blink of an eye. T'omar staggered, but kept going.

So quickly was it over that I hadn't even raised fire to my fingers before our attacker was slumping against the wall with a look of surprise. T'omar was on the floor, curled around a wound I couldn't see.

The rifle shot had attracted attention. I could hear the

sound of running feet in the corridor. Swearing in a way
to make T'omar proud, I slammed the door, drew the
bolt across and lay a temporary ward across the woodwork. I felt Serein's presence brush over the room, and
held the scry-block tightly over us.

There was blood on the floor. Blood on hands, clothes,
stones – and I didn't even know whose was whose.

Kneeling down by T'omar, I pushed his hands away
from where a crimson stain was seeping through his side.

His face was pale, but he wore a triumphant smile. 'I
got one bastard, then.'

'You couldn't have got him more quietly, could you?
Lie still!'

He obeyed, a mad gleam in his eyes. 'Get out of here,
Kite. You've still got to fry Serein.'

There came a hammering on the door. I exclaimed,
'For a great bloody tactician you've got a crap sense of
timing.' *How to get out, what to do, don't panic, don't panic* . . .

I hauled the black robe over my head, and began
tearing long strips off it. 'Why the hell did you do that
anyway, or shouldn't I ask?'

'That man was the one who took Mountpoint.'

'Alone?'

'He was the general who defeated me.'

'And you let professional pride get in the way of the
mission? I know you too well for that.'

'It wasn't professional, Kite. He deserved to die.'

I gave T'omar a calculating look, ignoring the hammering on the door as best I could. Someone began to
pick away at my wards.

He strained to turn his head, and looked at the
window. 'How are you at air-mastery?'

'Flying? Fine when I don't have to sustain two scry-blocks, a basic ward and a reflection shield.'

'Not the window, then . . . If you give me the rifle . . .'

'Not a chance. You're going under this bed, to stay there until I'm dead, or Serein is.'

It took several seconds for realisation to sink in. 'Kite! For dreams' sake! How will it sound when they sing of our exploits and say, "While one saved the world the other stayed under the bed"?'

'Damn good when they mention how much blood you lost. The bullet may have hit a lung, and the pressure of time and nightmare mean I can't risk a healing spell.'

'You mean I'm dying.'

'No, I bloody don't!' I was angry. Angry at T'omar for being so damnably brave, angry at myself for not being equally strong, angry at Serein for existing. And full of rage at not knowing what to do!

'You are an incredible stubborn man, Kite.'

The anonymous necromancer picking at my wards was making me angry too. I strengthened the magic in my wards and thrust outwards with a strand of thought, to grip his heart in a hand of ice. He flailed ineffectively, his shields crumpling before the force of my anger, and suddenly there was no more necromancer to pick and pull.

I pulled a knot tight, making T'omar gasp with the pain.

'We're in deep trouble, aren't we?'

'You're the tactician. You tell me . . . Put your hand on this.'

He obeyed, pushing hard against the wound.

I glanced at the door and saw what he meant. Despite

my wards, the bolt was straining. 'I'm going to push you under the bed, pull a few sheets down, enough to hide you from the most glancing of glances. Don't make a noise, don't attempt anything heroic, just remember to keep pressing and breathing.'

Something acid began to eat away at the door. *That's my trick!* I thought, and risked a probe. A tentacled monstrosity of some kind was sitting boldly in the corridor, squirting green slime over the wood. I felt the immense pressure of a Key as it fought to dissolve the reality around me, and resisted with every last drop of magic I could find.

Hurriedly I pushed T'omar under the bed, and pulled the sheets down around him. A blood-stained hand caught my sleeve and his pale, sweat-drenched face peered at my own. 'Kite, I'm sorry I wasn't more help.'

'When we get out of here and you're thinking straight, you'll know what a dream-sent blessing you are.'

He hesitated, tried to smile and let me go. Although I had no alternative I felt guilt at leaving him alone and unprotected. I slipped a probe inside his mind, and triggered the deepest trance I could. His eyelids flickered, then closed.

So now I was alone in a castle intent on blowing me to bits. I raced to the window and flung the shutters open.

Serein was somewhere nearby, watching it all. I could feel his presence hammering at my scry-block. *What the hell, he knows where I am anyway* . . . I let the spell go, leaving only a layer of defensive shielding in place. From the bottom of the keep, thorns began to grow, climbing the stonework ever faster until the whole massive structure looked like a square hedgehog. Clearly someone didn't want me to try climbing. They were going to force me to fly . . .

In the open sky, three dragons were waiting for me to do just that. The floor creaked as Serein struggled to undermine it beneath my feet. I felt the touch of the Key once again, stonework cracked . . .

But didn't fall.

'The Key is yours.' *A twisted ball of red fire, trying to pull in two, little bolts of lightning burying themselves deep in its heart, striking from an unseen corona.* I could feel Serein's burning anger and confusion as the Key refused to obey a direct command. I laughed out loud. Haven was on my side! Sure, he could summon thorns to tear my hands if I climbed, and dragons to turn me to dust, but he could *not* directly harm me with the Key!

The door buckled, began to crumble. *Alternatively, he could destroy the door and let his guards do it instead* . . .

I ran across the straining floor, grabbed the rifles of T'omar and his unknown enemy, slinging one across my back and placing the other against my shoulder. I reached the window again in two strides, took aim . . .

I'm not a particularly good soldier, and bad with a gun. But a dragon is a big target, and one of the last things these creatures expected from a desperate mage was a non-magical attack. The first dragon roared as a bullet struck home. The second dragon dived desperately out of the way, but there was a satisfying rip of leathery wing as it flew into a salvo. The third dragon snarled, fire in its mouth, and plunged straight towards me. I fired at point-blank range, but the creature still emptied a stomach full of sulphurous flame over my barely functional fire-ward. My eyes watering and half-blinded, I saw the blurred shape of the dragon plummet to earth, three bullets buried in its skull.

Now seemed as good a time as any to risk flying. I pulled myself onto the window ledge and leapt into the air. The magic didn't catch at first. Twenty feet from the ground, I swooped upwards again, to the sound of gunfire and the shouts of guards who'd only just woken up to the reality of a magical battle of unprecedented proportions.

Lightning arced out of the sky, narrowly missing me and drawing a scorched line of fire across the ground. The rain hammered down, plastering my clothes to my skin and driving the sudden cold into my bones. I couldn't stay flying much longer. Angling upwards, I sped towards the top of the keep, burning magic at an alarming rate to fuel my ascent. Swerving from side to side probably saved my life as the two sentries on the rooftop took pot-shots at me. I crested the top of the keep in a shower of magical sparks, and landed between the two guards. With what little force I could muster, I summoned two walls of magic, and sent the sentries tumbling over the edge. Lightning struck all around me, but never once touched.

'You're cursed, Serein! The Key won't respond to you! It'll burn you, eat you, devour you from within!' I screamed to the sky. I was trembling with the cold, soaked through and exhausted, but from the top of the keep I could see all across the city. I saw the elementals, renewed by a respite in the Void, swooping in from the shimmering barrier between possibility and reality, screaming magical death on their enemies. I saw the churning mass of flimsy order in the centre of the city, where a weak web of Key-bound magic barely restrained the still-open Void-rift from devouring everything. I saw the mob of furious people charging from street to street, storming the mages' towers and the guardhouses of the dark knights. I saw the massed armies of Silverpoint, Waterpoint, Westpoint and a dozen other kingdoms, rise seemingly out of nowhere on every road around Haven, like ants crawling out of cover. Saw them turn towards the ravaged and divided city, and charge.

'You're going to die, Serein! You and all of yours!'

A roar of wind that felt like knives tore me off my feet and sent me sprawling on the stone floor. Guards were running towards me from the towers around the keep, carrying rifles and swords. I mustered the last of my energy, seeking to open a Void-rift beneath my feet that would destroy the palace, me, T'omar, everyone within a one-mile radius and, most importantly, he who ruled the nightmare, in a single swipe of deadly magical force . . .

And someone hit me.

I don't think I was swimming in the big black sea of unconsciousness for very long. Certainly the guards dragging me along hadn't reached the great hall by the time I woke up. My first thought was, where'd I put that book I was reading in Stormpoint, before all this fuss started? I suppose that's the kind of thing you think when you've got mild concussion. The second thought that managed to crawl its way into the spinning forefront of my mind was, 'I wonder if T'omar is still alive?' Since I had no means of answering that question, I decided not to think about it, and focus on the problems of self.

Problem. I'm being dragged along a corridor by a bunch of guards with big guns and swords. Problem. I've cracked my skull and am not really thinking straight. Problem. I'm soaking wet, freezing cold, stink of sewers, am covered with blood and just want to go to bed, possibly with a bath on the way. Problem. I can't move my hands thanks to this bloody rope, and my legs feel as if they're about to go to sleep. Problem. I'm going to die.

Hold on! That's not a problem, that's a future possibility! It only becomes a problem when it reaches present tense, and then you won't have to worry about it anyway!

Truly I wasn't thinking straight.

However, old habits die hard, and the instincts of a thousand similar situations took over. I slumped in the guards' arms, tuning what little magic I had down to a minimum, and let all but the most basic of shields relax. The resulting effect made me look a lot deader than I felt.

The great hall was a little different from how I remembered it. For a start, it was hotter. A mad demon-designer had come up from the nether reaches of hell and been let loose on the massive room. Gone were the long trestle tables where plots were hatched and lovers matched. Gone were the massive tapestries showing various wonders from Haven's history. Gone were the bright stained-glass windows where eagles spread their wings.

Say hello to bubbling pits of flame and screaming slaves. I shut out the various sounds of suffering around me, and wondered if the fire-ward I'd inscribed on my hand was still in force.

There were two narrow walkways surrounded by lava, I realised at last. Where they crossed in the heart of the room someone had chiselled a massive star, with a throne, guards, etc . . .

In the middle of the seas of lava around this central star were smaller islands, also in the shape of a five-sided star, where people who'd pissed off the new lord of Haven sat naked and trembling, their eyes the wide stare of someone who yesterday thought they'd seen everything and today knew that everything was very little indeed. High gothic windows and walls carved with pictures of suffering, of death, of fire, and, I noticed, of Serein holding aloft the Key of Haven triumphantly as all his enemies cowered before him provided little light and reflected even less. The place was like a sauna, and even the guards were sweating furiously.

Serein's back was to me, and I could hear the low murmur of voices as he talked with two of his generals. The guards strode right up to the throne and flung me to the stones on my knees.

I could throw a mage-bolt at him right now, I thought. *But he'd have shields raised, and I'd be shot dead before I could do anything more.*

Serein turned. He smiled to see his latest enemy on bended knee, soaked by the storm, scorched by fire and lightning, bloodied and cowering. 'Excuse me, gentlemen,' he murmured to the generals.

Eyes never leaving my face, he sauntered to the throne, and sat down like a peacock displaying his feathers. Most of the guards who'd dragged me in bowed and left the room, leaving two of their number with their rifles pointed at the back of my hanging head.

'And now you're going to gloat,' I sighed, barely noticing that I'd spoken out loud. 'It's all the same with you types. Gloat and sneer and never quite get round to killing because you're scared that if you kill me my ghost will haunt you or some such crap.'

'On the contrary,' he said, looking flustered nonetheless, 'I'm not about to make the mistake my father made.'

'Oh yes, your father. Now, didn't he have me at his mercy on the road in the Void, saying, "I'm not about to make the mistake my necromancers made" before I threw him into the abyss?'

I sensed a twitch of anger. The Key was working against him, and Haven was being torn apart. He had too many things to focus on at once. If only I could push him just a little further . . .

'You are a brave, if stupid, man.'

'The two often go together. By the way, shouldn't you be fighting a rampaging army?'

'I intend to. Bring him nearer.'

I was kicked and shoved forwards, until just a few feet away. Serein concentrated – and I felt reality change.

The star began to rise beneath us. The two guards lurched with the sudden movement, but to my disappointment didn't fall off. Up through a roof that was suddenly as substantial as dust, up into a sky where rain sliced the air, up until we could see the whole city stretched out far below. The star expanded, the throne still at its centre, but with several yards of empty space added on. And into that empty space . . .

I felt my stomach churn. Fear, real fear, gripped me and made my heart struggle to beat. A gallows, a single noose swaying in the wind, waiting patiently for its next victim, built itself out of nothing, and confronted me.

The whole city would see their living legend die.

Forget what I said earlier. names do count. They would all see a name die, and all that had kept the battle raging would die with it.

It didn't matter that it was to be my body dangling from the noose. What difference did it make if it was me, or the anonymous boy who'd just fallen to them beneath a black knight's blade? The person behind the name meant nothing. Only the past mattered, in this battle to decide the future.

The two guards dragged me towards the gallows. *What a way to go*, I thought bitterly. *At least the devils will really have to exert themselves, to get this high up and drag poor old Kite into hell.*

The elementals, seeing their master in danger, broke off their attack on a stormcloud of struggling dragons, and turned towards us. Serein laughed, and a yard-thick glass-like bubble surrounded us, supported on nothing. A few bullets bounced off the sparkling ball, but it didn't even crack.

A beam of light broke through the clouds to illuminate our little scene. *Yes, let everyone have a look, you bastard . . .*

'You kill me, you'll never get control of the Key,' I rasped as I was forced up onto a rickety stool that I could imagine turning beneath my feet to little more than a wispy maybe.

'You're wrong. When you're dead the curse on the Key will have nothing to focus on, and will dissolve to nothing. All those stupid spies of your precious Consortium who've been causing me so much trouble will slink off into the shadows which spawned them, and the elementals will flee to their own places within the Void, confused without the guidance of their master. The people will be demoralised, no other mage will dare stand up to me, and the dreamer you no doubt used to get you inside Haven will die. Everything will be shattered.'

However I tried, I couldn't find a single reason why Serein might keep me alive. Usually there's something these mad monarchs want, but this guy was as cool as a cat, smiling faintly as the guards pulled a noose over my neck. I gasped as the heavy knot bumped against the back of my head. The pressure of the rope against my neck felt a thousand times greater than I knew it to be. Serein smiled to see me so afraid. No great speeches, no bravely staring at the face of a beloved and dying with a proud smile for the tear in a child's eye – I was too scared even to pretend bravery. *Thisisityou'regoingtodie*.

The mob, specks on the distant ground, were hammering at the gateway to the palace. Soldiers fell like flies as the attackers shot them down with guns stolen off the dead. Serein laughed as he saw my expression of fascinated horror. 'Oh yes, my soldiers will die. But it doesn't matter, because I'm up here and they're down there, and I can summon a thousand dragons to kill all my adversaries. Haven will be turned to nightmare, Stormpoint will fall, Skypoint, Silverpoint – dreams will die.'

The stool was unsteady beneath my feet, the noose harsh around my neck, breathing fast, heart faster. The elementals drew back in slow horror, their forms flickering as reality began to wear down on them. Then as one, they fled, leaving me suddenly alone. The sympathetic crowd on which I'd so depended had been forced to flee. Serein was winning every battle.

'You're a fool, Serein!' I cried. 'If the dream dies Earth falls into despair. Our worlds are so closely bound together that one depends on the other. You'll plunge not only this world but the next into darkness; Earth will be haunted by endless nightmare. It will seep into their world, and when Earth fights they fight with real guns! They'll drop nuclear bombs on each other, and there won't be a mage in the Void to summon more people, or a magical artefact in some lost kingdom to save them. There'll be no infinity of maybe to summon a new Haven. The humans will annihilate themselves, and when there are no more humans there will be no more of this world. No more imagination, no more dreamers, no more kingdoms. Earth and the Void are too closely bound, there must be balance!'

I prayed that just this once he'd recognise the truth.

'The great mage reveals all?' he asked wryly.

'The great mage thinks you're a bloody fool!'

Serein's eyes flashed. 'And who is the great mage to judge that? What is the great mage that he can see more clearly than any other? How *dare* you presume that you see, feel or perceive what no one else can! How *dare* you presume that you can lecture kings! You know what you are, *Laenan Kite*?' There was something in the way he said my name that made my blood freeze. As though he had said it many times before, with the same curse on his breath. 'You're an illusion of a mage. You're an empty vessel in which people can shape their hopes and aspirations and say, "Yes, here is proof that it can be so"! But it's gone to your head, *great* mage. You believe that you can see what we cannot, that you can preach what no one else can, that you can be a hero and somehow pull through. You fool! You're nothing more than a canvas on which other people love to paint.'

He was breathing fast, little muscles twitching involuntarily in his face. I stared at him for a long, horrified while, trying to feel hatred or anger or both. All that rose up was pity, whether for him or me I could not tell. 'No,' I said finally. 'Illusion I may be, *mortal* I may be. But it is not arrogance to say I see these things. What kind of arrogant fool would want to see as I see, feel as I feel? If I truly was such a great fool, I would have blinded myself to the truth as you have, and in that blindness found contentment. There must be balance, Serein! You think it makes me happy to say so, to realise that the world can never be pure white or black but only a dodgy shade of grey? There must be balance, in this world and the next! Dreams above, I wish I were a fool so that I need not see the destruction that will come from this as clearly as I do! You bloody idiot, you murdering, bloody, stupid idiot!' I spoke with a seeming anger that in truth my heart was past feeling.

For a second Serein seemed to hesitate. I saw something in his eyes almost of recognition, and my heart leapt. Then it died and the raw anger, tainted with madness, was back.

'Kill him,' he hissed. 'Kill him now!'

Is that it? Not even a 'You're wrong' or 'I'm not a fool'? Just 'Kill him'?

I closed my eyes. This is where you stop being a rational human being and let the slight genetic alteration that makes you a mage show through. This is where the untapped power of emotion comes to the fore, in a tide of blind chaos annihilating all order that dares stand in its path. All you have to do is find the key to that untapped madness, let it flow, let it grow . . .

The stool shook slightly beneath my feet. I leant back, desperate to keep it steady beneath me while I kicked out with one foot. The heel of my boot connected with something satisfyingly soft, a soldier gave a grunt of pain and retreated. The hot pain across my back as his comrade lashed out with his rifle butt, and the stars which burst around my eyes, proved once again how futile the fight was. *I'm going to die . . .*

Let it flow, let it grow . . .

'What are you waiting for? Kill him! Let everyone see him die!'

And if that madness is unleashed, it will draw more madness. Madness from the heaving Void-rift in the centre of the town, madness from the skies above.

Someone pulled my head back by the hair, and the crazed eyes of Serein met mine. 'You are so hard to kill, Kite! Need I dissolve the chair beneath your feet?'

All I needed was the key . . .

Renna.

My eyes flew open. If ever I'd found a symbol to unlock unseen powers, it was now. Renna was the link between worlds, the proof of what I'd said – that there had to be balance between Earth and the Void. She was proof that only by dreaming was there a chance, however slim, of becoming something more. We *had* to dream, else our little mundane lives would suck us down to where we all lived and died but never changed anything, never became something new. Renna was the proof that both worlds had to dream, else all was lost . . .

A guard raised his foot to kick the stool out from under my feet one more time, Serein backing behind the throne to watch the scene from a critic's standpoint. This time I didn't kick out or struggle, but let the anger rise up like a tide. I let the hatred and the pain and the resentment of five hundred years' lying and fighting for others, be they smiling king or cunning or sincere prince of honour, pour out of me. It was a stream, suddenly filling with the meltwaters of the mountains and bursting into an unstoppable churning river that crushed the tallest trees in its path. The stool came away beneath my feet, the rope tensed around my neck . . . and broke. I landed lightly on a point of the star and raised my hands. The rope that bound them snapped and fell away.

I screamed, with a burst of magic that I didn't know I had left. It was fuelled by emotion that I had never felt before and could never feel again. The chaos of that magic alone wasn't going to be enough though, and through instinct alone I bound it with science in a world where even the rules of gravity or pressure or light can be bent. The guards' noses began to bleed, and they collapsed to their knees, hands over their ears. With a scream that matched my own the glassy sphere cracked, strained, and shattered into a myriad glittering pieces that erupted outwards and became just another sparkle with the rain. The throne crumbled and exploded into shards of stone that whizzed through the air and filled the sky with grey powder catching the sunlight. The gallows creaked, and ruptured outwards in a thousand splinters.

A piece of stone, flying outwards, caught me across the side of the face. The scream faltered and broke, the spell it had woven breaking too. Stars played across my eyes, tears poured down my face, mingling with blood and rain.

Where are the elementals when you need them?

The sunlight turned blood red, the same colour as the heaving, gaping Void in the centre of the city. The rain returned, bringing a horrible sense of reality. Slipping on the stone, there was nothing romantic or graceful about us. Soaked adversaries, about to fight for our lives, on a surface that was suddenly less than stable.

The only sound was of the rain and the faint echoes of a scream, dying away. Everyone in the city had fallen silent. Dark knights, swords locked with nomads from Westpoint, turned their eyes, mid-thrust, to the sky. This was a fairy-tale kingdom, after all, and the story required that the representatives of good and evil fight each other to the death. The nomads, with a more pragmatic view of life, took the chance to slay their opponents.

But even the nomads then turned their attention to the star of stone, hanging in the sky. They saw the two figures, one soaked and bloodied, facing each other.

The two guards lay dead on the stones, their insides turned to jelly by the combined forces of science and magic. Curiously enough, I felt more guilt over them than for anyone else in the whole war. Perhaps it was the reality of seeing them lie before the one who should have been the only corpse.

Serein, the powerful, the evil, the cunning, lowered the shield that had protected him. In one hand he raised the Key. The division in its centre was there for all to see. The lightning within it was like another, unbroken layer.

'It doesn't seem to respond to you, Serein.'

'Not now. Not with you so near.'

It was then that I collapsed. There was nothing I could do to stop my head flopping onto the stones. The Key might not be responding, but neither were my legs.

'They're watching us, Kite. They know who you are, what you did to my father.'

'You're a blind idiot,' I croaked.

'Get up.'

'Can't.'

'Get up!' There was magic in those words, forcing me to obey. I staggered upright, facing Serein. He wasn't even scratched, and his magic blazed bright and clear. He smiled again. I was too tired to be unnerved.

'Listen. Everyone's gone silent. They're all watching us. Waiting for one of us to fall.' He pointed at one dead guard, then the other. The two corpses blazed into human torches, then turned to ash.

'You always were too arrogant, Serein,' I murmured. 'You should have summoned a sandstorm full of knives, set it roaring about your palace. But no, you left yourself open to attack, thinking you could easily defeat anyone. You, the great conqueror who took Haven. And now look at you. There's a mob down there, thousands of troops from dozens of kingdoms. Hundreds of mages, just waiting to strike. And the Key of Haven doesn't respond to you, because in taking it you were just too presumptuous. You're doing to die, Serein.'

'If I die, I'm going to take you with me.'

Through a haze of exhaustion I heard my own voice whisper resignedly, 'But you don't know whether I've got an ace up my sleeve.'

I struck, then and there, not caring what happened. A bolt of pure white light erupted out of my opened hands, and smashed into Serein's shields. He laughed, and summoned a swirling cloud of black and red energies which bore down on me like a plague of flies. I didn't bother with shields, but dived to one side, falling hard against the stone. The magic exploded in the empty air.

I retaliated from where I lay, sending mutterings into his mind. So small and simple it is to send thought, but such a underestimated weapon. <Your father was weak, easy to kill . . .> Images went with the thoughts, images of a lord of nightmare catching my wrist, pulling me to the edge of the road. Memories of looking down on his face lined with terror, memories of his fingers slipping, of the face disappearing into the fog . . .

Serein roared with rage and sent a wave of fire out-wards in all directions. I ducked beneath it, but it still scorched my hair and brought tears to my eyes. The fire-ward, poor abused thing, flared in a brave final defence of its master, and gave out. But, for the moment, that last defence had been enough to save my life.

Yet still the avenging son from hell pressed home his advantage, making the stone beneath me burn red hot. I pressed a blanket of entropy down on it, willing the atoms to be still and silent. For a moment, Serein did not understand what was happening. He was using tra-ditional spells, the time-honoured magics of ancient duels. Like so many mages before, he wasn't used to the fact that science and magic could work hand in hand.

I used that second of hesitation to kick out, catching him across the ankles. He staggered and fell forward, hands glowing with blue lightnings to catch my throat. I raised a shield and shoved him off before he could touch me, then rolled away and onto my feet.

He was up too, his greater strength and agility easily bouncing him off the stones. Against his shields I hammered a volley of spells. He staggered but resisted, flinging them aside.

I found myself raising my hands in self-defence against a serpent whose deadly, stinging tail passed straight through me like the illusion it was. But that second of diversion was enough for Serein to strike with a force that sent me winded to my knees.

Another bolt of magic, barely deflected, followed by an ice lance. Frost crawled along my skin and clung tight. I tried to crawl away from Serein's advancing figure of death, and my fingers found themselves groping the rim of the stone star. I was poised precariously on the edge. Serein came towards me again, picking his way across the slippery stone. 'This is only fair, don't you think?'

'Stupid question,' I muttered.

'You didn't have an ace up your sleeve, then?'

I grinned. 'You'd be amazed.'

In a sudden movement I reached forwards and up, grabbing Serein's clothes and pulling him towards and over me. His hands tightened around my arms, burnt my flesh with the power playing over them. I felt the slippery stone slide beneath us, felt the world take a sickening one-hundred-and-eighty-degree lurch, and we were falling head over heels through the storm.

I was walking down a road covered with ice. The spirits turned as I approached. 'But he did fight, your mage of fire and anger,' I heard them whisper. 'He did win.'

'Earth is too closely entwined.' My lips moved, vibrating with the passage of sound, but even then . . . 'I can't break free.' *Not my voice. How is this possible?*

'You have already broken free. You think a human, a dreamer with a body, could find their way here? You can turn back.'

'I am dead.'

'Nightmare wills you to be dead. Dreams will you to be alive.'

'Nightmare rules the dreams.'

'Nightmare falls in dreams' arms. You can turn back, and save dreams. Dreams, your dream, is with you even now. Watching through your eyes.'

Was that a tear, rapidly turning to ice? I couldn't control my body, but while I felt every nerve and muscle, I felt no pain. I wasn't drenched with sewage, I wasn't bloody or soaking or dead or dying.

'He is going to die. When he dies, then I really won't be able to turn back.'

'Then save him. He has driven nightmare from the city of dreams, now you must save him.'

'We did not find paradise!'

'You did. The Journey is complete.'

'But I am a dreamer! I cannot find my dream!'

'You have found your dream, your paradise beyond Earth. *He* is your dream. Paradise does not have to be a time or a place. You never dreamed of a time or a place. You dreamed of your husband, so your husband was here. If you die, he dies, because there will be no dreamer to sustain him. If he dies, you die, because the nightmare will truly rule you. He is here! He is with you now, for you are too closely bound for one to survive without the other! He is your dream, created by you, *part* of you, just as you are part of him!'

And I was turning, the ice fading to nothing, my *body*

fading to nothing, taking with it the memories of a world utterly unreachable. I was a free mind, bound only by the limits of imagination . . .

Serein's fingers dug deep. Neither of us could let go of the other – we were both too terrified. The crowd was roaring below us, a circle clearing where we would fall. Soldiers of nightmare staggered in confusion, too shocked to fight as their master plunged to certain death. The crowds were wailing the loss of a legend. Better if they'd been wailing for me, but I was willing to settle for second best. I faced Serein once again, the only thing which wasn't spinning wildly. <Two one to dreaming!> I sent.

<The legend dies, the hope dies!>

And we were falling, reality changing as the Key recognised the certain death of its master and dissolved all but the most basic of works. The dragons roaring overhead gave out one last blast of fire, and died. The vampires sucking blood from another victim burst into showers of ashes, the goblins and the ghouls shrieked their last.

And still we were falling.

But the clouds were parting, the sunlight trying to shine through. The Key, suspended on the stone, flared bright red, then returned to its normal pink, the lightning around it fading to nothing. The watching crowds and desolated city went from ground to sky and back again in a matter of seconds, but . . .

But their movement was slowing. I found I could move my fingers beyond the paralysis of fear, and forced them open. Serein fell away from me, ever faster, as if I

were a feather and he a ton of lead. The city returned to
being the ground, then froze in motion.

This is it, I thought. *You've died and now there are angels
taking you up to heaven.* I felt hands grip me under the
arms. Hands glowing with silver light. *See? Angels' hands.*
I felt warm breath tickle the back of my neck, the rain
stopped completely, the sunlight broke through. *And now
you're going off to heaven.*

I craned my neck, curious to see what it was that held
the crowds so rapt. I wasn't the least astonished to see a
shining figure of light wearing pure white robes with
golden wings. Nor was I very surprised to notice the perfection of every feature, the fire in the eyes, the mystical
wind which the angel rode like a dream.

The hiking boots were out of place, though.

'Renna?'

She smiled softly. 'You won.'

'I did?'

'Uh-huh.'

'Did I win in time?' I asked carefully, not totally sure
what was happening but asking nonetheless.

'Oh, yes.'

'And . . . you're an angel, right? Doesn't that mean
you're dead?'

She snorted. 'Angel? No such thing as an angel!'

'But . . . the wings? And you're hovering in mid-air
without magic or anything.'

'Not an angel. A dreamer, remember?'

Something went click – an extraordinary thing at two
hundred feet, with the world spiralling in a purple haze.
'We got the nightmare out of your head, didn't we? You
were able to wake up.'

'I was able to die, Kite. But I was here, and here looked attractive. So I've decided to move in for a while, see if there's anything interesting to do.'

A mind, without a body, I thought, and wondered at the implications of that. What could a mind do without a body? What couldn't it do, for that matter?

'Are you going to make everything better now that you're . . . you're . . .'

'Call me a builder.'

'What do you build?' I was still losing blood, wasn't thinking in straight lines. *I know the answer to all these questions, why am I asking them in the first place?*

'Realities.'

'Oh.' What was the question again? Oh, yes . . . 'Are you going to make it all better, now?'

'No. You've got to do that.'

'Can't it be done tomorrow?' I just wanted to sleep. Everything had happened too fast and now that it seemed at a climax I didn't want to know. As far as I was concerned I'd done my bit and reality could look after its own affairs.

'And disappoint the crowds?' Oh yes, the huge crowds of so many colours, straining to look at us, all spread out in neat little lines, separated by the houses.

Without a word of warning we were standing at the top of the main gate, looking across the square in front of the palace. Every street leading to us, every window and every rooftop was full of people watching and waiting, hypnotised by this creature who wasn't human any more, but wasn't anything else I'd ever encountered. Renna let go, and I sagged to my knees. *Just want to sleep . . .*

The Key hovered in front of my nose, looking as innocent as a ball of possibility could after it had helped Serein to get me beaten black and blue.

I glowered at it. 'Oh look. Now you're trying to be apologetic too.' Without even a flicker across its surface the Key nonetheless looked suitably contrite. 'Okay, since Lisana isn't here . . .' I reached out with shaking hands, and took it into me.

It took a few seconds to grow adjusted, in which time I saw Renna smile. Not Renna, I reminded myself. Something more.

My legs were going to sleep. My head throbbed. The air stank of death, but all the monsters Serein had summoned were gone, vanishing with their creator. Or possibly it was to do with Renna. I was just too tired to perceive which, or even care. What was it I had to do again? Oh yes, that.

Sighing, but with a sense of achievement that surpassed anything I'd ever felt, I raised my hands to the now bright and glorious sky, closed my eyes, and summoned the full force of the Key.

It began to rain. Golden droplets of growth started pouring down, like fairy dust, only without the inconvenience of a chittering horde of the annoying creatures. Where the magic struck, it healed, warmed, renewed.

It burnt away the bodies of the dead, raised flowers through the rubble of buildings annihilated by fire. Seeped into the bloody wounds of the injured, bound them up with clean bandages. Burrowed into the bitter black thorns that surrounded the keep, turned them to green-leaved ivy.

Danced towards the red, glowering sun that squatted

on the horizon, played and spun around its surface, and became one with it. There were ruins and fires and gaping holes in the fabric of reality and mourning and tears – but Renna's hand on my shoulder was enough to tell me all I needed to know. I'd done my part. This once, someone else could finish tidying up the mess.

Morning broke, on the city of dreams.

Epilogue

There's not much left to say. Dreams grew big and strong, Nightkeep lost nearly half its territories, and withdrew to lick its wounds. We lost maybe two thousand people, soldiers and civilians alike, in battles in and out of Haven. But as T'omar said when they dragged him out from under the bed, we would have lost a lot more without the Consortium.

Stormpoint is more or less tidied up, and back to nearly its normal size and population. A group of nomads is staying by the river for a time, and a bard is with the elven court trying to write a ballad describing the Consortium's great victory over Serein. I've given instructions to the elves to keep the man busy for a very long time.

The Consortium will never really be the same. It's come out into the open, and when T'omar gets out of hospital he'll have to do some serious thinking about

the nature of his organisation. I don't mind though.
Secret police can be a mixed bunch, and it's probably
best for everyone that in this case they're secret no
more.

The greasy patch that was Serein has been dissolved
by the healing showers I summoned when the Key was
inside me, before I gave it to Lisana. She received the
Key graciously, and one can almost forget how often
she's behaved like a right pig after the last bucket of
grain.

So now Lisana is on the throne in Haven, where the
court lives in terror of a queen who's just beginning to
reveal the true meanness of her temper. Those of us
who've been dreaming of Earth for long enough compare
her to Elizabeth the First of England, who was famous
for being a right madam when she wanted, but one hell
of a queen. After so long, it feels weird to be on good
relations with her, and even weirder to think that I
helped her onto the throne. But it was either her, failing
the illegitimate Talsin – such a noble, noble bastard – or
me. Perhaps things might have been better another way
round. Perhaps not. Though I pretended otherwise, I
still wonder what was lost by the death of Talsin, the
finest noble idiot that ever was.

Haven responds well to her. If I'd kept the Key any
longer, the place might have become a madhouse, since
my head was in such a state. As it was, she was very nice
about everything. She sat by my bed where an extraor-
dinarily stern matron specially dragged in from
Healpoint had told me to stay put for a week, and shared
gossip and generally seemed willing to let bygones be
bygones. I thought forgiveness was something I

should've bestowed on her, not the other way round. But it's such a rare quality that I thought I'd better cherish it on any terms.

Windsight is back in Skypoint. Recently there've been tensions in our friendship, but time the great healer, and an explanation from Renna, will hopefully relax things. He survived the Void-rift relatively unscathed, thanks to my beloved elementals, and is considering settling down once and for all. Perhaps at last he'll get married. Saving the universe can be that much more stressful when you're a bachelor, especially for a gentle man like Windsight. Nasty people, such as I, have less trouble.

Saenia is back at Haven. There's little changed about her, save that she smiles a bit more and has led thousands of refugees across dreams. She's still my bigger, better sister and I'm still the little boy running to her to cry. I asked her how she did it – how she got so many people out so quickly. She just tapped the side of her nose and said, 'You're not the only one who invents spells, Kite.' I haven't asked her again.

Renna. We had to get to Renna sooner or later. To tell the truth, I've no idea where she is. She appeared in my room in Stormpoint the night I got back, and we talked for a while. But she wouldn't tell me where she was going, nor what she planned to do.

She's not what she was. Well, obviously not. For a start she can summon her own chairs, even inside a reality controlled by me. And she can change her shape at will, and make real food without having to step into the Void, and do all kinds of things. She tried to explain how to me, but I didn't understand too much of it.

But if, as people say, the new creature that is Renna

was made by my victory, then I believe I've created a fledgling goddess.

And me. Well, nothing new there. Besides, after seeing the defeats and victories I've been dragged through, you might describe me in different words from those I'd use. I might say clever, you might say stupid, I might say kind, you might say cruel, and so on. I'm biased about myself, but who isn't? Gits think they're nice, nice people search their soul in quest of fault. There may be parts of this story which my ego has exaggerated, and some which my pride has understated. A few mistakes may have been scrubbed out, some brave deeds written in. But then, unless Earth gets a lot closer to the real world, I don't think you dreamers will ever learn the truth about me and Haven. It's probably a good thing.

Shakespeare was the guy who summed it up best:

> *If we shadows have offended,*
> *Think but this, and all is mended,*
> *That you have but slumbered here*
> *While these visions did appear.*

But then, Shakespeare was talking about fairies.

I never dreamed again of the hospital where Renna had slept, nor of my doppelganger, David Kiteler. They were but dreams to me, as I must appear to you.

I think I'll go out to the Void today, and see what the possibilities of two worlds can bring forth into one.

And when you sleep tonight, dream of me.

I may well be dreaming of you.

Laenan Kite *will* return. . .

About the Author

Catherine Webb was just fourteen when she wrote her extraordinary debut, *Mirror Dreams*. With several novels already in print at nineteen, Catherine has quickly established herself as one of the most talented and exciting writers in the UK.

Look out for Catherine Webb's thrilling new novel

The Extraordinary and Unusual Adventures of Horatio Lyle

The Bank of England robbed! Murder on the Streets of London!
Hypnotism! Mystery! Pursuit! Saint Paul's Cathedral ablaze!

Welcome to the world of Horatio Lyle . . . When Mystery
beckons, he gathers his courage, sharpens his wits and fills
his pockets with things that explode

On Sale February 2006

PRAISE FOR CATHERINE WEBB

'If I were a teenage fan of Terry Pratchett or Philip
Pullman, I would love this book'
Telegraph

atom

MIRROR WAKES

by

Catherine Webb

The stunning sequel to Mirror Dreams

Laenan Kite repelled the Lords of Nightkeep,
but he could not destroy them. Now, with
deadly spells igniting across Haven, Kite must
prepare for battle once more. But is Nightkeep
really the source of the trouble, or could Kite be
facing a new enemy? Someone who's learned the
secret to harnessing a Dreamer's power.
Someone from much closer to home . . . ?

WAYWALKERS

by

Catherine Webb

The opening volume in a breathtaking series

Sam Linnfer works part time at a London University. He's a quiet chap with a real skill for ancient languages and an affection for cats. He's also immortal and the Son of Time. You might know him better as Lucifer, Old Nick, or the Devil . . . And with all the Gods in Heaven about to go to war over ownership of Earth, you're going to be extremely glad he's not exactly the person history portrays him to be.

Waywalkers is an absolutely stunning new novel. You'll come face to face with Jehovah on a cold Moscow night, walk the Ways between Earth and Heaven with Buddha, take a hair-raising cab ride with Adam (yes, *the* Adam – only he's into denim now, rather than fig-leaves) and find yourself trusting the one person you never dreamed you would.

Because in a war between Gods, where Earth is the battleground and humans are expendable, you'll need to have more than just sympathy for the Devil.

TIMEKEEPERS

by

Catherine Webb

The thrilling conclusion to the series

Sam Linnifer returns to continue what he started in
Waywalkers and rid the world of the deadly plots and
schemes of the elder gods. But with Seth, Jehovah and
Thor now in control of the dread Pandora Spirits, Sam
knows Earth's only hope may rest in his unleashing the
Light.

But the power bestowed upon him at birth by his father
Time could have deadly consequences for Sam himself.
For in unleashing the Light, Sam must touch the minds
of every human on Earth. To save the world, Sam may
have to destroy himself . . .

Timekeepers is the stunning follow up to the acclaimed
Waywalkers. You'll meet Firedancers in London on a
rainy summer night, walk the Ways between Earth and
Heaven with Buddha, hole up in a sleazy German bar
with Adam,. and find yourself trusting the one person
you never dreamed you would. In a war between Gods,
where Earth is the battle ground and humans are
expendable, you'll need to have more than just sympathy
for the Devil.

FROM THE TWO RIVERS

Part One of The Eye of the World

By Robert Jordan

The Wheel turns and the greatest fantasy adventure of all time begins . . .

Life in Emond's Field has been pretty boring for Rand Al'Thor and his friends until a strange young woman arrives in their village. Moraine is an Aes Sedai, a magician with the ability to wield the One Power, and she brings warnings of a terrible evil awakening in the world. That very night, the village is attacked by blood-thirsty Trollocs – a fearsome tribe of beast-men thought to be no more than myth. As Emond's Field burns, Moraine and her warrior-guardian help Rand and his companions to escape. But it is only the beginning of their troubles. For Moraine believes Rand Al'Thor is the Dragon Reborn, and that he is fated to unite the world against the rising darkness and lead the fight against a being so powerful and evil it is simply known as *the Dark One*.

atom

TO THE BLIGHT

Part Two of The Eye of the World

By Robert Jordan

The most incredible fantasy adventure of all time continues . . .

Despite the magical aid of Moraine Sedai and the awesome fighting skills of the warrior Lan, Rand Al'Thor and his friends have been unable to throw off the foes that pursue them. Even a detour through the ghosts of the ruined city of Shadar Logoth has failed to deter the Dark One's minions. Now the companions have a Trolloc army at their rear and eyeless shadowmen, known as Myrddraal, laying ambushes on the roads ahead. Worse still, the Dark One has dispatched his most feared general to ensure that Rand will die. Aginor is the powerful magician whose dark magic first created the Trollocs and he will stop at nothing to fulfil his master's bidding. Unless Rand can unlock the secrets of his extraordinary destiny, Aginor will destroy him and the darkness will triumph forever.

atom

WINTER ROSE

by

Patricia McKillip

They said later that he rode into the village on a horse the colour of buttermilk. But I saw him first – as a fall of light. And then as something shaping out of the light. So it seemed. There was a blur of gold: his hair. And then I blinked and saw his face more clearly . . .

From that moment, Rois is obsessed with Corbett Lynn. His pale green eyes fill her thoughts and her dreams are consumed by tales of his family's dark past. Of son's murdering fathers, of homes fallen to ruin, and of a curse that, as winter draws in, is crawling from the frozen forest to engulf them all.

at●m